A DRAMATIC NOVEL

TUESDAY to BED

I0628684

Francis Sill Wickware

WILDSIDE PRESS

Chapter 1

STANTON WYLIE, lying on his back in bed, with one arm crooked around his head on the pillow, opened his eyes slowly and wondered why he was awake. For a split second he even wondered where he was. He had one of those peculiar alarm-clock minds, and before dropping off to sleep at night he could tell himself what time he wanted to wake up in the morning and be sure of doing so with a very narrow margin of error. This was a trick which he simply accepted without attempting any psychological explanation, and the results often puzzled him. This Friday morning, for example, he awoke at eight-twenty (having set the mental alarm for eight-fifteen the previous evening) and from beneath half-closed lids obliquely regarded the curtains ballooning out from the windows with no immediate comprehension.

He licked his lips and stirred, aware of a feeling of strain in the crooked arm. Then his gaze—veiled by eyelashes which looked as thick as tree trunks in that strange focus —wandered from the curtains to an oblong of brown sole leather which seemed to be resting on the blanket at the foot of the bed. He vaguely recognized it, after a while, as the top of his overnight case, and he wondered what it was doing there. Then something snapped, and he remembered . . . Chicago; the Century this afternoon; the speech. Words began to parade through his mind. "Mr. President, Members of the Committee, ladies and gentlemen of the convention . . ."

He sat up, stretching mightily, yawning, running a big-fingered hand through tawny hair, and making the bed seem preposterously inadequate to support him. He reached out and automatically turned off the switch on the cord trailing from the blanket, then looked automatically toward his wife's bed. It was empty. The covers were thrown back, with the top sheet piled into a little mountain—a brown sheet, with a diamond-shaped pink monogram, "E.B.W."

What is Betsy doing up so early? he thought, and then reached out for the switch on her blanket. She never remembered, never would remember, he thought, but indulgently. She wouldn't be the same if she did remember, and he didn't want to change her. He caught the whiff of her perfume from the sheets as he leaned toward her bed with his hand on the switch, and he experienced a sensation of tingling gladness as sudden and exuberant as a bursting skyrocket. The speech has got to be good, he told himself. I want her to be proud of it.

The room was cool and dim. The brown carpet looked purple in the early light, and the pink walls were gray. Outside, a boisterous wind galloped across a slate-covered sky, and Stanton watched the lashing branches of the willow tree beyond the windows. Then he pushed two switches in a panel on the bedside table. Something hummed in the wall, and the windows slowly closed, with the curtains flapping once or twice before they resumed their sedate vertical folds. From above came a scratching, sputtering sound as the fluorescent tubes hidden behind the window valences abruptly flooded the room with daylight. Stanton touched a third switch, and the curtains rolled together like closing gates. The room—as Stanton blinked—came to life and color, with the mirrors in Betsy's dressing alcove shining pink and brown and blue and reflecting sharp little facets from the bottles grouped on the mirrored top of the kidney-shaped dressing table skirted with the same pink-and-brown curtain material.

On the brown carpet between the beds Betsy's nightgown made a small rippling pile of pink silk, and Stanton picked it up and smelled the fragrance of his wife. He worked the fabric between his fingers, thinking of the relative tensile strengths of silk and nylon thread, then pressed the gown to his face and inhaled Betsy's perfume. Nylon was a fine invention, he decided, but it didn't have the personality of silk. It was too cold. It couldn't absorb the essence of a woman's body and hold it and send it out again like silk. Somewhat incredulously he held the nightgown at arms' length and studied it. Although he had been married to her for nearly fifteen years, Stanton never had lost his sense of wonder that anyone as lovely as Betsy could be his wife—or

4

his wonder at the lovely, fascinating, mysterious garments she wore. I am a very lucky man, he told himself, and immediately added: The speech isn't good enough. I've got to do something about it.

Then he let the pink silk splash back onto the carpet, and swung out of bed. In the bathroom he flicked switches again and there was a blaze of ultraviolet. He passed a cobra-headed electric shaver around his cheeks and chin, shed his pajamas and stepped into a glass-inclosed shower, where he pressed one of a row of insulated buttons on the wall and bathed in a spray automatically regulated to seventy-eight degrees Fahrenheit. ". . . ladies and gentlemen, to say that this is one of the proudest moments of my life would, of course, be an understatement," he orated above the hissing of the shower. No, too self-conscious, he told himself. The beginning shouldn't be so formal. Now how about this? . . .

He continued the rehearsal while drying himself with monogrammed towels which repeated the color combination of the sheets, continued while he dressed, abstractedly selecting a light gray tweed suit, blue chambray shirt and a navy tie with vivid red compasses, protractors and T-squares—Betsy's find. ". . . We stand on the threshold of a new era," he said to the mirror while he straightened the tie and adjusted a gold collar pin. I'll say we do, he added to himself. His glance shifted from the mirror to a black wooden frame hanging a foot or so to the right, and for a moment all the life seemed to be blotted from his face. He stooped a little, and furrows stretched across his forehead and were gouged in slanting lines from the corners of his mouth. He was a big man, sparely built, and in that particular attitude he suggested one of the old Brady photographs of Lincoln—kindly, thoughtful, perplexed by a responsibility too vast for one man to face. Yet in the black frame he only saw the top third of a newspaper page, already starting to fade and yellow. It read: *Oak Ridge Journal* above a roaring black headline: IT'S ATOMIC BOMB!!!, with the dateline August 6, 1945. Attached to a corner of the frame was an oblong green plastic badge—MANHATTAN DISTRICT PROJECT—*Stanton Wylie*—some personal particulars, a cloudy thumbprint. That was all.

Impulsively he put out a hand as if to pull the frame from the wall. Betsy always had objected to it—said it was morbid and out of keeping with the rest of the room, which it was. They had had quite an argument about it, with Betsy saying: "I don't see the *sense* in it, Stanton. Why not hang it, if you must, in your office, or out in your workshop? Why *here?*" But he had insisted: "This is something easy to forget because we would like to forget it—or I would," he had told her. "But I haven't the right to forget it. I need to be reminded every day when I wake up and get dressed. Then maybe I'll——" He never finished what he might have said, because Betsy shrugged impatiently and walked out of the room. "Oh, all *right,*" she said from the doorway. "Hang it there if you *must,* but it will just *ruin*——" The frame stayed on the wall, and neither of them mentioned it again. His hand stopped less than an inch from the badge. Then he dropped it to his side, and looked back into the mirror. ". . . stand on the threshold of a new era," he repeated. "And it is up to us to see that it is the era of . . ." In the corner of his eye he saw the headline: IT'S ATOMIC BOMB!!! He shook his head in a puzzled way, and the lines deepened in his face. Betsy was so deft, so intuitive, so swift at forming opinions and grasping ideas, yet he never had been able to make her see what he meant, and he was sorry for that because he very much needed someone who would understand. But the last thing in his mind was blame of Betsy. No, it was his fault, he just couldn't explain things very well, and anyway why should a woman who was such a wonderful wife be asked to think about such things?

His mood changed back to cheerfulness as soon as he turned away from the mirror and the black frame was out of sight. ". . . up to us to see that it is the era of achievement and promise—promise of a—" he proclaimed loudly on his way downstairs—"promise of a following era of even greater achievement. We can't do all of it, ourselves, in our generation. But we have the tools at hand and the know-how in our minds and we can—— Damn!"

It was an old house, built for average Americans of the post-Revolution period, and since then average Americans had added several inches to their stature. When he wasn't watching for it, Stanton invariably bumped his head against a beam halfway down the staircase. He often had determined to remove the beam and enlarge the shallow tunnel of the stairway, and after saying "Damn!" and rubbing his forehead he decided again to have the place ripped apart.

Then, as the pain in his forehead subsided, he studied the beam and thought: No, I can't touch you or change you. I'll let you be a reminder. You were right for the people who built this house and lived in it. They could walk under you, otherwise they wouldn't have put you there. And when I bump my head, you remind me that people are bigger than they used to be. Not only bigger in body, but bigger—he paused—in mind. Perhaps not that even—bigger in hope and belief. . . . He stared at the wrinkled black slab, wondering whether his own words were true. . . . Hope and belief; hope for the future, and belief in the integrity and creativeness of man. As long as you remind me of those things, stay where you are.

". . . promise of a following era of even greater achievement," he said aloud. ". . . Not only for us, but for our children, the children of our children, and——" His brain soared; it would be a great speech, he decided—hope and belief, that would be the keynote. He would make them see, make them build, make them create, and he would go one better: he would build for hope and belief. He would build something white and shining and tall and triumphant which would dwarf even the ugly mushroom cloud which he had helped to slap across the face of heaven.

". . . children of our children, privileged either to live in a world of beauty, striving and accomplishment," he continued, ducking under the beam, "or foredoomed to hate, destroy and be destroyed. Because we are too stupid to appreciate our own cleverness. Because we are afraid of our own cleverness—afraid to let it work for us, to let us build and make and create what we should——"

At the foot of the stairs he was interrupted by the passage of a large, dark individual wearing a white apron and carrying a silver tray.

"Peace!" this personage cried, with an ivory smile. "Morning, Mist' Wylie. Just toting your breakfast in for you."

7

"Good morning, Supreme Love," said Stanton. "Where's Mrs. Wylie?"

"Mis' Wylie? Why, I b'lieve—" she looked up at him, and for a moment—or did he imagine it?—the bland, black face wore a crafty, unfathomable expression—"she's on the telephone. Now, you come on in and eat. I got that creamed chipped beef you been hollering for."

She lumbered flat-footedly toward the breakfast room, calling back, "Now you come on, Mist' Wylie. Don't you let your food get cold."

Stanton was about to follow Supreme Love when he heard Betsy's voice around the corner from the living room. It was a rich, warm, husky voice, but now it sounded strained and urgent. ". . . Yes, yes, I'll call you later, can't talk now. Yes, *later*. Good-by." He heard the hollow sound when she dropped the receiver back onto the base of the telephone, then the hurrying rustle of her *moiré* dressing gown. He called, "Betsy, I think I've got it. The speech is all set, and I want you to listen to this——"

Suddenly she appeared, saw him, and stopped as though she had run into an invisible barrier. "Why, Stan—I don't know—how long have you been here?"

"Hope and belief, Betsy—that's what I'll tell them. To build, make, create—that's the theme. We *must* believe, we *must* have hope, because otherwise we destroy ourselves. Do you see what I mean? Do you think it's good?"

He paused, looking at her and waiting for her verdict, the way a dog might look at a man or a child at his mother.

Betsy took a deep breath and rustled toward Stanton. In the interval of those few feet he stretched his arms and hopes through the roof of his home, through the familiar atmosphere of his visible world, through the singing wilderness of space toward some undiscovered star sailing in pure seas of rightness and wonder.

As she approached him, Stanton thought, Everything I build is for her; she's so lovely.

Actually the years were beginning to leave their imprint on Betsy. She was acquiring a matronly fullness around the bust, and though her legs were still youthful her ankles were perceptibly thicker. There was a prediction of sagging in the line of her jaw, and the corners of her mouth were starting to make a permanent downward curve which gave her an almost petulant expression.

But Stanton saw none of this. His indelible vision of Betsy was of the girl he married when she was two years out of Farmington, one of the notable beauties of the Eastern seaboard, and perhaps the most sought-after debutante in the entire platinum triangle between Cambridge, Hanover and Annapolis. Other girls maneuvered for Yale, Harvard and Princeton prom bids, and even bought them, one way or another. But Betsy was the kind of girl whose acceptance immediately conferred a social accolade, and for the really important parties she never had fewer than six or eight invitations to choose from. Those were the enchanted years when the music never stopped and the stag line stretched from the Meyer Davis orchestra playing "You're the Cream in My Coffee" in the Boston Copley to the Meyer Davis orchestra playing "I Can't Give You Anything but Love" in the smilax bowers of the New York Ritz, and magnums of Heidsieck were presented to departing couples at dawn because the hostess had ordered too much and the waiters would drink it up if it wasn't given to the guests, and that would be bad for the waiters. Everyone—including the waiters—talked about United Corporation, Commonwealth and Southern, and General Motors. It was the best of all possible worlds, although up in the balconies where the chaperons sat there was some indignant muttering about the radical policies of that fellow Hoover.

Whether Betsy had been created for this bright, tight little dream world or the world for Betsy would be hard to say; at any rate, they complemented each other perfectly. Betsy then was as slim and graceful as an arrow. She had a radiant halo of straw-blonde hair and the most extraordinary eyes—in color almost a true violet, with black lashes. Her dancing was just short of Broadway professional standards. When she had a good partner and decided to cut loose with him, it was something to see. In no time all the other dancers would stop and form a big circle around them; Meyer Davis would waggle his baton for something especially intricate; and at the end there would be general applause, with Betsy blushing prettily as though she hadn't realized anyone was watching.

In addition, of course, she had a good deal of money—not a real wad, according to the peculiar yardstick of the times, but enough to interest any number of young men accustomed to using the Social Register and Dun & Bradstreet the way a horse breeder uses the studbook.

The brightest picture Stanton carried of her was not Betsy surrounded by stags at a coming-out at the Ritz, or even Betsy at their wedding on the vast, sheep-cropped lawn of her family's place in Southampton, where she again was surrounded by tipsy gallants sweating under their frock coats on that hot June afternoon. He remembered her best when he had her all to himself, during their honeymoon in Venice, and he never looked at her without at least one flashing recollection of that fantastic summer when Elsa Maxwell was stage-managing the Lido and the Brenner Pass was nothing but an obscure and barren spot of the Italian Alps. He remembered Betsy in the bow of the mahogany speedboat dancing across the lagoon from the landing stage of the Danieli to the landing stage of the Excelsior Palace and back again . . . Betsy breakfasting with him at Florian's . . . wild strawberries and hot chocolate, the wintry shadow of the campanile flung across the hot glare of St. Mark's Square, and the fuzzy-legged German trampers thumbing their Baedekers . . . Betsy posing for snapshots in front of the candy-cane columns of the Doges' palace, looking as dainty as a Dresden shepherdess in a stiff white piqué dress with a blue-and-white polka-dot sash . . . Betsy on the marble floor of Chez Vous, the candlelighted sunken garden night club on the Lido, dipping and wheeling to the music of the Argentine tango orchestra playing *Adios Muachos, Plegaria,* and *Mama, Yo Quiero Un Novio* . . . Betsy curled against him beneath the canopy of the gondola tied to the music barge in the Grand Canal, guitars and throaty singing . . . and Betsy lying in flushed, tender sleep under the mosquito netting while the fan whirred on the ceiling. . . .

Stanton never realized—it would have shocked him to realize—that by only remembering her as his bride he completely insulted her as his wife.

"Why, Stan, it's wonderful. That's a wonderful theme." Betsy still had the violet eyes and the black lashes. But she looked down and turned her face aside when he kissed her, and her hands in the rustling sleeves of her dressing gown merely brushed his shoulders. When he put his arms around her she stiffened and backed away.

"Who were you talking to?" he asked.

"Talking to? Oh, just now—on the phone? Is that what you mean? That was . . . uh . . . Mrs. Hazen, about the Red Cross Drive. Come on, Stan—breakfast's on the table, getting cold."

"Do you really think it's good?"

"Good? Good? What—?"

"My speech. The idea, theme ——"

"Oh." There was relief in her voice. "A marvelous idea, Stanton, really wonderful. I'm so glad you finally have it straightened out. You've been worrying over it all week, haven't you?"

"I've had it on my mind," he admitted. He was a little disappointed that she had nothing definite or positive to say about the speech; he wasn't looking for easy words like "wonderful" and "marvelous," but for something indicative of critical interest. Besides, she seemed abstracted by something, an abstraction which he had detected more and more often in the last few months, baffling and inexplicable. His mood of elation dwindled; probably it wasn't any good after all, and Betsy was just trying to be nice.

"It's the first speech I've tried to make since prep school," he said. "I wish you——"

"You haven't made it yet, Stan," Betsy interrupted. "Come on, let's have breakfast, shall we?"

She lightly slipped an arm through his and let a slender hand rest lightly on his wrist while she guided him toward the breakfast room.

It was silly to buy a house, Stanton reflected, only because you wanted a single room, yet the breakfast room was the reason Betsy had settled on the place. The original builders had located it on the summit of a long, low hill which stretched in a compass-true line from east to west, and along the entire southern exposure of the house they had installed a brick terrace with colonnades up to the second floor, which projected over the terrace. This arrangement had endured with only minor alterations until Betsy snapped her fingers and decided on the breakfast room. The colonnades were removed, although the contractor swore that without them the house would collapse in the first strong wind. The old bricks in the terrace were taken up and used to extend the side walls out to the line of the projecting second story. After some Herculean engineering, huge plate-glass windows which stretched from floor to ceiling were installed across the whole exposure. These could be raised or lowered at the touch of a button, and would disappear completely into the floor—a spectacular feature which had involved an awe-inspiring expenditure.

Betsy had decorated the room in stark white from end to end. The walls were whitewashed, and the floor was covered with a white fur rug made up of dozens of squares of goat hides which Betsy had imported from Mexico. The breakfast furniture was white wrought iron, and she even had found a white sideboard. In fact, the only relief from white was the vines spilling from the flowerpots hung every few feet along the back wall—these, and a pair of Marie Laurencin pastels in white frames. Stanton never cared for the room; it always made him feel as though he were having breakfast on a movie set, and aesthetically it displeased him because it was so out of keeping with the rest of the house. But Betsy wanted it that way, and that was that.

Otherwise, the house was comfortable and unpretentious —even modest, for Fairfield County. It was the kind of house which would be appropriate for a fairly minor advertising account executive, say, during the interim period of his career before he hit the really big money and moved on to a shore-front estate with stables and a private dock.

This was precisely what the former owner had done. Stanton occasionally ran into him at the country club, and never ceased marveling at the way the world rewarded a man for fanatic loyalty to things in which he didn't believe. At least, Stanton didn't see how it was possible for the man —who was reasonably intelligent—really to believe that his agency's particular brands of tooth paste, breakfast food, and whatnot were any better than any others, yet he had heard him fervently proclaiming in the country club bar that Popsies (his breakfast-food account) was virtually the salvation of America's children. But then, Stanton reflected, it was natural enough, because Popsies had put him on top of the ladder.

The man—his name happened to be Smith—was the first person in the whole evolution of the human race to realize that the basic thing about breakfast food ("basic" was Smith's favorite word) was not flavor or nutritional value, but the amount of noise it made in a bowl of milk. Smith not only had had the luminous inspiration of advertising Popsies for sound instead of substance, but had developed a special microphone technique so that the actual sound of Popsies popping in milk could be broadcast as the theme introduction to the Popsies Parade radio program. Surely genius of this order deserved at least a fifty-foot ocean-going yacht, the shore estate, and a four-year psychoanalysis. Which Smith had.

As he entered the breakfast room Stanton perceived that Smith's trail crossed his own glass-topped table, with the geraniums blooming in the pots attached to the white wrought-iron legs. Popsies were popping in the bowl in front of Jeremy, his son, named for an uncle of Betsy's who conceivably might leave something. Jeremy was wearing Brooks Brothers suits to school. He had something of Betsy's hair and eyes and more than a little of her manner.

"Hello, Dad," said Jeremy. "There's another story about you in the paper this morning."

The white wrought-iron chairs with the white leather cushions were not designed for anyone of Stanton's dimensions, and he settled himself with difficulty into one of them.

"Morning, Jerry. What are they saying about me this time?"

He glanced at the folded copy of the Westport *Herald* lying beside his plate, and saw the headline: WESTPORT MAN TO RECEIVE COVETED ARCHITECTURAL AWARD; WILL ADDRESS CHICAGO GROUP. He read the story perfunctorily: "Mr. Stanton Wylie, of Crestview Road, Westport, departs this afternoon for Chicago, where he will attend the annual banquet of the American Association of Architects and Industrial Designers, to be held tomorrow night at the Hotel Stevens. The banquet will be marked by the formal presentation of the Association's 1947 annual award for the most distinguished contribution to American architecture. Considered the most coveted prize in the profession, the award this year went to Mr. Wylie for his plan and model of 'the ideal American city,' which was four years in preparation. Mr. Wylie, still in his thirties, is the youngest architect to receive the award since it was first established in 1910, and in an unprecedented decision, the Association's prize committee voted unanimously for his entry. . . . Four thousand contestants . . . Award consists of a scroll, a gold medal and $1,000. . . . A native of New York City, Mr. Wylie has been a resident of Westport for a number of years and is prominent in numerous civic and charitable activities. . . . A graduate of Harvard University and the Harvard School of Architecture . . . Worked on the Manhattan District Project at Oak Ridge, Tenn., during the war. . . . His wife, Elizabeth Wylie, is active in club and society affairs throughout Fairfield County and is well known as a charming and popular hostess. . . ."

"Dad, is your speech going to be on the radio?" Jeremy asked.

Stanton looked up quickly. Not, he noted, *"Is your speech going to be good?"* but *"Is it going to be on the radio?"* Why? He hated the fact that of late Jeremy was beginning to irritate him, and mostly because of questions like that. Why?

"No, thank Heaven, it won't be," he said. "I wouldn't want my friends listening in. I may make a fool of myself."

"No you won't, Dad. I'll bet you'll wow them."

"Well, I'm glad you have so much confidence in me. Come to think of it, I did win a debate once, when I was at Ely."

"When will the article about you be in *Life,* Dad?"

"I'm not sure," Stanton said. "When they called me the other day, the girl told me they wanted it ready to go to press Tuesday. They sent the photographer yesterday, but here it is Friday, and I haven't even met her yet. I don't see how they can do it so fast."

"She's meeting you on the Century this afternoon, isn't she?" Betsy asked. "What's her name?"

"Mm . . . Mainwaring, I believe," he said. "Nancy Mainwaring. Now," he added severely to Jeremy, "please don't go telling people in school about this."

"Why not, Dad?"

"Because—well, for one thing, it may not appear at all. It hasn't even been written yet, and I'm hanged if I know what they can find to say. Furthermore, I don't care much for the idea of being written up in a magazine like that. I'm not used to all this fuss."

"Oh, that's silly, Stan," Betsy said. "You can't expect Jeremy not to be excited about his famous father. Why, I've told all my friends about the *Life* article."

"Well, I wish you hadn't."

"Oh, Stan, they're *so* jealous! It does my heart good, after listening all these years to them yapping about the big deals *their* husbands put over, to be able to say that *you* are going to hit *Life*."

Stanton frowned. "Betsy, I don't like to be thought about in those terms. Or talked about."

"Don't you want us to be proud of you, Stan?"

It was on the tip of his tongue to say, Are you proud of me, or proud of the publicity I'm getting? But instead he said, "I rather hoped you were a little proud of me already."

"Oh, Stan, don't act like a wounded child! You know perfectly well what I mean."

"Yes, I suppose so. But—oh, let's not argue about it. I want my breakfast." He started to apply himself to his grapefruit, then looked up at her. "I'm sorry, sweet. Didn't mean to bark. It's just that everything has happened so suddenly."

"I know, Stan. It's all right." She reached over and ever so lightly squeezed his hand. In return, he took hers and held it in a firm grip. He saw her again only as the slim blonde sprite with bouffant skirts whirling in the Ritz ballroom with the crowd circled around her, saw her—in short —as a child.

"I wish you were coming with me, Betsy," he said gently.

Jeremy, having disposed of his Popsies, observed his face and said, "Hubba, hubba!"

"That'll be enough out of you, Jerry," Stanton said. "I've told you before I don't want you to use that expression, least of all in——"

"Oh, Jerry didn't mean anything, Stan," Betsy said. She detached her hand. "It's just the way they all talk."

"I'm sorry, Dad," Jeremy said quickly. "I forgot."

"Well, don't let it happen again, hear? Being sorry isn't any excuse, and neither is 'I forgot.' "

"Yes, Dad."

"How about it, Betsy? Won't you come along?" Stanton continued. "I can change my space on the Century and get a bedroom. Or——" Or you could even share the roomette with me, two of us squeezed into the same berth, the way we used to travel. But he checked himself; Betsy wouldn't consider anything like that.

"I'd just be in your way, Stanton," Betsy said.

"No, you wouldn't. You wouldn't be in the way at all. Why would you?"

"You're going to be involved for hours with the *Life* girl, being interviewed," Betsy said. "Then you'll be dashing around Chicago all tomorrow, pillar to post. Then you'll want to have some time with your mother. You're going to see her, aren't you?"

"She's meeting me for breakfast at the Ambassador. But what difference does that make? And what difference does my schedule make? You've got plenty of friends you could spend the day with."

"There isn't a soul in Chicago I care about seeing," said Betsy. "Besides, Stan, it's out of the question. I can't just pick up and leave like *that*. I've got a dozen things I simply have to do tomorrow."

"Such as what?" Stanton inquired.

"Why, there's the Community Chest meeting for one thing, and the social-events committee of the country club is getting together to go over the plans for the Halloween party. Don't forget," she added pettishly, "*you* were the one who wanted me to get into all these activities."

"Was I? I certainly don't remember advising you to get on the social-events committee. It takes up more of your time than all the other things together. Oh, well," he sighed, "I guess there isn't much point. I did hope——"

The appearance of Supreme Love with the creamed chipped beef put an end to the discussion. It was Stanton's favorite breakfast dish, but for several minutes he left it untouched. He sat back as far as the wrought-iron chair would allow and studied his wife. The Lincoln lines crept back across his face. He was remembering the old, gay, careless days when Betsy would have gone with him—anywhere, any time—like a shot, brushing aside objections and obstacles with a shrug of her shoulders or the toss of her head. It was very puzzling. He knew that the mood of two people in love is a fragile thing, ephemeral as a rainbow, having no more substance than a cup of air, as fleeting as December sunshine on a hillside, yet when people loved and lived together why shouldn't the mood become stronger and more binding instead of more illusory?

"Don't let your beef get cold, Stan! I practically had to bribe the manager of Gristede's to get it for you. What's the matter?"

"What?"

"You were looking so peculiar."

"I was thinking."

"Thinking? Thinking what?" Betsy sounded impatient. "Stan, I'm sorry I can't go to Chicago with you, but that's no reason——"

"I wasn't thinking about that, Betsy."

"Well, then what?"

Stanton straightened up in his chair and applied his fork to the chipped beef. "I was thinking about something I seem to have lost, and wondering where I lost it. The beef is very good, Betsy. Thank you."

"Something you lost? What was it?"

He looked at her levelly, and after an instant her eyes wandered to some distant spot on the landscape beyond the vast windows of the breakfast room.

"I'm not sure that I know," he said. "Perhaps it never existed. It doesn't make any difference."

"Really, Stan!" Betsy exclaimed. From Jeremy came a sound which might have been a suppressed snicker. Stanton glanced at him, but Jeremy had a napkin spread over most of his face, and bent his head.

They proceeded with their separate breakfasts in silence. Then Betsy said, "Oh, by the way, Stan . . . uh . . . what time are you getting back?"

"I don't know yet," he replied. "It depends on how late the banquet goes on and whether I can get a plane afterward. There was some talk about a get-together with the committee after the banquet. An informal celebration, or something. If all goes well, I'll be here for late breakfast Sunday morning."

"Oh." Betsy sipped her coffee demurely. "I thought you said you were going to stay over and spend Sunday in Winnetka with your mother?"

"Yes, I was planning on that, but Mother's busy all day Sunday, so what's the point? Anyway—" he looked at her in surprise—"how did you remember that? I only mentioned it once, and that must have been two weeks ago."

"Why, I don't know. I have a reasonably good memory, Stan."

"No, I'm coming back just as soon as I can. Let's make Sunday a real day, Betsy—go off somewhere together, what do you say? You know what I'd like to do? I'd like to put the car on the Bridgeport ferry and go over to Long Island. We could drive out to Montauk and take a look at the ocean. I haven't seen any real ocean for months. Then we could have a big shore dinner on the way back. What do you say to that?"

Jeremy and Betsy exchanged glances.

"It sounds lovely, Stan, but we can't do it this Sunday."

"Why not? What's to stop us?"

"Well, Jerry's got a date to go riding with the Johnson boys in the morning, and then in the afternoon there's the Hopkins' cocktail party."

"Oh, Lord! You didn't accept, did you?"

"Certainly I did. They always give wonderful parties."

"As far as I'm concerned, no suburban cocktail party is wonderful, or anything like it."

"Well, I enjoy them," she said, again with the pettish tone in her voice. "Just because you can't drink is no reason why I shouldn't see my friends."

"There's no need to be so tart," Stanton said. "Especially in front of Jerry."

"Well, I think you're unreasonable. I really do. You never want to go *anywhere*."

"I beg your pardon. I just got through suggesting a trip to Montauk Sunday. Every week end it's the same routine —cocktail party Friday afternoon as soon as I get off the train; dinner party Friday night; Saturday, two or three cocktail parties in the afternoon, dinner dance at the club and a few nightcaps at somebody's house afterward so that we don't get in until four or five; Sunday, the same thing—buffet luncheon, drink, drink, drink all afternoon until time for another cocktail party. It seems to me that once in a while we might do something different."

Being a nondrinker put Stanton at a painful disadvantage in Fairfield County, where social life is fueled almost exclusively by alcohol. He would wander miserably through these affairs, with a celery stalk in one hand and a glass of ice water or ginger ale in the other, maintaining a fixed smile as long as he could and wishing that he was back in his library or out in his workshop. Meanwhile the air grew thicker, the martinis warmer and more potent; the canapes dried out and began to curl at the edges; the voices became louder and shriller, and the talk less and less coherent. Someone invariably let a cigarette burn out on the living-room rug, and someone else invariably spilled a drink on an antique table and forgot to wipe it up. The hostess would bite her nails and scream that it didn't make a bit of difference, honestly! Hurry up and get a rag, John! Don't just stand there.

But what Stanton mostly objected to was the behavior—after a certain point—of the women. He doubted whether the fine old Eskimo custom of wife trading was quite as widely established in Fairfield County as some of the talk he had heard would indicate, but in the later stages of the cocktail parties a goodly proportion of the wives seemed to be doing their best to make it universal. There was a certain type of woman in the station-wagon set—usually a woman in her middle or late thirties, with two or three children—who by day shot golf in the eighties or showed prize setters or served as expert crew on her husband's International Class boat in the Saturday afternoon races, and who looked wholesome and healthy and chaste as a statue. By night, after eight or ten drinks, the same woman would begin to lurch and slobber, repeat unspeakable limericks and locker-room stories to the party at large and twine her pudgy arms around the neck of the nearest male. As often as not she would disappear with him and come back looking smeary and disheveled—and then disappear with somebody else. All of which seemed to be taken for granted by everyone but Stanton, who stood by and watched and listened with a mixture of amazement and disgust. Looking at these women, he always had the feeling that they probably were leaking from every aperture.

Whenever they stayed late at a party—and Betsy rarely wanted to leave early—Stanton endured assaults by one or several of them. They would lurch up and lean against him heavily, spilling part of their drinks on his sleeve, and saying something like: "H'lo, big boy, let's play house, just you and me. . . ." He would never forget the night when he had been quietly reading on a sofa and the drunken wife of one of his neighbors first planted herself in his lap, then swiveled around, lay down across him, pulled her knees up until they nearly touched his face, and spread them apart. . . . He saw her on the station platform the next morning, prim and pure as a daisy. She and her husband waved to him cheerfully, as though nothing whatever had happened. Betsy of course knew about the incident and thought it was funny. That Stanton couldn't understand.

Of course Betsy had nothing in common with these women. Her conduct was above reproach. But she never expressed any protest against the conduct of the others. And Stanton did, at least to himself.

"Stan, I'm not trying to drag you out against your will, just for my own entertainment," Betsy said. "It's for your sake, too."

"For my sake, too. I see. Or, rather, I don't see."

"Look, Stan, you know the Hopkinses. Everybody will be at the party."

"Yes. Including the usual contingent of bright young ad-men."

"Exactly. And why not? That's the point. You're famous now. They'll——"

"They'll all want to meet me, is that it? And now they'll want to commission me to design new labels for their canned tomatoes or whatever it is? Why, do you know that Bill Smith asked me to design a new box for his damned Popsies? He wants me to design a box with a top that pops when you open it. How do you like that?"

"What's the matter with that, Stan?"

"What's the matter with it? Do you want me to design Popsie boxes?"

"It would mean a good deal of money, wouldn't it?"

"Oh, certainly. A new pop-top box for Popsies, probably worth five thousand. But——"

"With your name, ten thousand. Think—designed by Stanton Wylie, winner of the 1947 award for the——"

"Just a minute. If the award means anything at all, it means that maybe I'm capable of creating something worth while. At least, I hope that's what it means. Anyway, I'm not going to pervert it for the benefit of breakfast-food manufacturers who may think that my name will help them sell more of their sawdust. Of course I turned down Smith's job. I should think you would have wanted me to."

"Oh, Stan, you're so silly about some things. You know I admire the idealistic approach, and all that, but is there anything wrong with money?"

"No, but there's a lot wrong with some ways of making it."

"I suppose that comes close to being an epigram, doesn't it? Very neat, Stan. But just remember, you're always taking on assignments that pay nothing. You wasted most of last week on those plans for the youth center."

"Was it wasted? I don't think so. In view of the delinquency rates, it seemed to be important to design an attractive and usable place where boys and girls would like to go instead of hanging around dance halls and street corners."

"Stan, I'm not arguing about that. It was a wonderful thing to do, and you can do it again. But at the same time, here's your chance to cash in, and why not? What harm is there in picking up five or ten thousand for a box top? You could do it in a day!"

"Yes, and be pegged as the guy who accidentally won the big prize and sold it to anyone with cash to buy it. Like Shakespeare writing Sunday-supplement articles. Would you like that?"

"Nobody would say that, Stan. You're in business. You're supposed to be making money."

"Maybe nobody else would say it, but I'd say it to myself, which amounts to the same thing."

"Well, you might think about my side of it." Betsy sipped her coffee and sighed in a resigned way. "After all——"

"Don't say it, Betsy," Stanton interrupted. "I've heard it

before and I don't want to hear it again. You're spending your income and dipping into your capital to keep this place running the way you want it. You don't need to. My income is enough to support any sensible family, and anytime you want to live on them, I'll be delighted——"

Supreme Love darkly reappeared in the doorway. "Jerry, yore school bus is outside, tootin' the horn for you."

"Tell the driver to hold it a minute, will you please?" said Stanton. And to Jeremy he added: "Sorry, old boy, I didn't mean to have all this bickering."

"It's all right, Dad," said Jeremy, finishing his cocoa.

"No, it isn't," Stanton said. "I don't know why we seem to—— Well, let's have the Long Island jaunt next week, shall we? Let's plan it for Saturday. Invite one of your friends, if you'd like to. How about that nice little girl you had at the birthday party—what's her name?"

"Anne," said Jeremy. He stood up. "I b'lieve Mom has something planned for me Saturday. I better go now, Dad, or the bus will leave me." He presented a fresh, cool cheek for Stanton's kiss. "Hope the speech goes over with a bang. 'By, Mom."

After he had gone Stanton sat without speaking for a minute. Then he said, "So Saturday's out, is it? What's the reason this time?"

"Why, Stan, I talked to you about the series of children's matinee concerts at Carnegie Hall, didn't I? Next Saturday is the first one."

"I don't remember your mentioning it. And Sunday?"

"Sunday the school is having its annual charity bazaar. For which particular worthy cause I can't remember. Anyway Jeremy's going to be in charge of the pies and cakes booth."

"I see. How often are these concerts?"

"I told you—Saturdays."

"Every Saturday?"

"Yes."

"And how long does the series last?"

"Oh, I don't know. Sometime in April I think. *Now* what's the matter, Stan?"

He looked at her and said, "I should think you could figure that out for yourself."

"Well, I can't." Betsy shrugged impatiently. "I suppose you're annoyed about the concerts, is that it? It's high time Jeremy started to learn something about musical appreciation. It's just as important to his general education as arithmetic and grammar, and I should think——"

"You don't need to go on," Stanton interrupted. "It isn't the concerts themselves. I have no objection to your taking him to concerts—I suppose you *will* be taking him, won't you?"

"Of course. I can't very well send him to Carnegie Hall with Supreme Love, can I?"

"No, I suppose not." Stanton stared at his coffee. As he often did when he was preoccupied, he tapped on the table top with the heavy gold seal ring which he wore on his left hand.

"Please don't do that, Stan. It's nerve-wracking."

"What? Oh—sorry. I didn't realize." She often had chided him about his unconscious habit.

"And I wish you wouldn't look so *moody*," Betsy said. "Why do we have to start the day this way?"

"I don't know," Stanton replied. "I certainly don't enjoy it."

"Well, then, let's be cheerful."

"I was very cheerful when we started breakfast," he said. "Don't you see, Betsy? I'm worried about Jerry. I never have any time with him. When he was a little boy, I kept looking forward to when we could do things together—the three of us, or Jerry and I by ourselves. The things that families are supposed to like to do together, but never seem to get around to doing. Before the war he was too young for much of that. Then during the war I was away so much there was no opportunity. And since I came home—well, it's the same. Either Jerry's always busy, or you are. We never have a chance to do things together."

Betsy said nothing, and Stanton continued: "He's enrolled in camp for the summer, and next fall he goes away to prep school. Between these concerts and his social engagements the week ends are knocked out all winter and spring. I . . . all I'm saying is that I'd like to be able to get to know my own son. And apparently that isn't going to be possible. When he goes away to school it will be a break with home. I'll see him an hour or so, now and then, between parties during his vacations. There's nothing in that sort of relationship. No, it's a strange situation for me, Betsy, and I don't like it."

"Oh, Stan, you're just being *morbid*," Betsy said. "The child isn't going into exile; you'll have plenty of chance to see him whenever you want to. We're simply trying to give him some of the advantages you had. Why, when you were Jerry's age, you . . ."

She went on talking in a quick, strained voice, but Stanton was oblivious to what she was saying. He perched on the uncomfortable wrought-iron chair, blinking in the glare of light coming through the windows and peered around the garish breakfast room almost as if he never had seen it before. He was conscious of a peculiar and most disconcerting sensation—one which he had experienced more than a few times lately—of being completely alone in his own home even when he was surrounded by people. It made him feel as though he were standing on the edge of a vast canyon and trying to shout across it to someone on the other side, but never getting any answer except the echoes of his own voice. Strange, strange, that it was possible to move so far away from those who were supposed to be so close.

"Stan!" Betsy's voice broke through his remoteness. "Aren't you listening to me?"

"Yes, dear, of course."

"Well, why not answer me then? I said, if you want to catch the nine fifty-five we'd better be getting ready."

"Oh." He glanced at his wrist watch. "Yes, you're right." He drained his coffee cup and rose. "Do you want to take me to the station, or shall I call a taxi?"

"No, I'll be glad to take you," Betsy said.

"I can just as well get a taxi, if it's any trouble."

"No, I have to go in to do the week-end marketing anyway. I'll slip into a dress while you finish packing," she said, on her way out of the breakfast room. "Everything's in your bag except your dinner jacket. Now come on, Stan, or you'll miss your train."

"Yes, dear," Stanton said, and followed her.

Chapter 2

At the Westport station, Betsy pulled into the line of cars disgorging husbands for the nine fifty-five, and stopped opposite the door of the waiting room. She flicked the gearshift lever and pressed her foot down on the brake pedal. She put her hand on his shoulder and turned her face toward him. "Well, Stan, here we are. Don't you want to kiss me good-by? You've scarcely said a word since we left the house."

"Of course I want to," Stan muttered. "Pull ahead a bit, Betsy; let's talk for a minute or two. I have something I want to tell you."

"All right, Stan." She eased the car ahead a few feet. In front of them other cars were backing and turning in the narrow roadway, and from behind came a staccato honking. "We can't stop here," Betsy said. "There's nowhere to park."

"Pull over by the side of the platform, just for a second," he told her. "They can squeeze by, if they have to." The honking grew insistent, and he added: "I guess they don't want to, though."

He put his arms around her swiftly, drew her close and brought his mouth against hers. For a moment she pressed herself toward him and parted her lips for his kiss, with her fingers clasping the back of his neck, behind his ears. The paisley bandana she had been wearing slipped down, and he ran a caressing hand over her shining blonde hair. Beneath his arms he felt her body tremble, and from her throat came something like a sob. Then she drew back.

Stanton grinned at her. His spirits had risen immeasurably during their embrace, and the sense of aloneness which had come over him at breakfast suddenly lifted. She was his girl again; still the wonderful, beautiful Betsy he had married.

"I couldn't leave you that way, darling," he said. "I'm sorry I was grumpy at breakfast—probably just worried about the speech and everything, subconsciously."

"It was mostly my fault, Stan. I'm sorry."

The honking behind was growing in volume; a police whistle shrilled. At the corner the red-faced cop who was on duty at the station during rush hours shouted, "C'mon! C'mon! You can't stay there! You're blocking traffic!"

"What I wanted to say is, when I get back we'll have a man-to-man talk Stanton said quickly; "take a little inventory of ourselves and look at these things we argue about, and we'll see that they're not worth the time of day. Because we don't have anything at all to really argue about, Betsy. Do we?"

"No, dear," said Betsy. "Of course we don't."

The whistle shrilled again, and the cop started to approach from the corner. Stanton opened the door and got out, dragging his suitcase. Then he leaned across the seat, and Betsy again tilted her face for his kiss and put her hands on the back of his neck. "All the luck, Stan, dear. I know it will be great. I *am* proud of you."

"I love you, sweetheart," he said. "You make me very happy."

He closed the door reluctantly, and the car slid away. The approaching cop stopped halfway from the corner and said, "Lovebirds!" in a disgusted voice. Stanton smiled at him, and waved once at Betsy just before she turned and went out of sight.

He strode into the waiting room, picked up a *Times* at the newsstand and emerged onto the platform just as the eastbound Boston express went roaring past, sucking a small cloud of dust from the ballast on the roadbed and causing everyone on the platform to squint and retreat an involuntary inch or two. A cold, damply penetrating northeast wind was blowing, and against the solid gray sky the lower clouds bobbed about and collided with one another. Stanton rather liked mornings like this. He pictured the Sound, a wet field of rugged gray-green furrows, and the muddy whitecaps slapping on the diminishing beaches in front of the summer cottages. It wasn't real ocean, of course; salt water, but not ocean. He could nearly visualize and hear the real thing—

the booming oncoming crash and the retreating sigh of the sledgehammer breakers pounding the granite abutments of North America along the Atlantic coast. It would be nice, he thought, if Betsy arranged so that next week end we could——

"Morning, Stanton," he heard a voice at his side. "Keeping bankers' hours these days, I see."

Stanton recognized the voice, and turned. "Oh, good-morning, Mr. Hazen. Is this your regular train? I usually get the eight-thirty."

"Why don't you drop the Mr. Hazen and just call me Chester?" Hazen inquired. "We've known each other a long time. I'm only old enough to be your father, after all. Why make me sound like your grandfather? Next thing, you'll be calling me 'sir,' and I'll have no more to do with you."

"How about Sir Chester, as a compromise?" Stanton suggested. "An interim arrangement, until I get used to the Chester?"

Hazen chuckled. "Agreed. Lawyers always like a compromise—if it's favorable."

Stanton chuckled with him, but he was not quite at ease. Chester Hazen was a local pillar of society and one of the first citizens of Westport, and it was true that Stanton had seen a good deal of him as a fellow member of several political and civic-improvement committees which Hazen either inspired, or financed, or both. But they had associated only as fellow members, not socially. The Hazens belonged to a much older, wealthier and infinitely more settled community within the concentric communities of admen, brokers, successful artists and writers and miscellaneous entrepreneurs. There was plenty of traffic to and fro between the outer concentric rings, but virtually no social penetration of the hard, permanent core of Westport life represented by the Hazens and a few other families like them. Stanton worked constantly with Hazen on committees, yes, but the Hazens never had invited the Wylies to dinner, and the Wylies never had invited the Hazens because it went without saying that the Hazens would have prior engagements. So why, Stanton wondered, the sudden Chester? He was not the sort of man—indeed, the last sort of man—to be impressed by anything like the Chicago award.

Some people in Westport—mostly on the outer concentric rings—said that Chester Hazen was nothing but a rapacious old Wall Street lawyer who had stolen millions in his heyday and now was trying to atone for his former depredations with a pretense of good works. Stanton didn't know whether it was true or not, and didn't care a great deal. It seemed to him that what Hazen was doing at present for the general welfare mattered more than what he might or might not have done forty years ago. Anyway, he was a cultivated and engaging old gentleman who looked as though he might have stepped out of *The Pickwick Papers* or just climbed down from the top of the Liverpool-London stage in one of those old prints. He had a merry face—bright pink cheeks and clear blue eyes with white tufted brows which sprouted like spring tulips. He was half a foot shorter than Stanton, and he had a massive, leonine head of white hair which gave him the appearance of a wigged English barrister. Stanton never saw him without thinking of the lawyer in Conrad's *Youth:* ". . . fine crusted Tory, High Churchman, the best of old fellows, the soul of honor. . . ." Hazen also happened to be a senior partner in a Wall Street law firm with clients like DuPont, Standard Oil and General Electric; Hazen himself had won a million-dollar patent suit for one client within the month. Even at his age he was a bit of an exquisite. He carried a cane, which he didn't need, and he tapped Stanton's suitcase and said, "Off to Chicago, eh?"

"Yes, Mr.—Sir Chester." Stanton smiled.

"Ha! Sir Chester, well, that's all right. Not going to congratulate you again, Stanton, about your honors, know all that. Think I told you last week how pleased—it's great, great!"

"Thank you. I don't know how great it'll be after tomorrow night. I'm supposed to make a speech."

"Speech! Nothing to it!" Hazen flicked his cane. "Listen —tell you a little trick. Something I learned a long time ago, when I tried cases in court. It's a banquet, isn't it? The speaker will introduce you?"

"Why, yes, I suppose so," Stanton said. He was now quite perplexed. Why should Chester Hazen—?

"All right! After you're introduced and stand up, don't start talking right away. Wait a few seconds. Look them over. Look slowly—*slowly,* mind you—from left to right across the audience and then back and forth so you cover as many faces as you can. Then wait another second or two. That makes them wonder whether you're stalling, or whether you've forgotten what you wanted to say, or whether—anyway, you have their attention, main thing. It works. It always works."

"Is that the secret of your success?" Stanton said, smiling. "Hypnotizing juries by staring at them?"

"Never mind. Remember what I say when you stand up behind that table."

"I will," said Stanton. "And thanks for the tip. It certainly comes from one who knows." He expected Hazen to withdraw at this point, but the old gentleman showed no disposition to leave.

"Don't you usually go south about this time of year?" Stanton inquired. "You're not going to sit out one of our Connecticut winters, are you?"

"No, no, I'm too old. The cold gets into my bones, and I stiffen up like a board. No, as a matter of fact, I'm leaving Sunday—be back once or twice a month, of course."

"Mrs. Hazen going down with you, I suppose?"

"Mrs. Hazen? Oh, she's been down all week. Left last Monday with her sister, to open the house."

Stanton frowned in a puzzled way. "That's funny," he said.

"Eh? Funny? What's funny about it?"

"Not her being down South, of course. It's just that I thought I heard Betsy—Mrs. Wylie—say she had been talking to her on the phone this morning, about the Red Cross Drive. I must have misunderstood."

Hazen's head was tilted back. He seemed to be making a concentrated inspection of the thick black power lines strung between high black steel towers marching along the right of way. He half turned to Stanton and started to say something, then stopped. "What's the news this morning?" he asked, glancing at Stanton's paper.

"I haven't looked at it yet." Stanton unfolded his *Times.* The significant headline—the one over the two right-hand columns—read: GROMYKO AGAIN REJECTS U. S.

ATOM PROPOSAL. SAYS BOMB MUST BE SHARED WITH ALL.

"Same thing," he said. "The Russians are still saying 'no.' " He paused and scanned the first paragraph of the story. "I wish that once in a while the peace news could be as good as the war news used to be. Remember the war headlines toward the end? Advance, enemy routed, successful invasion, new landings—victory? Now what have we got?"

"Hmph, see what you mean," Hazen agreed. "Still, I had the idea you were more or less pro-Russian, Stanton? You don't sound it."

Stanton laughed. "A good many people seemed to get that idea. It started with a letter of mine that was published in the Westport *Herald*. I simply pointed out that thirty years after the American Revolution we were a pretty cantankerous and self-conscious nation ourselves, and that maybe the newness of the regime over there had a good deal to do with the way the Russians are behaving. I wrote the letter because I thought it might cut down some of the violent talk I'd been listening to around here, but of course it didn't. People began talking about me as though I were in the pay of the Kremlin.

"No, I'm not pro-Russian," he continued. "I'm not especially anti-Russian, either. I just have no patience with self-righteous dogmatists, whether they're Russians, Republicans, Baptists or anything else. Here's our train," he added, as the blunt green nose of an electric locomotive came into sight down the track and rumbled across the drawbridge over the Saugatuck. Stanton had seen occasions when all traffic on the New Haven was blocked at this point so that a couple of kids in a sailboat could go through the bridge.

He was positive that Hazen would bid him adieu as they boarded the train, but instead the old lawyer said, "Mind if I sit with you?"

"Of course not," Stanton said. "I'd be delighted."

"I'm glad I ran into you," Hazen said, after they were settled. "I nearly called you at your office yesterday."

"So?" Stanton smiled. "I can guess what about—those plans for the youth center, isn't that it? Actually, I drew them up in rough last week, but I haven't submitted them yet because I'm waiting to hear what we can get in the way of materials. You know, we talked about glass brick for the façade? I'm afraid we'll have a tough time getting any before late spring, and we want to have the center finished by then. Of course we could put up a temporary wall and replace it later on when the glass brick is available. How does that strike you?"

"Eh? Yes, yes, I'll recommend it." Hazen coughed in an embarrassed way and looked out the window. "I'd never worry about you doing the plans, Stanton, or anything else you said you'd do. Always know I can depend on you. Not like some of these other fellows we have on the committees, all promises and no performance." He paused. "No, there was something else I thought I might want to discuss with you."

"Well," said Stanton. "Here I am. Shoot."

Hazen shook his head. "This wouldn't be quite the place, I'm afraid. Anyway, it may turn out to be nothing at all."

"You're being very mysterious."

"Am I? Well, that's a lawyer for you. However," he said carefully, "I may want to get in touch with you later today. You going to be in your office?"

"Yes, until traintime. I'm taking the Century."

"Mm. Ah . . . got a pretty busy day ahead?"

"No," said Stanton. "I'm going to answer my mail, if there is any, and then polish my speech a bit—oh, and practice looking at audiences, slowly, left to right," he added with a smile. Hazen did not smile in return. "I don't think I could keep my mind on any work today."

"Well, as I say, I may call you toward the end of the morning. In fact, I might want to drop around to see you. Be all right?"

"Why, certainly." Stanton's expression was bewildered. "But . . . I wish you'd give me some idea of what this is all about?"

Hazen again shook his head. "No, not now. It's just— something. Perhaps nothing. I'll know later. Mind if I look at part of your paper?"

They read in silence until the train paused briefly at 125th Street, then rolled through the jungle of Harlem tenements. From the elevated tracks it was possible to peer down into the bleak, uncurtained windows and glimpse the most intimate and sordid vignettes. Stanton never saw these mean, barren little rooms and the stark, crumbling ugliness of the tenements without a sense of inner protest. What conceivable reason or excuse was there for people living that way, in Manhattan, in 1947? Yet he knew that these buildings along upper Park Avenue were veritable palaces compared with the tenements he had seen in some other slum sections.

"Ah . . . by the way, Stanton—" Hazen's voice startled him—"seen that actor fellow lately?"

"You mean Billy Paige?"

"That's the one."

The train rocketed into the long tunnel leading to Grand Central. Some of the more impetuous commuters stood up and started putting on their coats and hats, moving toward the vestibules.

"Why—" Stanton considered—"I saw him a little while last Sunday. He came out for tennis and stayed for the cocktail party afterward at the club. What makes you ask about him?"

"Just happened to think of him," Hazen replied. "What do you think of that chap, anyway?"

"Well, I don't know. I never thought much about him, one way or the other." Paige was a little too deft, a little too facile, a little too well-dressed, a little too aggressively handsome for Stanton's taste, but he was pleasant enough and seemed to know a lot of funny stories. He was about thirty and had rather suddenly become a prominent Broadway figure on the strength of the leading part in the first big hit of the season.

"These theatrical people—I don't seem to have much in common with them," Stanton said. "They live in a world of their own and they don't have much interest in anything else. At least, I find it hard to talk to them. But Betsy—Mrs. Wylie—gets along with them pretty well. She's interested in the theater."

He reflected that her interest of late had become almost irritating. Betsy pretended a superior knowledge of all phases of stagecraft from playwriting to baby spots, had dragged Stanton to any number of bad plays he didn't want to see, and at times referred to people like the Lunts as "Lynn and Alfred" although she never had met them.

"Paige is sort of a lightweight, if you know what I mean," Stanton went on. "But he's all right; I like him well enough. He's a very good dancer, too—at least, that's what Betsy says. You know, she's very keen on dancing, and I'm much too tall for her. She likes dancing with him."

Hazen's eyes were half closed, and his expression was inscrutable.

"Grand Central!" a conductor bawled from the end of the car. The train slid to a stop alongside the gray concrete platform. Stanton and the lawyer edged into the line of passengers and were propelled through the vestibule.

As they were climbing the ramp to the marble floor of the terminal, Hazen said: "Where'd you meet this Paige fellow, Stanton?"

Stanton had almost forgotten about Billy Paige. He glanced quickly at the lawyer, but Hazen was looking at the floor of the ramp. Stanton said, "Mr. Hazen, why are you so interested in Paige?"

"Oh, just wondered about him—seen him around," Hazen said. "Where'd you meet him?"

"Well—" Stanton had to think about just when he had met Billy Paige—"in Westport, early in the summer. They opened the Playhouse with a revival of *Private Lives*, and Paige had the lead—the ex-husband of what's-her-name, Anna? Something like that."

"Amanda," Hazen said. "Very amusing part."

"Yes. He was good in it, very good. Afterward——"

They passed through the gates above the ramp and emerged in the vast stir and turmoil of the station. They stood there, making a little eddy in the stream of people issuing from the trains.

"Afterward, somebody—I think it was the McRaes—gave a party for the cast. We were invited, and that's how we met Paige. Why, Mr. Hazen?"

The lawyer seemed to be pondering the animated signs on the station walls. On the near side these urged the smoking of Chesterfields and the drinking of Four Roses; on the far side, Alka-Seltzer was recommended for that headachy feeling. Against the tall eastern windows the New Haven had erected a photo-mural glorifying an autumn vacation in the Berkshires. Overhead, golden gods sprawled on the blue vault of the ceiling and tossed casual golden stars back and forth.

Hazen tapped the marble floor with his cane and said, "Ah . . . you will be in your office all morning? Definitely?"

"Yes."

"Well, you may hear from me. Nice to see you anyway, Stanton. I'll get a cab out here. Too old for these subways, you know."

"Mr. Hazen——"

But the old man only nodded, and stepped spryly into the moving crowd. Stanton stared after him for several seconds, frowning. He was conscious of a vague feeling of disquiet, even apprehension, as he walked slowly toward the Lexington Avenue doors and crossed the street to the Chrysler Building. Why should Chester Hazen even be aware of the existence of Billy Paige, let alone have so many questions to ask about him?

Chapter **3**

STANTON's secretary, Miss Rice, was in a fine flutter when he arrived at his office. She was a small, pert, birdlike girl who generated an almost incandescent enthusiasm.

"Oh, Mr. Wylie! So many exciting things are happening to us!" she greeted him. "You should see the morning mail!"

Stanton grinned at her. "You know, Helen, I wish I got as much fun out of this business as you seem to," he said. He tossed his coat and hat onto the sofa and went over to his desk. "Well, what's the score?"

"All sorts of wonderful things!" she gushed. "Here's one from the Civic Improvement League of Omaha. They want you to make a speech out there the first week in November. This one's from the Royal Canadian Society of Engineers, inviting you ~~to attend~~ their convention in Montreal December third and fourth, and make a speech too."

"Gad!" Stanton protested. "There seems to be a general conspiracy to make me stand on a platform and make noises. I'm no lecturer! Anything else?"

"Yes." Miss Rice giggled. "The Harvard School of Architecture wants to know if, as a distinguished alumnus, you would deliver a series of lectures. There's a note from the headmaster of your old school, offering congratulations, and inquiring delicately whether your son isn't about ready for prep school. Are you sending him to Ely, incidentally?"

"No," said Stanton. "Mrs. Wylie decided on St. Paul's."

"Here's an answer from Corning about that glass brick you wanted. They say they can't promise anything less than eight weeks ahead. This one's a query from something called Pacific Industries, in Los Angeles. They want to know if you will help them design what they call a packaged kitchen. They're getting out a line of interrelated equipment to be sold as a unit. . . ." She paused for breath. "This is a letter from a book publisher, asking if you could do a book on new trends in design, what the world will be like twenty-five years from now. . . ."

"Will there be a world twenty-five years from now?" said Stanton. "That publisher is an optimist. Anyway, Walter Teague's already written the book."

"Well, they want another. Why shouldn't there be a world twenty-five years from now, Mr. Wylie? Of course there will be." Miss Rice was not notably gifted with imagination. "Oh, that reminds me—the young lady from *Life* called and asked what space you have on the train, so she can find you this afternoon. And a man called from the *Herald Tribune* asking for an interview they could print in the Sunday edition, but I told them about the *Life* article, so he said they'd wait awhile. We *are* getting famous, aren't we?" she exclaimed, looking flushed and happy.

"Ah, yes," Stanton agreed. "I suppose that's the main thing, isn't it? Well, there must be a few headaches in the midst of all this sunshine. What's the bad news?"

"I was coming to that. Mr. Sanderson called from Long Island, just beside himself, and said the plasterers had walked off the project because of that prefabricated wallboard you ordered—honestly, after the local agreed to use it only a week ago! And the electricians are kicking because those sinks have an electric garbage-disposal unit in the drain. They claim *they* ought to install the sinks, not the plumbers, and the plumbers say *they*—— Really, it's so infuriating! With thousands and thousands of people trying to find a decent place to live, these *fools* haggle over things like that!"

"I know," said Stanton. "They're cutting their own throats, but they don't know it. Well—" he shrugged—"I'll go out to the project Monday and try to persuade the plasterers all over again. If I don't, I suppose I'll have to cancel the wallboard order and let the boys put the houses together with sticks and mud, like the Pueblos. . . . The Pueblos at least finished theirs. I wonder whether we'll *ever* finish Happy Homes. What else, Helen?"

"Oh—oh, yes, General Electric. A letter from Mr. Browning in Schenectady, about that eccentric gear you designed for the magnesium elevator. He says the engineers don't think it's possible to make a sintered part that large, with so many stress points."

"I don't agree with the engineers," Stanton said.

"Well, they're willing to try, but they won't guarantee anything, and they estimate that the die alone will cost $10,000."

"Ouch! The client won't swallow that. What else?"

"The blueprints for the new Galveston airport building. They were blurred; and they have to be done over. . . . The model maker wants another two weeks on that truck job. . . ."

"He's a month late now. I'll give him one more week, no longer. What else?"

"Monsanto—positively no Lucite before the first of the year. And the Airfoam for your self-adjusting theater seat, not before April. But—" Miss Rice looked at her pad— "Lear Avia *can* deliver those quarter h.p. motors you wanted. I guess that's all."

"Hm." Stanton glanced at the pile of letters. "I'll call Sanderson, and you can tell Wilhelm that I want that truck model not later than next Friday, or it's the last work he gets from me. I'll let everything else ride over the week end.

I want to work on my speech. I'd like to give you the day off, Helen, but I may need you for typing later on. But you can leave early."

"Oh, Mr. Wylie—" little Miss Rice stood in front of the desk, twisting her stenographer's pad between her hands—"I *want* to stay as long as you need me. It's so wonderful, the way everything is clicking," she said, rushing her words together. "I'm so proud to be working for you, and I *know* the speech will be sensational."

There was an embarrassing amount of adoration in her eyes and her voice, and Stanton pretended to hunt for something in the file drawer of his desk.

"Can I help you, Mr. Wylie?"

"No, no, Helen." He stood up. There was too much invitation in the girl's manner; he didn't want her behind the desk. "Jake here?" he asked casually.

"Yes, he's in the shop. Mr. Wylie, I wondered——"

"Yes, Helen?"

"After you've made the speech you won't need the manuscript any more, will you?" she said very fast, looking at the floor and twisting the pad. "I wondered—" she faltered—"I wondered whether you'd autograph the original for me and let me keep it. I'd like to have it so much," she finished, almost with a gasp. "You see, I——"

"Helen, of course you can have it," Stanton said gently. He thought, She's behaving like a child, behaving the way I thought Jerry might behave, but never did. This is a bad situation, he added to himself. He turned to the windows and said, "Suppose you call Wilhelm for me now, Helen? I want to talk to Jake for a minute."

"Yes, Mr. Wylie."

It was a small office, too small for Stanton's needs, but the best he could find, and the first office he ever had had for himself. The reception room was not much larger than a closet, and Stanton's own office barely accommodated his necessary furniture and a drawing board, with a few square feet of clear space by the windows where he could pace back and forth when he had a problem on his mind. There was a third room which they called the shop, although it was too cramped for any real production. Stanton's ambition was to get enough space so that he could have his own model department, instead of sending jobs outside, because model building was the part of the work which he most enjoyed.

He walked into the shop and greeted Jake Bundy, his young assistant who had come to him during the summer, fresh out of Harvard. Jake was an agreeably homely, pug-faced youth with black-rimmed glasses and a crew haircut. He was now rummaging about in the racks where they kept samples of new materials.

"Morning, Jake. What's the word?"

"I'm looking for something else to try," Jake said. "I fiddled around with spun glass, but it won't work. See."

Stanton went over to the workbench under the fluorescent-light fixture. There were two oblong pieces of blue Koroseal stretched across the bench, and a fluffy pile of spun glass. The bench also held a small power saw, and an electric drill.

"It's too bulky, for one thing," Jake said. He spread a layer of the glass over one piece of Koroseal, then placed the other strip on top of it. "You see? And I can't figure out a way to bind the glass to the plastic. It would all bunch up every time you put the top up or down."

Stanton usually had several experimental projects going, and this was one of them—a Koroseal top for convertible automobiles. Koroseal had any number of advantages over the conventional rubberized canvas material. It was practically impervious to weather, could be matched to any finish color, and could be kept immaculately clean with a minimum of effort. The problem was to find a durable filler material that could be used between layers of Koroseal to serve as insulation and make the top opaque.

"No, that's no good," Stanton said. "I heard about a new DuPont fabric that might be just the thing—heavy parachute nylon impregnated with styrene. I should think several thicknesses could be laminated."

"Yes, that would do it. We wouldn't have to worry about binding it, either. The Koroseal would fit over it, like an envelope."

"Give DuPont a ring Monday morning, Jake, and have them send us some samples. I don't know what they call the stuff, but Harrison will tell you. Now, why don't you knock óff for the rest of the day? I'm not going to do anything, and there's no reason for you hanging around."

"Well, if you don't need me——"

"No, not a thing. This isn't a good day for working, somehow. Why don't you go out to the track?" he suggested, knowing that Jake had a fondness for improving the breed. "Where are they running now?"

"Empire," said Jake. "I might do that. I've got my eye on a nag in the fifth."

"Sure, good idea," said Stanton. "While you're at it, how about putting down a little bet for me?" He took out his wallet and handed Jake a ten-dollar bill. "I'll split with you."

"Okay. I hope the nag doesn't run backward."

Miss Rice appeared in the doorway. "Mr. Wylie," she said. "The secretary of a Mr. Hazen is on the wire, and wants to know if he can come and see you at two-thirty. She says it's very important."

"Oh, yes," Stanton said with a quick frown. "Tell her I'll be expecting him. Well, good luck, Jake," he added. "Come back from the race with a bundle."

"I'll try," said Jake. "Thanks for letting me off, and the very best to you in Chicago, Mr. Wylie. Not that you'll need any luck out there, of course, but still we'll all be chewing our nails tomorrow night. So long!"

Stanton returned to his office and sat down at his desk. The much edited manuscript of his speech was in front of him, and he leafed through the pages, holding one of the thin brown architect's pencils which Miss Rice kept needle-sharp for him. But he couldn't seem to concentrate, and after a while he got up and moved to the windows. He stood there, looking out at the gray sky and listening to the muted roar of the city which ascended thirty stories from the street. What's the matter with me? Stanton said to himself. Probably one of Hazen's clients has some job or other, and the old man's excited about it. But why—?

Chester Hazen arrived almost on the second of half past two. He seemed to show his age much more than he had in the morning, and there was no merriment in his face when

Miss Rice led him into the office. She helped him off with his coat. He nodded thanks to her, and shook hands with Stanton.

"Sit down, Mr. Hazen," Stanton said. "That armchair there is an odd shape, but it's comfortable."

"No—no, think I'll stay on my feet. *You* sit down, Stanton, wherever you usually sit." He produced a handkerchief and ran it across his forehead. "I hoped I wouldn't have any occasion to make this visit, but I . . . well, here I am."

"You certainly managed to puzzle me a good deal," Stanton said. "I've been wondering what this is about."

"Yes. I'm sorry for that, but I had a reason. Stanton—" the lawyer faced him across the desk—"you aren't going to like what I have to say any more than I like saying it. In fact, it's the hardest thing I've had to do for years."

There was a tap at the door of the office, and Miss Rice entered.

"Yes, Helen?"

"There's a man on the wire from the *American Weekly*," she said. "He's writing a feature story about the new UN development, and he wants to know whether you think there's any way of making the buildings so that they can survive an atom-bomb attack."

"Certainly," said Stanton.

"There is?" Miss Rice asked in surprise. "How?"

"All they have to do is to construct the buildings so that the top stories are a quarter of a mile underground."

"Oh, Mr. Wylie! You don't really want to tell him that, do you?"

"No, I suppose not," Stanton said. "Tell him—tell him there's no possible way of building an atomproof skyscraper. And Helen——"

"Yes, sir?"

"No more calls or interruptions, please, while I'm with Mr. Hazen."

"All right, Mr. Wylie."

"Now?" said Stanton, when Miss Rice closed the door. He sank into his desk chair. "Go on, Mr. Hazen."

The lawyer again used his handkerchief. "You'll have to be patient with me, Stanton, if I seem to tell you this in a round-about way," he said. "I can deal with proxies, and

SEC filing patent litigation, that sort of thing, but this is——"

"Go on, Mr. Hazen."

"Well, to begin with, you understand that my firm handles corporation accounts exclusively. We don't do any criminal law, or any divorce work."

Stanton said nothing. The office suddenly seemed quite chilly, although Hazen's face was shining pinkly.

"But once in a while a client comes to us, and says he wants a divorce, and what should he do about it?" the lawyer continued. "And we help him out to the extent of referring him to a divorce specialist—fellow named Woods. He's honest, and reliable. I. . . I guess I make lawyers sound like doctors, don't I? Talking about referring people to specialists?"

He made a poor attempt at a laugh, then went on: "Anyway, this fellow Woods collects pretty heavy fees from the clients we send him, as you can imagine. It's a valuable connection, and he appreciates it. In return—" he paused—"he occasionally passes along confidential information that he picks up in the course of his own practice and thinks we might be interested in. You follow me?"

Stanton nodded. "What are you trying to tell me, Mr. Hazen?"

The lawyer put up a hand and said, "Be patient with me, Stanton. I want you to understand how I come into this, how it all happened, do you see?"

"All right, Mr. Hazen, I'm sorry."

"Tuesday afternoon I was talking to this Woods about something personal. He asked me if I knew you."

"If you knew me?" Stanton repeated.

"Yes. He had read the newspaper stories about you and noticed you lived in Westport. I told him I knew you pretty well, and he came up with some news, something he'd heard by accident."

"What was it, Mr. Hazen?"

The lawyer took a deep breath. He avoided looking at Stanton. "There is a young person in New York," he said. "Her name is Dreamboat McKenna." He seemed to pronounce the words with difficulty. "Dreamboat McKenna."

"Dreamboat McKenna," Stanton repeated.

"Yes. . . ah . . . her professional name, that is. She formerly was a dancer on the stage, in musical comedies. She now is a . . . ah . . . divorce co-respondent, for hire. You know, the lady in the lacy black negligee who is apprehended in the midtown hotel room with the erring husband?"

"I've heard," Stanton said. "Go on."

"In private life—" the lawyer hesitated—"she is Mrs. Billy Paige."

Stanton stared at him.

Mrs. Billy Paige," he said. "I didn't know Paige was married."

"No. Well, I'm not surprised. They used to be a theatrical team, but for the last few years they've been separated, more or less."

"More or less?"

"They aren't legally separated, but they've been living apart, except when their . . . ah . . . mutual inclinations draw them together, if I may put it that way."

"And—?"

"Apparently they had a bad time together when they were on the stage—starved most of the time, I gather. More than that involved, but I don't know what. Then Paige suddenly hit the headlights, in this new play of his. What's the title?"

"It's called *The Lonely Road.*"

"That's it. That's the play. So it appears that Mr. Paige has been neglecting his wife, this . . . ah . . . this Dreamboat person. Financially, and . . . ah . . . in general. And she——"

"Yes?"

"She is distressed, shall we say? She is planning to do something about it, get revenge on her husband, and——"

"And what, Mr. Hazen?"

"She is getting ready to divorce Paige, Stanton, in New York. You know what that means?"

Stanton nodded.

"She has a lawyer—I might call him a scavenger of the law," Hazen said. "Bad chap, no doubt about it. One of those people we have on the fringes of the profession. Our man Woods doesn't know whether he's put her up to it, or whether she thought for herself and told him to. They haven't done anything yet."

"What is she planning to do, Mr. Hazen? You said she was going to divorce Paige."

"Yes, Stanton. In New York. For adultery. You know, that requires a . . . ah . . . partner."

Stanton reflected that it inevitably took two to break the Seventh Commandment. Reflected idly, at mental arm's length, because he didn't connect with what Hazen was saying, didn't quite understand what he heard.

"And this Dreamboat person is going to sue for divorce and name . . . Stanton . . . name your wife as co-respondent. Having gone that far, I'll tell you the rest of it," Hazen said with a rush. "Woods doesn't know whether they have blackmail in mind, or whether she's a jealous, vindictive woman. . . . Stanton!"

"It's all right. Go on."

"You looked so white, are you—?"

"Yes, yes, go on."

"Here's the worst of it," the lawyer said. He was standing in front of the windows. "They've outlawed alienation of affection suits in New York, but there's a law about . . . adultery. They call it unlawful cohabitation, Stanton, and it's a criminal offense. It could mean a prison sentence, and . . . blackmail would be simpler, Stanton. But this Dreamboat person *may* be one of those women . . . vindictive . . . and the lawyer—— She *may* want most of all to put Paige in jail. And she can do it. And if he goes, there's a chance that your wife might go with him. At least, your name would be—— It's an awful mess, boy."

Stanton had the stunned, dumb, uncomprehending look of an animal.

"You see, when I heard this from Woods, I couldn't believe it. I told him it was impossible, but . . . he knew what he was talking about. We have a fellow in the office, smart fellow, use him as an investigator when we need to. I sent him out to check up, Wednesday. He gave me his report Thursday morning. I . . . I'm afraid there's no argument, Stanton. Your wife has been coming into New York to see this Billy Paige fellow, and——" He sighed. "Don't ask me to go into details, Stanton."

Stanton said nothing.

"This morning, when I asked you all those questions about Paige, I wanted to find out if you knew the situation. It was a . . . possibility. I've been ashamed of myself for imagining it, but—well, lawyers have to think about those things. In one way I hoped you would know about it, condone and so forth, because that—— Well, I wouldn't be here, telling you all this. But of course you didn't, knew you wouldn't, not a suspicion, was there? I nearly called you yesterday afternoon," he went on hastily. "Told you that, didn't I? But I wanted a double check before I talked to you, so I waited to get a second report from our investigator. . . . Oh, Stanton!"

"It can't be true." Stanton spoke from the depths of a nightmare. "It just can't be true. Not Betsy—Mrs. Wylie——"

"I knew that would be your reaction," Hazen said. "It does you credit. Stanton, you're one of the best men I ever knew, last chap in the world that a thing like this should happen to. If there was any doubt whatever I wouldn't have said a word—especially today, when you're ready to make this speech, and all that. I wanted to put it off until next week, but Mrs. Hazen's expecting me down South, and I wasn't able to change my train reservations. So I came today. I thought if you had to know, it would be a little easier coming from a friend than from a stranger. Perhaps I was wrong. As I say, I'm completely out of my depth in this sort of business."

"Not Betsy," Stanton murmured. "Not Betsy."

"I know. Stanton, people can be awful disappointments. Sometimes the people who owe you the most let you down the hardest. See it all the time in the law. Seen it in my own family, for that matter. . . . Take my boy Freddie—a drunkard. Never be anything else. In a sanitarium one month, out for a few weeks, back in the sanitarium again. No good to himself or anyone else. . . . Take my daughter Cynthia—she's in Reno now for her third divorce, says she's going to marry one of those fake cowboys who live off rich fools—I don't mind saying it—like my daughter. That's why I called Woods the other day," he added. "See if he could put a stop to this cowboy idea."

"I'm very sorry, Mr. Hazen. I didn't know."

"Well, there you are. Children brought up with everything in the world—everything, that is, but a few guts and a few brains and a sense of decency. I know I sound bitter; I *am* bitter. I don't know. Maybe it was my fault—mine and Mrs. Hazen's. Maybe we did too much for the kids, or too little, or something. I know we did our best, though, and it wasn't good enough.

"But I think there's something more than that—something we couldn't control," he went on. "I have a feeling there's an evil thing loose in the world. I don't know what it is, but I see it at work all around me—my children, my friends, and——" He left the sentence unfinished. "Something chiseling away at people's values, making a joke of honor and honesty—even of God. I suppose I'm old-fashioned," he continued. "I know it's smart to make wisecracks about the fuddy-duddy ideas of my generation. But at least we had standards and values that we believed in, and when I look at people today it seems to me that what most of them need most badly is faith—faith in something—yes, even the ones who would laugh loudest at what I'm saying. . . .

"We all seem to be living in the shadow of something evil, something terrible," he said with a sigh. "Stanton, I have to leave you now. I'm very tired—an old man, you know. This has been a strain. Here—" he placed a slip of paper on the desk—"here's Woods' phone number, and the address of this . . . ah . . . Dreamboat person. I told Woods you might call him Sunday morning. You can reach him at home until noontime. Well, nothing more I can say, I suppose. Except—" he leaned across the desk and put his hand on Stanton's shoulder—"don't let this get you down, Stanton. You're a very decent man, and there aren't many of us left. We can't afford to lose you."

Stanton scarcely was conscious of the old lawyer's departure. He sat at his desk in a trance. Miss Rice came in and said something to him, but he didn't hear it. His eyes ran back and forth across the first line of his manuscript. "Mr. Chairman, Members of the Committee, Ladies and Gentlemen . . ." but the words made no sense. He was quite surprised, presently, to find himself holding the telephone to his ear. The voice of Supreme Love cried "Peace!" He must have called his home, he supposed, but he had no recollection of it. Supreme Love repeated "Peace!" and Stanton managed to say, "Is Mrs. Wylie there?"

"Who this?" the maid demanded.

"Mr. Wylie."

"Mist' Wylie! Well, I never! You don't sound like yo'self, Mist' Wylie."

"Is Mrs. Wylie there?"

"Mis' Wylie? Why no, the madam ain't home."

"Do you know where she is?"

"You feeling all right, Mr. Wylie? You don't sound——"

"Where is Mrs. Wylie?"

"Why, sir, I don't know."

"She didn't say where she was going?"

"No, sir." Supreme Love sounded frightened. "She came back to the house from the station and changed her clothes. Le's see, some gent'man called on the telephone from New York, and right after that she went out again."

"Didn't she say anything?"

"She just said she wouldn't be home for dinner—at least, that's what I *think* she said. Is something wrong?"

Stanton didn't answer. He looked at the receiver for a moment, then carefully put it down on its base. He pressed a button on his desk, and when Miss Rice came in he said, "Do you have a newspaper out there, Helen?"

"Yes, I do, Mr. Wylie."

"I wonder if you would look up the theatrical section, and find out if the play called *The Lonely Road* has a matinee this afternoon?"

"It doesn't, Mr. Wylie. I happen to know because my aunt wanted to see it this week, and I tried to get tickets for her, but they were sold out. Matinees are Wednesdays and Saturdays."

"I see. Thank you, Helen."

She hovered in the doorway, looking at him with a curious expression. "Thank you, Helen," he said again, and she closed the door.

Somehow he found himself at the windows. He didn't know why he was there, didn't even remember walking across the office from the desk. He stared out, seeing nothing, not blinking his eyes. Backed by the solid gray of the afternoon sky, the window glass dimly mirrored his face. He said to himself, His Betsy. His wonderful girl. God, it was funny. Venice, and Betsy, and the music of the tango orchestra those nights at Chez Vous. Betsy, lying under the mosquito netting. Those beautiful memories of her, those thoughts of her which filled his mind every day, those dreams. God, it was funny. So she was talking with Mrs. Hazen on the telephone, about the Red Cross Drive. Hah! So she couldn't go to Chicago with him, she couldn't just pick up and *go*, like that, because she had so many things she had to do. Hah! The social-events committee. Hah! So Jeremy had to go to the concerts at Carnegie Hall, and Betsy had to take him. Hah! So she was proud of him. Hah! So they would have a little man-to-man talk and they would see that they had nothing to argue about, really, did they? Did they? Did they?

Stanton said these things to himself mechanically, with neither anguish nor passion. He felt nothing, nothing at all. He caught the faint reflection of himself in the glass and tried to find some kernel of thought, or sensation—anything —within himself. But there was simply nothing at all. Absurdly, his mind wandered back to a hot morning in August when he was very young, when he had gone to the dentist to have his first extraction. He remembered the dentist pushing the needle into the roof of his mouth with a little crunch, the acrid taste of the novocain, and everything feeling numb and strange and his tongue wandering across the unfamiliar surfaces, and . . .

The thin, sharp wail of a siren stabbed upward from the avenue. A police emergency truck was scurrying like a green beetle between the traffic lines on Lexington. Somebody is dead, Stanton thought. They send out those emergency trucks only when somebody is dead; the siren is like women keening at a wake; it must be the loudest siren in the world. Now, who can be dead? Is it a man who fell on the subway tracks? Is it someone who turned on the gas and blew up an apartment? Is it another fashionable murder in Turtle Bay? Is it a woman who jumped out a window? Is it a child who accidentally swallowed Drano instead of milk of magnesia, and they suspect infanticide? Is it a bloated corpse someone spotted bumping the piers in the East River?

Or is it me? Stanton asked himself. Are they coming for me? Am I dead?

He felt something jerking at his sleeve—didn't feel it, really—but became conscious of it, became conscious, too, of a voice close by mounting to a scream louder than the siren.

"Mr. Wylie! Mr. Wylie! What's the matter?" It was Miss Rice. "Oh, Mr. Wylie, are you all right?"

"Yes—yes, Helen, I'm all right," Stanton said. "What is it?"

"Oh!" The girl gasped with relief. "You've only got fifteen minutes to make the train, Mr. Wylie. I came in and told you three times, and you didn't seem to . . . I was afraid something was . . . afraid you were ill. Oh, Mr. Wylie!"

"No," said Stanton, wondering at his ability to say anything, since he was dead. "Everything is fine. I'll go to the station."

Chapter **4**

Stanton did everything mechanically—riding down in the elevator; standing on the curb until the lights changed on Lexington Avenue; walking across the street; handing his bag to the red cap; weaving through the crisscrossed lines of people rushing with bent heads and folded afternoon newspapers toward their collective destinations; noting the time on the four-faced clock atop the information desk; pausing while the conductors checked his tickets at the gates; following the porter down the long red carpet stretched on the platform beside the train; entering the vestibule of a long, silver-gleaming car which—he noted irrelevantly—was named "Corinthian Palace"; tipping the porter—overtipping him, to judge from his smile—in the boxlike roomette; hearing the "Boo-ard!" repeated down the line; seeing the latecomers scrabbling into the nearest cars they could reach, their porters tossing baggage into the vestibules after them and grabbing their tips; then the gentle forward lurch of the train, lights on the platform first lazily swimming past the window, then quickening to a run, then flicking; darkness—the brilliant red and green rosettes gleaming everywhere in the jumble of switches, the blurred glass front of the train dispatchers' office, with the shirt-sleeved men and the instant sight of the black control panel behind them, the deepening roar in the tunnel beneath Park Avenue, the accelerating *click-click* of the trucks over the rail points, sounding like steel crocheting needles. . . .

There is primeval excitement in the departure of a train, and even a man as lost as Stanton felt some of it. The Century didn't hesitate, or halt, or proceed diffidently, like ordinary trains. It rolled into the tunnel with vast power and assurance, hit the elevated tracks, and shot through 125th Street with an impact which made the whole station tremble. Ahead, red and amber signals changed to green, and the Century streaked like a silver serpent across the Harlem yards.

A switch engine whistled mournfully on a siding, while in the closing gloom a quivering blue neon sign spelled the name of a celebrated laxative.

Stanton closed the door of the roomette and locked it. He sat down on the couch and stretched out his legs. He leaned against the window and stared down at the rushing steel tracks. Then he closed his eyes. There was some obscure solace in being in that locked steel compartment moving across the land; at least, nothing more could happen to him while he was there.

It was nearly night when he opened his eyes again, roused by a persistent tapping. The train was racing along the banks of the Hudson, and the black surface of the river darkly reflected the scattered lights on shore. Stanton finally opened the door and was confronted by a porter.

"You Mr. Wylie, sir?" the man inquired.

"Yes," Stanton said, and added to himself: I suppose so.

"Young lady in the club car sent you this note," said the porter. He waited in the corridor while Stanton unfolded the paper and read:

"Dear Mr. Wylie: If you feel strong enough to begin the ordeal, I'm holding down a table in the club car, and thought you might like to join me here. But if you'd rather stay put, just tell the porter, and I'll come right back—provided, of course, you're in the mood to start. Nancy Mainwaring, *Life* magazine."

Written against the swaying of the train, the words staggered across the page, and Stanton read the note three times before comprehending it at all. The *Life* article was only a dim and quite fantastic memory. His eyes lingered on the phrase "provided, of course, you're in the mood to start."

"You want to send a message to the young lady?" the porter said at last.

"What? Oh, I—I'll go to the club car."

Stanton handed him a tip, and for no reason at all folded the note into a perfect square and carefully placed it in a vest pocket.

"Thank you, sir," said the porter. "Club car's three cars back."

Stanton moved like an automaton through the narrow corridors, and when he reached the club car he paused in the vestibule, making an aural study of the intricate tapestry of sound inside. He heard the steady *chuck-chuck-chuck* of ice in a cocktail shaker at the bar, the *slip-slap, slip-slap* of cards being shuffled, cards being flipped from gin rummy hands, and the splinters of conversation which rebounded against the muted background roar of the train: "Honestly, my dear, not a *thing* to buy in Paris or London. I really believe Fred when he says either New York or Los Angeles will be the fashion capital. . . . Bought Vanadium at 16, just before . . . And if you can't keep the God-damned schedule any better than that, I told him, I'll take you off the picture and put Abrams on it. . . . Yeah, but wait until the '48 elections. Every time that guy Taft opens his mouth, the Republicans lose 50,000 votes. I'm for Stassen. . . . So I said to the union, okay, I said to them, I said I'll shut down before I'll sign for a closed shop, that's what I said. If you Reds think it's such a cinch to run a business these days I'll turn it over to the union, I almost said. . . . Contract or no contract, before I'd let a daughter of mine behave like *that* with *that* old goat . . . Oh, Wallace, for

Christ's sake. He can go . . . Did you see the crack about Madge and Alex in Hedda Hopper's column this morning? . . . Why, this talk about a recession is nonsense. Prosperity depends on capital goods, and the backlog in heavy industry can carry us for five years regardless of export. It's all a political maneuver, because Truman . . ."

Stanton listened to these fragments of talk without any understanding. He made an absurd translation from his ear to his imagination: he visualized each fragment as a bright little tropical fish darting across the reservoir of sound made by the train, a reservoir filled with components like the long, slow, sad whistle from the engine ahead; the smooth grind of the wheels on the tracks, sounding like a stream of water from a tap; the hollow rush across culverts; the quick sound under bridges like surgical plaster being torn from skin; and the rhythmical break in the symphony as the cars rolled over the rail joints with a tiny coughing sound.

"I don't care *what* they say about these long skirts, my legs are still good enough so——" He heard a woman's voice, and pictured a fat goldfish, all wavy fins, floating up to the reservoir window and bubbling the words. Then a lean, cruel, long-jawed fish darted up and announced: "I'll break her, see? I'll break her. My lawyer——"

The car was foggy with tobacco smoke and crowded from end to end, but Stanton didn't see anyone who looked as though she might be a *Life* writer. Sitting alone at one table was an uncommonly handsome girl with a dramatic streak of white in the deep brown of her hair, but she was much too pretty and much too well-dressed to fit his somewhat shadowy idea of a female journalist. He was the more surprised, then, when she nodded, smiled, and held up a brown mailing envelope with "LIFE" printed in big block letters on one corner. Stanton approached the table, and said, "Miss Mainwaring?"

"Yes," Nancy replied. "You're Mr. Wylie, of course." Her handclasp, Stanton discovered, was surprisingly warm and firm. "I recognized you right away from one of the old pictures in your Harvard yearbook. I must say you haven't changed much."

Oh, but I have, thought Stanton. Aloud he said, "Where

on earth did you find that relic? I haven't seen it for years."

"Oh, we have practically everything in the *Life* morgue."

"How appropriate!" Stanton murmured.

Nancy gave him a brief, questioning glance, and said, "Won't you sit down? Here——" She shifted herself along the circular settee behind the table. "Sit on this side, if you like. There's plenty of room, and I think it'll be easier than talking across the table. It's suddenly awfully noisy in here."

"Yes, it is," Stanton agreed. Somewhere in the car a radio was playing, and the chorus of a song was superimposed on the mingled sounds of the train. Stanton slid into the deep gray cushions beside Nancy. Just as some of the atavistic thrill of the Century's departure had penetrated the wall around his feelings, so he experienced a small, deep involuntary response to the proximity of this girl. Nancy was wearing a tan gabardine suit and a ruffled white silk blouse with smoky mother-of-pearl buttons, caught at the throat with a crescent-shaped gold pin set with diminutive pearls. Her brown alligator pumps obviously were brandnew, and so was her matching brown alligator bag. But in spite of the newness and obvious costliness of her clothes and the general perfection of her surface, she somehow avoided the hard, kiln-baked, enameled look of contrived elegance which steals so much femininity from the women who are able to afford it, making for the robotlike beauty of models in the fashion magazines, embalmed, machine-made, precision-fitted. Their patina is so exquisite that it is self-defeating; around their necks they wear invisible placards which say: DON'T TOUCH!

Stanton always was vaguely frightened by such women; more important, they left him cold. But this girl, this Miss Mainwaring, this female with the firm, warm handshake, this girl had the small, superficial, significant flaws which made her a human being instead of a painted marionette, just as certain flaws make a perfect emerald, while a flawless stone invariably is a counterfeit. The white splash in the hair above her temple was a flaw, he supposed, yet it made her brown hair even browner, more glistening. The slight tilt of her brown eyes was another flaw, but it only intensified the snapping aliveness of them. The old ivory tint and smoothness of her skin was flawed by tiny lines on her forehead, yet somehow they emphasized the petal-like quality of her complexion. Her face wasn't really pretty— the wan, almost rueful little-girl expression was a flaw— but it was a humorous, sensitive, articulate face with tremendous vitality, and when it was activated it became beautiful, or so it seemed to Stanton.

He decided first that Nancy must be a very comfortable sort of person. Then he decided that she was a very real, adult person; next, that she was more than that—a woman, a very real woman, warm and earthy and fragrant with sex, very sure of herself, very much aware and proud of the fact of her sex. She was the antithesis of those stereotyped, denatured doll-women in the magazines. Everything she did or felt or said or thought would be a reflection of her sex, and every part of her, every pore of her, not only cried to be touched and caressed, but was redolent with warmth and promise. Into Stanton's mind as he looked at Nancy came the words of Shakespeare's timeless description of Cleopatra:

> *Age cannot wither her, nor custom stale*
> *Her infinite variety: other women cloy*
> *The appetites they feed, but she makes hungry*
> *Where most she satisfies: for vilest things*
> *Become themselves in her, that the holy priests*
> *Bless her when she is riggish. . . .*

He didn't immediately realize that Nancy's voice in a way mirrored the whole woman. It was flawed by a slight roughness in the lower registers, but it was warm, alive and eager, drenched with the promise of her sex, and when she spoke again it struck a chord which vibrated some sympathetic string in Stanton's consciousness.

"I hope I didn't disturb you, Mr. Wylie, sending the porter back with my message? I was afraid you might have forgotten all about the interview."

"As a matter of fact," said Stanton, "I had."

"What! Forgotten you were to be interviewed by *Life!*" Nancy exclaimed. She gave him another swift, questioning glance and saw that he wasn't joking. What's wrong with this man? she asked herself. Where is he? He seems so far away, so removed, so remote.

"I'm afraid so. I—I've had a good deal on my mind this afternoon."

"Those are harsh words, suh. You are speaking of the publication I love."

"No offense, Miss Mainwaring. Frankly, I don't think it's going to be much of an interview. I don't see how you can make an article out of anything I have to say."

"Well! This is certainly new and different," Nancy said.

"Is it? Why?"

"Oh, for one thing, most of the people I interview think that they're giving me the biggest story I ever heard. They pretend to be modest about themselves for the first ten minutes. But I can always tell. They're usually shaky and overawed by the prospect of a *Life* interview. But——" But I guess you wouldn't be shaky and overawed by much of anything, would you, Mr. Wylie? she reflected.

"How about a drink?" she asked. "What will you have?"

"Well——" Stanton hesitated. "Won't you have one with me?"

"Later perhaps. The first five rounds positively must go on my expense account. Anyway, my editor particularly told me to buy you a drink. Steward!"

On the chromium stands the highball glasses rattled with a noise like snare drums. The white-coated Filipino traversed the narrow aisle between the outthrust feet with the agility of a cat walking a fence, effortlessly balancing a tray on his right hand. He paused at Nancy's call and said "Please?" with an agreeable white smile.

"What'll it be, Mr. Wylie?"

"Why——" Stanton again hesitated. "I'll take a Scotch and soda."

"You will?" Nancy asked in surprise, and immediately added: "Two Scotch and sodas. Ballantine for me, if you have it. Does that suit you, Mr. Wylie?"

"That will be fine. Anything."

"Yes, miss." The steward resumed his feline progress along the aisle, and Nancy said, "By the way, Mr. Wylie, did our photographer get the pictures yesterday?"

Stanton nodded. "He came to the office yesterday morning," he said. "He was there about two hours."

"Oh. Who was it—do you happen to know? I haven't been in the shop the last two days, and I don't know what's been going on."

"I should know, but I'm afraid I don't. He was quite tall, with red hair, and he brought in dozens of gadgets. I asked him about them, but he didn't seem to hear me. I thought he was deaf."

Nancy laughed—a warm, cheerful sound—and Stanton edged a bit closer to her.

"You were quite right, Mr. Wylie—he *is* deaf. That was Ossip Brancowski, one of our more eccentric staff members."

"Well, at least, he looks like a *Life* photographer," Stanton said. "Whereas you——"

"Whereas I what?"

"I was going to say, you surprised me. You don't look like a *Life* writer."

Nancy laughed. "Just how should a *Life* writer look, Mr. Wylie?"

"Oh, I don't know," Stanton said uncomfortably. He felt a tendency to blush. "I pictured someone rather dowdy, I suppose."

"I get it!" Nancy hooted. "The intrepid girl reporter at the end of a hard day in the city room, is that it? Scraggly hair, and a chewed-up pencil behind her ear? Dandruff on her collar, dirty fingernails, and perspiration stains under her arms? Stocking seams not straight? But a wild light of triumph in her bloodshot eyes because she's just turned in the scoop of the decade? Something like that?"

"I have a suspicion that you're ribbing me," Stanton said. "Are you?"

"Why, Mr. Wylie, of course not! A sincere, respectful attitude is essential to the success of an interview—that's one of the first things we learn. I must confess," she added, "that this isn't my ordinary working uniform, and sometimes I *do* look like the intrepid girl reporter. No, I bought this outfit for a trip to Bermuda. I'm actually supposed to be on a vacation now, but it was washed out at the last minute."

"Not on my account, I hope?"

"Mm. Well, partly. It doesn't make any difference, really, I'll go down next week instead of this, that's all."

"Still," Stanton objected, "I hate to think that I'm responsible for you sitting here instead of on a beach in Bermuda."

"The beach will keep."

The Filipino steward arrived opportunely, gliding up as silently as a canoe. "Your drinks, miss," he said, first placing the highballs on the table, and then a check.

"Please let me do this, Miss Mainwaring," Stanton said. "I'd feel better if——"

"No," Nancy said decisively. "My boss would be offended, and you wouldn't want to offend him, would you?" She had the money ready in her hand, and gave it to the steward. "Thank you, keep the change," she said, and to Stanton: "You know, I didn't expect you to order that."

"Order? Order what?"

"The Scotch and soda. I more or less expected you to ask for a lemonade, or a Coca-Cola."

"You did? Why?"

"Oh, I interviewed an old friend of yours this morning. He told me you never touched the stuff. Is that true?"

"Well, ordinarily——" Stanton began. "Good Lord!" he exclaimed. "I knew you people were very thorough, and all that, but I—who was it?"

"A man named Frank Bassett."

"Bassett! *Shrimp* Bassett! Why, I used to room with him at prep school, at Ely."

"Yes, I know. Apparently he thought a good deal of you."

"But I haven't seen him for years. Where is he? What's he doing?"

"He seems to be doing very nicely. He has a paint and varnish business in Newark, and he lives in Red Bank. That's where I was this morning, interviewing him at home. He has two daughters and a very attractive wife."

"I'm glad to hear it, but——" Stanton was mystified. "Of all people, how could you smoke out Shrimp Bassett for an interview? And why?"

Nancy laughed and picked up her highball. "Here's to you, Mr. Wylie," she said, clinking her glass against his. "You know—I hope it cheers you up a little—I'm beginning to be glad to be sitting *here*. I talk to so many pretentious bores in the course of the job, it's reassuring to interview a man who seems to be so—" she paused, searching for a word, and looking at him squarely—"genuine," she finished. "By the way, that's a very handsome ring you're wearing." She glanced at his hands. "May I see?"

"Surely." Stanton drew the ring from his finger and passed it to her. It was a heavy gold seal ring, the face deeply etched with a device of a dragon transfixed by a lance.

"Most impressive," said Nancy. "What's the motto?"

"Nil nisi bonum."

"Mm. That means 'The best is none too good,' or words to that effect, doesn't it?"

"Not quite," Stanton replied. "It means 'Nothing unless it is good.'"

"Oh, yes. My, that takes some living up to, doesn't it? How do you make out, Mr. Wylie?"

"Is there any answer to a question like that?" He raised his glass. "Here's to *you*, Miss Mainwaring. I'll try not to be a pretentious bore, but I can't promise anything." He sipped the highball. The sharp, sweetish liquid prickled his unaccustomed tongue, burned the back of his throat. He grimaced, and put down the glass. "To get back to Shrimp Bassett, I'd still like to know how you came to interview him?"

"Elementary, my dear Wylie. I had your Harvard yearbook, which told me where you prepped. I didn't have enough time to go up to Ely, but I called the school and talked with a couple of masters who were there during your era."

"Who?" Stanton inquired.

"Coming to that. One was named Vail."

"Oh, the Frog! We called him the Frog. He was the French master for the upper forms."

"Yes. The other was a Mr. Byer."

"Johnny Byer! Is *he* still there?"

"He seems to be."

"He used to teach math, and coach the football team."

"Yes. He said you were pretty good in both departments. Anyway, he volunteered to send me some old copies of the

Ely Register. Very revealing, Mr. Wylie. You were a well-rounded character, according to all accounts. Head prefect in the sixth form; captain of the crew; fullback on the football team; voted the man who had done the most for Ely; winner of the Founders' Medal for public speaking——"

"Oh, stop it! That's enough! Where does Bassett come in?"

"Why, the *Register* said you roomed with him for three years, and in those very obscure items in the section called 'School Notes'—inspired title—there were a lot of references to you and Bassett: pranks and midnight pillow fights and so forth. He sounded like a logical man to interview on the subject of Stanton Wylie—so I did. Satisfied?"

Stanton laughed and said, "At least, I understand now the way *Life* digs up those odd little facts in the close-ups. I've often wondered. Do you always use this Scotland Yard technique on your subjects?"

"Yes, more or less, and when it's a rush assignment, like this, we have to. You know this piece is in an early form that has to go to bed on Tuesday. Anyway, I'm glad I met your old roommate. He's awfully nice."

"Yes," Stanton agreed. "I feel conscience-stricken, not having seen him in all these years. I'll make a point of calling him next week. It's so stupid, the way we let old friends drift away."

"I know he'd appreciate it," Nancy said. "I gather he was something like a mascot of yours, in school."

"Mascot?"

"Oh, mascot, or hero-worshiper, or whatever you want to call it. You see—" Stanton could almost feel the deep-brown kinetic gaze of Nancy's eyes—"he told me about the barrel."

"The barrel?"

"Don't tell me you've forgotten that—you couldn't. And Bassett certainly hasn't. He'll remember it all his life."

Stanton hadn't forgotten the barrel. On the contrary, he remembered it with the frigid clarity of detail of a Breughel landscape. It was a massive, antique, brassbound beer barrel which had been bought in England by the Rector and put to use in the common room at Ely as a wastepaper receptacle. And Shrimp Bassett was one of the smallest boys in school—small, quiet, with a gentle, studious face and a spinal deformity which ruled him out of athletics. He would just fit into the barrel, and one cold Saturday night in February after the monthly dance with the girls shipped down by bus from Miss Hall's in Pittsfield fifty or sixty boys in blue serge suits were horsing around the common room when someone shouted, "Let's put Shrimp in the barrel!" At first it was casual fun. Shrimp was a New Boy, and New Boys had to expect a certain amount of torment. No masters were in the common room at that time, that night, and Shrimp was hoisted aloft by half a dozen flushed and burly youths and was lowered into the barrel. There was a general yelling and uproar while Shrimp looked around with big, reproachful eyes and a sad, broken smile. Cheerful Hoover jazz drifted down from a score of wind-up Victrolas in the dormitory above. Then someone pushed Shrimp's head down and snapped the lid on the barrel. No one in the room had anything against Shrimp Bassett, but something like a lynch-mob spirit seemed to come over them. Someone else tipped the barrel over and gave it a push. . . .

Until then, Stanton—a New Boy, and Shrimp's allotted roommate—had hovered nervously on the outskirts. He didn't like what was going on, but he didn't know what to do—if anything. But when the barrel was tipped over, and pushed, and went spinning and caroming around the common room, with Shrimp inside it, Stanton acted, coldly, almost unconsciously. He pushed through the circle, caught the barrel, set it upright, opened the lid and released his roommate. Shrimp had bruises on his forehead, and he limped, retching, out of the common room. Then Stanton walked over to the boy who had started the business, and without saying a word punched him in the face so hard that he reeled against the wall and started bleeding from his nose and his mouth. . . . The bell rang then, and they scattered to the dormitories. Stanton went to his room feeling excited, and watery-weak in all his muscles. The cubicle was dark, and he lay down on the cot without taking his clothes off. Cold blue winter moonlight was pouring through the window, and Shrimp was huddled on the wall side of his cot, quietly sobbing. Stanton wanted to go over and say something, do something, but instead he gruffly said, "Bassett, shut up, will you? I want to sleep."

The sobbing stopped, but Stanton didn't sleep. The next morning after Sunday chapel, he said it again. Shrimp approached him as they were filing out of the stiff, chilly, High Church chapel. "Wylie, I'm sorry I kept you awake last night," he said. His voice was soft, his face was soft, his eyes were soft. "I won't forget."

"Bassett, shut up, for Christ's sake, will you?" Stanton barked. Bassett smiled at him, and Stanton smiled back. After that they were the best of friends. Stanton progressed to the more conspicuous honors which Ely offered, while Bassett earned the quiet distinction of making the highest College Board grades in the school's history. Besides, Stanton learned more trig from Bassett than he ever did from Johnny Byer. . . . And now Shrimp had a paint and varnish business in Newark, two daughters and a very attractive wife in Red Bank. It seemed an incongruous destiny.

"Let's not talk about the barrel any more," Stanton said.

"Have you been talking about it, Mr. Wylie?"

"Why——" He finished the highball, and Nancy flagged the Filipino. "No, I guess we haven't, at that. I was thinking about it, though."

"You were very far away, weren't you? I watched your face."

"You started quite a long train of memory," he said. "What else did old Shrimp tell you?"

"Oh, lots of fascinating things. About you singing in the choir, and being so good that you did a solo of a hymn at a Commencement service. What was the hymn, Mr. Wylie? Your friend Bassett couldn't remember it."

"Why, I don't know," Stanton muttered in embarrassment.

Nancy looked at him, and thought, Why, he's actually blushing! How sweet! Mr. Wylie, you're almost too good to be true. Do you know that?

"Come now, what was it?" she said. "I don't think you could forget the hymn any more than the barrel."

"I guess it was *'Ein Feste Burg'*—'A mighty fortress is our God.' I always liked that one. Do you know it?"

Nancy nodded, and said, "Yes. I've always liked it, too. 'A mighty fortress is our God, whose goodness faileth never.' Is that right?"

"Yes, that's right."

The steward reappeared with fresh drinks, and this time Stanton produced his wallet before Nancy could open her purse. "There, that's better," he said, when he had paid the check. "Now at least we're even."

"The next round is positively on me," Nancy said. She eyed his highball. "I've wondered whether these religious activities of yours had anything to do with your not drinking—or not drinking most of the time."

"No, there's no connection at all," Stanton said. "I don't mind telling you the reason, but I wouldn't want you to use it in the article."

"Well——" Nancy paused. "Ordinarily I don't like to listen to off-the-record statements."

"Ordinarily I don't make them," Stanton said. "But somehow you make me want to talk. You're very persuasive." This was only partly true, as he well knew. Something—possibly the whisky—was boring through the protective curtain of shocked numbness which had mercifully shielded his mind for the past few hours, and now he was fighting to keep his thoughts away from—that. Talk—incessant talk, talk about anything—was an anodyne.

"I *am* curious," Nancy admitted. "So if you want to tell me, I'll keep it off the record."

"All right," Stanton said. "Part of it is that I'm just not a good drinker. Maybe I'm allergic to alcohol. Anyway, back in the old days whenever I had much to drink I always seemed to end up doing foolish things."

"Such as?"

"Oh, just damn fool things. Climbing flagpoles. Trying to steal the Sacred Cod out of the Boston State House. Breaking windows. Riding cab horses in Central Park. Getting into fights. Insulting people. You know."

"I don't believe that last item, begging your pardon, Mr. Wylie. I don't think you'd ever insult anyone, drunk or sober."

"Well, I did. Lots of times. That was part of the reason I decided to stop. It wasn't any great sacrifice, because it

61

never made much difference to me, one way or the other. But the real reason I stopped was that I had an accident."

"Automobile?"

"Yes."

"Were you hurt?"

"No, not much. A gash in my head, and a couple of broken ribs. But the girl with me——" He paused and sighed.

"Was it bad? Was she killed?"

"No," Stanton said. "It was worse than that. She went through the windshield, and it tore her face to pieces, and she landed with a broken back. She hasn't walked since." He sighed again and went on quickly: "I wasn't drunk, you understand, but she'd come down to Cambridge for the Yale game with me, and we had a few drinks out of a flask in the stadium, and a few more afterward at a tea dance at the Copley, and then we went to the football dance and had a few more, and then . . ."

His face was grim. "She was at Smith, and her family were spending Sunday with her, so she wanted to get back to Northampton that night. We missed the last train, and . . ."

"And you drove her to Northampton?"

"Almost to Northampton," Stanton said. "It was a cold night, a hell of a cold night." He remembered it so vividly that he hunched his shoulders, and almost shivered. "I had the flask in my coat pocket, and a bottle in the glove compartment, and we had several drinks on the way, just to keep warm. I suppose I was driving too fast. Then there's a bad curve about eight miles out of Northampton on the turnpike, and . . ." With devastating clarity he could see the long patch of glare ice on the road in front of the headlights, could feel the nauseating sideways spin of the car and could hear the shriek of the tires when they left the ice and burned across the asphalt. Then the plunge across the shoulder, sickening impact against the tree trunk, sound of breaking glass, smoke and fire from the motor, and then . . . blood on the snow, a grotesquely twisted figure in a black evening dress moaning quietly at the base of the tree, and a red evening coat with a black taffeta lining hanging in shreds on the radiator cap.

"I honestly don't know whether the drinks had anything to do with it, but maybe they did, and I—just stopped, that's all. I don't like to drive a car, either. Never have liked to, since that happened."

"Do you ever see the girl?"

"Not very often, because she lives in Pasadena. But I write to her every month or two. She's amazingly cheerful. The last I heard, the doctors were going to try some new operation on her back, and there was a chance she might be able to get around on crutches—I don't know how it came out. So that's the story," he finished. "These are the first drinks I've had for—I can't remember how long. Except for a glass of champagne on New Year's Eve with my wife."

"Oh, yes," Nancy said. "I understand she's extremely attractive." Now what's wrong with *that* remark? she asked herself, noticing the change in his expression. "I hope the strain of the interview isn't responsible for knocking you off the wagon, Mr. Wylie?"

Stanton took a swallow of the highball and shook his head. "No," he said. "No. It's . . . something else."

Something you definitely don't want to talk about, Nancy told herself. So I won't ask you.

"What's that song?" Stanton asked suddenly.

Nancy listened for a moment, and said, "It's called 'Someone To Watch over Me.' Is it reminiscent?"

"A little," Stanton said. 'Someone To Watch over Me.' Just what I need, he reflected. Would you like to take on the job, Miss Mainwaring?

"It dates from the early twenties. Does it carry you back to your first kiss in the moonlight?"

"Something like that. It's a pretty song."

"Yes. 'Extraordinary how potent cheap music is,' as Noel Coward used to say."

"What? What's that from?"

"It's a line from *Private Lives.*"

"*Private Lives,*" Stanton repeated. "Do you happen to know it? Which character?"

"Why, I don't think I——" Nancy's forehead wrinkled. "Yes, I do, too. It was Amanda, in Act I, after she runs into

63

her ex-husband at the hotel when she's on her honeymoon. She runs out on her new husband and elopes with the old one. How's that for remembering?"

"Very good," Stanton said. His voice was barely audible, and Nancy looked at him and thought, Mr. Wylie, you baffle me, you really do. You are one of the strangest men I've ever met. What is it I say or do that puts that absolutely lost look on your face? What is eating you, my friend?

Stanton turned to the window and looked out with cloudy, disconsolate eyes. It had commenced to rain. The drops bounced against the glass and flew back in parallel streaks. The telegraph poles sprinted past, and a yellow gleam from the train windows raced along the taut wires. In the dark obscurity beyond, the landscape slowly rolled and heaved against the solid sky. The quiet farmland of western New York was hibernating in the autumn rain, and the dim lights of a house far out in the wet earth crossed the window like a distant ship at sea. Then there were more lights, closer, winking and flashing, and suddenly an echoing clatter as the train plunged through a little town, past a square red-brick station with a wet newspaper glued to the platform, and a man sitting on a baggage truck, swinging his legs. Automobile headlights flaring behind a white crossing gate, red blinker, faint sound of a bell . . . darkness, and again the long, slow roll of the sleeping fields.

Private Lives . . . Act I . . . "Extraordinary how potent cheap music is" . . . Amanda on her honeymoon, running into her ex-husband. That was Billy Paige. Stanton tried to concentrate on something which would keep him from thinking about Billy Paige, but it was no use now; the protective curtain had been torn away, and pictures of the actor flicked through his mind like frames in a strip of movie film. He saw him as he had seen him first, on the stage of the Westport Playhouse, tall and easy-moving, easy-smiling, wearing a white dinner jacket and a maroon cummerbund, and delivering Noel Coward's romantic nonsense in a tone so suggestive and caressing that even the most thoroughly dehydrated dowagers in the audience sighed and shifted in their seats and glanced speculatively at their more or less moribund spouses, who were pouchy and paunchy and had jowls of red-veined flesh hanging from their jaws and tucked up under their ears like velvet portieres tied back on windows. . . . Paige after the play, at the wheel of a little black convertible, top down; lovely, warm summer night; stars; and just enough breeze to make the treetops hum: Paige with his brown face, shining white smile and jet-black hair, careless strand out of place on his forehead, altogether looking like an accessory to the polished automobile, and Betsy saying, "Stan, I'll ride with Mr. Paige and show him the way," and jumping into the car before Stanton had a chance to suggest that Mr. Paige might find the way by following them in their own car. They had a ten-minute start before Stanton was able to get out of the parking lot, yet he arrived at the McRaes' ahead of them. . . . Paige at the McRaes' party, whirling beautiful Betsy in her white net evening dress with the little black patent-leather bows, after they had cleared the dining-room floor and turned on the phonograph. It was—he had to think of the tune when he had seen their heads and bodies so close— "Zing Went the Strings of My Heart." Extraordinary how potent cheap music is. The very late good nights, and the distance of Betsy on the drive home. It hadn't made any difference then. He'd been glad that Betsy enjoyed dancing with Paige, glad that she was so pleased with dancing with an actor, pleased that . . .

Well, this interview seems to have bogged down, Nancy Mainwaring said to herself. And I'm ravenous. She drained her highball, and said to Stanton, "Mr. Wylie, are you in favor of dinner? I missed lunch today." Mr. Wylie, Stanton Wylie, where are you? Nancy was thinking. What are you looking at out there? What's the matter? Can I help you?

Stanton pulled himself back from the window. He said, blankly, "What?"

"I just invited you to have dinner with me," Nancy said. "I'm hungry, and we can have another drink at the table."

"Fine," Stanton said. "Let's have another drink at the table."

He tried very hard to work up some great hatred of shining, black-haired Billy Paige, but he couldn't do it. After all, most of the men he knew were attracted to Betsy— paternally or flirtatiously—and he took it for granted that any man who met her would be as captivated as he had been all these years. So Billy Paige was just another man who liked Betsy. Betsy . . . Betsy . . . Betsy . . . How could you? How? How? Why? How?

And how, he asked himself, how could he, Stanton, have been so blind to what was going on? Granted that the injured party always seemed to be the last to learn the truth about affairs of this sort, how could matters have reached such a stage without his having the slightest suspicion? It was so easy now to look back and read the signs, incredible that he had totally missed their meaning. The number of times Betsy had gone into town to watch Paige rehearsing *The Lonely Road*. The number of times Paige had come out for week ends, and the way Betsy maneuvered things so that he quickly was accepted by their Westport group, yet remained her exclusive beau. The mysterious telephone calls abruptly broken off. The letters and postcards from Skowhegan when the play opened there in the summer theater. The sudden silence which had come over the men that Saturday afternoon when Stanton wandered into the locker room at the club; of course, they had been talking about Betsy and Paige, but at the time he hadn't paid any attention to their strained manner, or to the way they all seemed to clear out of the locker room when ordinarily they were so cordial.

And there were other things, too—small incidents which had been obscure or meaningless when they occurred, but now were painfully explicit. The Broadway first night of *The Lonely Road*, for instance, when Betsy had organized a Westport claque which filled the better part of three rows in the center of the orchestra and put on a demonstration noted by the critics the next morning, and which earned a scathing mention in Winchell's column a few days later.

Stanton had been out of town for ten days before the opening, didn't know anything about the preparations and was embarrassed to find himself part of a cheering section, especially since *The Lonely Road* was a good play, an obvious hit, and Billy Paige was perfectly cast. It was all juvenile, silly, unnecessary, and he had resented it, but when he walked out to the lobby with the group during the entr'acte he didn't say anything, because he was very weary, and besides he was thinking about the City, whether it was more efficient to have trucks unload in the subcellars of the skyscrapers around the park, or whether it would be better to have a separate utility center removed from the City, with freight packages routed on endless belts to the skyscrapers, through tunnels. That would be best, but it would cost too much, and he ruled it out. He was planning the City to be built, to be lived in, not to be dreamed about. And there were so many things that had to be compromised, because they cost too much.

"You'd like that girl, she's your type," Betsy had said to him in the smoky lobby. "That Barbara girl, who plays Billy's sister-in-law."

"My type?" Stanton said. "You're my type, sweet one." He knew he sounded banal, but he was too tired to care. "Betts, can we go home after the play? Do we have to go anywhere?"

"Why . . . uh . . . we're having a celebration at Sardi's, in Billy's honor," Betsy said. "We can leave after that. It won't be late."

But it was late, very late. From Sardi's they had gone on to the Stork, and from the Stork to Morocco, where Betsy created a sensation dancing with Paige, and everyone but Stanton ordered double Scotches when the bar service stopped at four o'clock, so that it was nearly dawn when they finally collapsed into bed in a room at the Plaza. Stanton hadn't given much thought that night to the curious persistence with which Betsy kept trying to pair him off with Barbara, the girl who was supposed to be his "type," but now he saw clearly enough that it was a deliberate attempt to promote an affair (which Barbara patently would have welcomed) so that she would have a freer hand with Paige and at the same time ease her conscience. That is, if she has a conscience, he added, as an afterthought. But I suppose she has, he reflected. He thought back over the enormous day, and speculated: I suppose all that quarreling at breakfast was intended to work up a lot of resentment so that she wouldn't feel so guilty about—— He checked himself.

Then there was that peculiar night when—on Paige's invitation—they went (or, rather, Betsy went, and Stanton tagged along) to the party in a murky Thirteenth Street studio, for the greater profit of something called the International Citizens' Committee for the Improvement of Negro-White Relations. The Committee was the usual Communist-front organization, more thinly disguised than most, and the party drew the usual astounding range of people.

There even was a bona fide Negro on display at the party, as well as a drunken girl who—no doubt inflamed by the recent writings of Sinclair Lewis—announced to everyone that she was one-thirty-second Negro, and that she intended to have a hysterectomy before she got married. Altogether, it was the sort of gathering which fastidious Betsy ordinarily would have fled from in horror, and Stanton kept fidgeting around the edges (trying to avoid a fairy who put a limp arm on his shoulder and said, "Don't think it hasn't been charming, old man.") and wondering why Betsy didn't want to leave, why she had to stay on until the party disintegrated and they dropped Paige at his hotel on the way up town.

Well, there was no more wondering about that, but what baffled him was the cold treachery of her behavior. Now, if Betsy had come to him (he told himself) and said I'm tired of being married to you, or I'm just tired of marriage, or—even—I've fallen madly in love with another man, I couldn't help myself, you see, it's just one of those things, he would have—well, he didn't exactly know what he would have, but indubitably it would be—well, anyway, he could have understood something like that, but the cheap, backsliding way this had come about he couldn't understand at all. What did people do in these situations? What were they supposed to do—grin and bear it? What was *he* going to do? Ah, that was the question, and when he asked it his thinking ran into a stone wall. From ahead he heard a dull whistle.

He was genuinely surprised to find himself stabbing at a chicken pie in the diner of the Century. The train slowed, and he felt the closing backward pull of the brakes. They came abreast of a fast freight, and he could read some of the names on the cars—Great Northern, Central of Georgia, Canadian Pacific, Canadian Pacif—New York Central, Pennsylvania, Pere Marquette, N. Y., N. H. & H., Nickel Plate, Burlington, Every Where West, Chesapeake & Ohio, Lackawanna, C., M., St. P. & P., Santa Fe, the Grand Canyon Route, Erie, Northern Pacific, Magnolia—G.A.T.X., Pacific Fruit Express, Pennsylvania, Baltimore & Ohio, Cotton Belt, New York Central, New York Central, Bangor & Aroostook, Baltimore & Ohio, Southern, Katy—the window fogged with steam as they passed the front end of the train, and Stanton heard the rasping pant of a 4-6-4 locomotive, then saw the yellow beam from the engine's headlight spilling along the glistening tracks.

"Mr. Wylie," Nancy said, "would you mind very much if I asked you what you were thinking just then? I was watching you, and I couldn't help wondering."

"Why——" He wondered what he actually had been thinking about as he read the names on the freight cars. Then he realized that deep down he had been thinking about a small boy named Stanton Wylie who was making his first overnight train trip and sitting for hours in the dark lower berth with his forehead pressed against the window, staring out with unblinking excitement at the kaleidoscopic panorama unreeling outside. To that small boy the names on the cars would have been more than names; they would have been symbols of the wealth and power of a nation, a continent, a hemisphere. But now, now it was just another freight train, passing in the night, and the names were only that.

"Why, I was thinking about that train . . . and how, when I was very young, I would have got a terrific kick out of it, whereas now I look at it and say to myself, 'There's a freight train,' and what of it? I suppose I was thinking that it's too bad we seem to lose so much capacity for surprise and enthusiasm when we grow up. Or at least men do. Is it the same with women?"

"What a very strange question, Mr. Wylie."

"Strange? Why?"

"Do you really think that men and women are so different? You're saying, aren't you, that the more experience you have, the less there is to discover?"

"Yes, that's about it."

"Well then, how could women escape that, any more than men?"

Stanton nodded, and said, "You're right."

"Of course, it happens in different spheres and different terms, since most girls aren't particularly interested in freight trains," Nancy went on. "But——" Then she was interrupted.

A sour, hate-drenched voice—the voice of a middle-aged woman on the verge of crying—announced: "Goddamn you, anyway!"

And the answer, thick and bibulous, came in a braying tone: "Oh, God damn me, anyway. Well, God damn you, you God-damn stringy old bitch!"

Then the crying, rasping rather than plaintive. It came from a table diagonally across from theirs, and Nancy and Stanton automatically looked around. In the discreet gray interior of the Century diner this unseemly dialogue and more unseemly outbreak of emotion were shocking in the extreme. All the well-behaved quiet folk turned and inspected the vulgarians.

Stanton saw a thin woman with a face out of a Grant Wood printing, bony, diamond-speckled hands clawing her bowed face while she sobbed and muttered and with her elbow knocked over a bowl of soup.

She was wearing an elaborate hat and an expensive dress of some stiff black fabric. Her husband—they were as obviously married as they were obviously drunk—was nine-tenths bald, and had one of those offensively clean-shaved faces, pink as a boiled ham, and with an expanse like the map of Asia, ornamented by a loose, rubber-lipped mouth which stretched and brayed: "Shut up! Shut up! Shut up or I'll push your teeth in, God damn you!"

Stanton was halfway out of his chair when the steward trotted along the aisle and soothed them in a worried voice: "Is anything wrong? Is anything wrong? Is there anything wrong with the dinner?" His collar had started to wilt, his dinner jacket was losing its press, and he was nervous. He took a napkin and fussily began to mop up the soup, but ham-face stopped him.

"Go 'way," he said. "Let her clean up her own mess."

Near by the table, the correct, bland-faced colored waiters in their starchy white uniforms studiously averted their eyes. They wore mysterious expressions, which might have been midway between pity and contempt.

"Charming young couple, aren't they?" said Nancy.

"Yes," Stanton agreed. "A fine, representative American family, demonstrating the joys of matrimony. An in-spiration to the youth of the nation."

"Still, even a row like that is better than those frozen married silences. At least, in my book. You know—you've seen them, haven't you?—sitting in a state of abysmal bore-dom and horrible politeness, not looking at each other and not saying anything more than 'Yes' and 'No' and 'Please pass the bread, dear' and 'Thank you.' They might as well be at separate tables, and you're perfectly sure they haven't slept together for years? Of course, these people here would like nothing better than to burn each other's eyes out with red-hot pokers, but, at that, there's action in hatred, isn't there? and give me action on any terms rather than that wooden-Indian business, if you follow me."

"Yes . . ." Action on any terms, action in hatred, he re-peated silently, seeing now—for the first time clearly—the glowing vitality of her face when she talked about some-thing which interested her. There were, he supposed, many women as pretty as Nancy, and a few—Betsy for one—even prettier. But he couldn't recall another who combined the prettiness with the aliveness of this girl. She was like—he groped for an adequate comparison, couldn't find one, gave up, and said, "It's a bleak choice, isn't it—sadism or si-lence?"

"What?" Nancy looked at him in astonishment.

"Isn't that what you've been telling me? American mar-riages end on one side or the other? They either have no mutual interests, can't find anything to talk about and en-dure it heroically for years and years, like wooden Indians —as you said—or else they amuse themselves with mutual flagellation, like this fine pair over here—isn't that what you said?"

And what refined forms it can take, he added silently.

"I was talking about unhappily married people. Not the happy ones."

"Are there any?"

Oh, oh, so that's it, wife trouble, Nancy said to herself. That's why he's been so lost. And what can I do about it, Mr. Wylie? Do you want to do anything about it, Mainwar-ing? Yes, plenty.

"Come now, Mr. Wylie, you make yourself sound like

Diogenes in modern dress, looking for a happy marriage. They aren't so hard to find."

"They aren't? I'm glad to hear it." His voice and eyes suddenly had turned cold, and he was tapping the table with his heavy seal ring. "Are you married?"

"No. Why do you ask?"

"You seem to know so much about it, that's all."

"Well——" Nancy looked down at her coffee. It was cold —she could tell by the way the cream was gathering on the surface—but she took a sip before she answered. "I was married, once. Once upon a time."

"And you were one of the happy ones?"

"Yes, very."

Stanton shrugged, his shoulders saying, It isn't possible.

"And then you went to Reno, I suppose?" he said.

"No." Nancy stared at the tawny coffee and quietly said, "My husband was quite—quite a wonderful man. He was one of those who didn't come home from the war."

It was she, now, who turned away and looked through the rain-streaked window at the rushing tracks, the heaving fields in the enormous wet night. And now it was Stanton who wondered what had happened, what he had said or done. He wanted to stroke the brown depths of her hair, but he didn't. Instead, after giving himself a mental third degree, he said, "Miss Mainwaring, I can't tell you how sorry I am."

"Don't try to, Mr. Wylie. I don't need it, really. I—oh, give me a cigarette, please, and let's get the hell out of here, and back to the club car, what do you say?"

Stanton nodded and gave Nancy the cigarette.

Chapter **5**

WELL, I wish we could just sit here and converse about life and things," Nancy said, when they settled back in the club car. "But I suppose I really ought to get on with the interview."

"Whatever you say, Miss Mainwaring. Where do we start?"

"Let's start with some background stuff. For instance, how you became an architect. Was it family tradition?"

"No, far from it," Stanton replied. "The family business was a stock brokerage, and if it hadn't been for the crash, I suppose I would have ended up in Wall Street. It seems odd now that stocks and bonds used to be so glamorous. Half the men in my class were headed for the Street—or thought they were—and everybody was going to make a million dollars and retire at thirty."

"How fortunate you didn't do it!" said Nancy. "Is the brokerage still in the family?"

Stanton shook his head. "It died a short time after my father died. That was thirteen—no, fourteen—years ago. The brokerage killed him, really."

"How so?"

"Oh, he was an exceptional type, for that business. In the first place, he couldn't bring himself to fire anybody. In fact, he wouldn't even cut salaries. So, after 1930 the brokerage was just eating its head off, and Dad was carrying the load out of his own pocket. But the real thing was that he had a bad conscience about people who had bought stocks on his recommendation, and then been stung when the break came. Of course it was no more to be blamed on him than on the man in the moon, but he felt guilty about it just the same, so he started trying to make good on all those losses, and the strain was too much for him. None of the rest of us realized how bad the situation was until after his death. At least, I didn't. Mother didn't appreciate the way most of the family fortune went down the drain, as she called it. She never said so, but I'm sure she thought Dad was a little crazy, making those refunds. She didn't have much in common with Dad," he added. "She never understood him very well."

"Is your mother still living?"

"Very much so. She married again about ten years ago—another broker, rich as grease, and one of the biggest stuffed shirts in the country. They live in Winnetka. I'm meeting her for breakfast tomorrow morning, incidentally."

"I take it there's no love lost between you and your stepfather," said Nancy.

"No—I have nothing against him, really. He's one of those arch reactionaries with a hide like a rhinoceros and something quite impressive in the way of a single-track mind. I don't suppose he's ever had a thought that wasn't connected with his bank account, one way or another. . . . Anyway, to proceed with how I became an architect. After the crash, as I say, it made no sense to go into the brokerage, and to tell the truth, I never wanted to. But I probably would have, except that Dad—who I guess had a pretty good idea of what was going to happen—told me that the firm couldn't afford to give me a job, and advised me to stay away from the Street entirely. Mother raised hell about that," Stanton said with a smile. "She thought it was indecent for a son of hers to be a Bohemian."

"Bohemian?" Nancy inquired.

"I'm afraid Mother thought anyone outside of banking and broking was a Bohemian," he answered. "And still does. No doubt that's why she likes Arthur—her new husband. He has roughly the same theory."

"You—" Nancy glanced at him, hesitated—"you resented her marrying again, didn't you?"

"Resented?" Stanton considered, and said, "Why, I don't know. I don't think it was resentment so much as surprise and—well, disappointment. I still don't understand how she can be married to Arthur, after having been married all that time to my father. I was quite close to my father," he added, very simply.

"Yes, I can see that," Nancy said.

"Since you asked me that, do you mind if I ask how you feel about marrying again, since you were so close to your husband?"

"*Touché*, Mr. Wylie. The question hasn't come up and I don't know the answer. Maybe we'd better get back to architecture," she said. "You were about to become a Bohemian architect. Wasn't architecture in a parlous state too?"

Stanton grimaced. "Parlous isn't the word. But it was something I thought I wanted to do, and it turned out I was right."

"What made you think you wanted that?"

"Oh——" Stanton again considered, and said, "Nothing very definite, except that I always had a lot of fun building

74

things—model trains and boats and houses, and whatnot. And I liked drawing fantastic plans of impossible machines and buildings. The usual things that boys do, but I kept it up much longer than most. I couldn't look at a blank piece of paper without wanting to get a pencil and make a design of something or other. Dad used to like the same thing, too, when he could break away from the office," he added, thinking of the intimacy of his relationship with his father, and the distance of his relationship with his son. "He fitted out a small machine shop for me, one Christmas, and he used to help me with the models on week ends. In fact, once he took one of my designs to a patent attorney."

"He did? What was it?"

"It wasn't anything. It wouldn't work."

"Please, Mr. Wylie, don't be kittenish. Little details like this are what make *Life* articles. Remember, you were asking?"

"Well——"

"And don't blush about it. You don't need to be embarrassed with me."

"No, I don't, do I?" Stanton said, smiling at her. "Well, it was an attachment that fitted on the end of an automobile exhaust pipe. The idea was, you could use the exhaust pressure to operate a jack, or to inflate a tire."

"That sounds fine. What happened?"

"Someone else had thought of it, and anyway it wouldn't work—not enough pressure," he answered. "I think Dad was more disappointed than I was."

"How about your son? His name is Jeremy, isn't it?"

Stanton nodded.

"Is he following in your footsteps, and so forth? Do you want him to be an architect when he grows up?"

"I don't know. I——" I've had almost nothing to say about him, past, present or future. Betsy—— "I want him to be whatever he wants to be," he said, and thought, Most of all, I want him to have some recognition of me as his father. And how that's going to be accomplished at this stage I'm damned if I know. "So far, he hasn't given much indication of any special aptitude." No, but his mother certainly has, he told himself bitterly. "By the way, do you have any children?" he asked.

Nancy shook her head, and Stanton, catching the wan, strained look which crossed her face, hastily said, "I'm so sorry, Miss Mainwaring. Please forgive me, can you? I promise to stay away from the subject entirely from now on."

Nancy smiled faintly. "It's silly of me, Mr. Wylie, and just too, too feminine for words. I shouldn't mind any longer, and most of the time I don't. But every now and then——— Do you think you can get the steward's eye? I'm about ready for a snifter."

Stanton gazed down the club car in the direction of the Filipino until he had his attention, then signaled him.

"Now back to architecture again," said Nancy. "You made the fateful decision and went to the Harvard School of Architecture?"

"Yes, I made a pretty fair record, and I actually managed to land a job, to everyone's amazement. With Robinson & Galbraith. It was mostly because one of the partners had been a friend of Dad's, so I had some drag. Twenty-five a week to start, later reduced to twenty-two fifty, but sheer charity, even at that. They were primarily residence architects, and there was just no building going on, as you no doubt remember. They kept me on a full year, and then they had to let most of the staff go, so, of course, I was among the missing."

"And were you starving in a garret all this time?"

"No, I'm happy to say that I was living in a good deal of comfort, not to say luxury. Dad had set up a trust fund for me, you see, and besides, my wife———" He stopped.

"Oh, you were married then?"

"Yes, several years." He spoke almost brusquely, through tight lips, with the lines again deepening in his face, and Nancy, watching him, thought, I am going to have to find out about this wife of his, and I can see that it isn't going to be easy.

"Anyway, that turned out to be a stroke of luck, in the long run," he went on quickly. "The straight architects were all going out of business, but the industrial designers were just beginning to establish themselves. In fact, the depression really was responsible for industrial design as an organized business. You see, it was so hard to sell goods, a lot of manufacturers began to realize that simply advertising the same old products in the same old packages wasn't enough, and for the first time they began to give serious thought to design and improvements, whereas before they'd just rolled along and had no incentive for changing anything. So, after a lot of finagling, I ended up working for Clarence Whitney. You've heard of him, of course?"

Nancy nodded.

"We didn't do much architecting, as such, but we certainly got into just about everything else. Everything from streamlined luxury liners to fountain-pen caps. Sometimes our jobs were simple product styling, but mostly Clarence wanted to tackle really fundamental stuff. He thought practically everything in the world ought to be torn apart and put together again. He was a terrific salesman, in addition to being a great designer, and we had more business than we could handle. Incidentally, did you happen to read his book *Prosperity Through Obsolescence?*"

"No, that's one I missed," Nancy said.

"Well, it's quite a book. I'll give you a copy next week."

"That's a date," said Nancy. I hope you mean it, Mr. Wylie, she said to herself. Then Nancy glanced away and made a pretense of searching for something in her handbag. The Filipino steward made an appearance, and after he had served the drinks, she said, "According to my notes, Mr. Wylie, you and Mr. Whitney designed the San Diego plant of Western Aircraft at the start of the war, and then you went to work on the atom project. Is that right?"

"Yes. I went down to Oak Ridge in 1934."

"What were you doing, Mr. Wylie? Or shouldn't I ask? Was it secret?"

Stanton smiled. "I would have been court-martialed if I'd done any talking," he said. "Frankly, though, I never had any clear idea of what I was supposed to be doing, or why. I found out later that most of my work was for the Union Carbide and Carbon plant."

"Carbide? Is that the big gray one, sitting all by itself?"

"Yes, that's the one. It's the most terrifying building in the world, I think. The most frightening thing about it is that you never see anything going in or out. It's just *there*, a quarter of a mile or so behind the wire fences, so big that when you look at it the walls seem to stretch away to the vanishing point, but absolutely no sign of life anywhere. . . . It's just as well they kept the project as secret as they did, because if they hadn't I'm pretty sure it never would have been finished."

"You mean sabotage?"

"Not that so much," he replied. "I think if we'd known what we were doing, a lot of us would have quit. A lot of technical men, anyway."

"Including you?"

"I don't know. I've often asked myself that. Oh, I suppose—" he frowned—"I would have stayed to help the war effort, but I *know* that hundreds of men would have hightailed it out of Oak Ridge as fast as they could." He paused, still frowning, then continued moodily: "I still feel guilty about even my little part in making the damned thing. I try to forget it, but I can't. It was—just *wrong*, somehow. I tell you, the morning I read the news about the Hiroshima bombing, and what had done it, and where it had come from, I was sick, that's all. I'm sure you've read John Hersey's article about Hiroshima, haven't you?"

Nancy nodded. "Of course it was horrible," she said. "But wasn't it supposed to have saved a million lives in the long run?"

"Yes, that's what they say. Who knows? After Pearl Harbor the Japs certainly weren't entitled to any particular consideration, but still it seems to me that since we boast about being such a humanitarian nation, we might have arranged a preliminary demonstration and then said, 'Look, now you see what we have, either quit right off or you'll really be plastered.' Something like that."

"They wouldn't have done it for us, would they, the other way around?"

"No, probably not, but is that any argument? I've never believed that what other people do or fail to do is any excuse for your own behavior. Do you?"

"Well . . . no, not in the abstract, but as it works out in practice it . . . My, you certainly are high-minded, Mr. Wylie! It's rather overpowering."

"I don't think it's being high-minded," Stanton said. He was feeling quite tight, and capable of formulating great philosophical truths. "I think it's a simple matter of self-preservation. Look, Miss Mainwaring, just because some African tribes practice cannibalism, is that any justification for *us* eating other people?"

Nancy smiled at him wickedly, but the arrival of the steward forestalled her answer.

"Last call for drinks, please?" he said. "The bar closes in ten minutes."

Stanton and Nancy simultaneously glanced at their empty glasses and simultaneously nodded. "Two more, please," said Stanton.

Well, well, Nancy said to herself. "As you were saying—?"

"I've been preaching. I'll stop."

"No, you weren't. Please go on."

"Why, there isn't much to say, except that I'm worried about the damned bomb. But who isn't?"

"You're a good deal more worried than most, aren't you?"

"I suppose, having worked on the thing, and knowing a little more about it than what's been printed in the newspapers . . . then, too, people seem to find it so easy to forget. Or, at least, they push it back into their subconscious minds, so they won't have to think about it."

"I can't get rid of the feeling that we've turned a flock of vultures loose on the world," he continued. "And sooner or later they're going to come flapping home to roost. In fact, I think some of them have come home already."

"Meaning?"

"I don't know whether I can explain very well. But the world is such a bad-tempered place these days, and the people in it are so confused and apprehensive about everything. There seems to be a general mood of hopelessness emanating from somewhere. Yes."

"Yes, what?"

"I was thinking about something a friend of mine told me." Dimly he recalled the words which Chester Hazen had spoken in his office, only that afternoon. "I have a feeling there's an evil thing loose in the world," the old lawyer had said. "Something chiseling away at people's values, making a joke of honor and honesty—yes, even of God. We all seem to be living in the shadow of something evil, something terrible." Could it be the bomb? Stanton asked himself. Was it the knowledge of that lurking, unpredictable horror which was undermining values and standards? Had people generally decided that the world was going to hell anyway, and there was no point in trying to make an effort any longer? Or was the bomb merely the most flagrant symptom of a disease already far advanced? Either way, was it possible that somehow there was some connection between the bomb and the fears and doubts which followed in its train, and the way that Betsy had—— He jerked his head sharply, as though to shake off the thought.

"I suppose," Nancy said, taking a sip of her fresh drink, "your model city represents a gesture of protest against all that, Mr. Wylie? A kind of compensation for your guilty feeling about working on the bomb? Or am I getting too fancy?"

"That might have been part of it," Stanton replied. "But not consciously. No, I think it was a straight and simple reaction to Oak Ridge itself. It was such an overwhelming place, and the way it was built was almost—well, stupefying, to say the least. No one—I don't care how dull—could possibly see it and not be permanently impressed."

"And a little depressed, too. Is that it?"

He nodded. "I think it's depressing that the Oak Ridges are always built under the stimulus of war. We talk about how much we want peace, but for really getting things done there's nothing like war, is there? So, after I chewed on *that* proposition for a while, one fine day I said to myself, 'All right, Wylie, suppose this were peacetime and suppose they came to you and offered you the same setup the Army has here—unlimited money, as many workers as you wanted, and complete authority to proceed as you see fit—and suppose they told you to go ahead, starting from scratch, and build a city that will stand as a kind of answer to Oak Ridge, a proof that the creative energy of man can be as potent and awe-inspiring in peace as his self-destructive drives are in war.' Does that make sense to you, Miss Mainwaring?"

"Perfect sense."

"You're very understanding, aren't you?" he said. He thought briefly and bitterly of the time he had tried to explain it to Betsy, who pretended to understand—probably just to shut him up—but of course didn't at all; she assumed

—he was positive—that he'd done the whole thing with the idea of eventually winning a prize for it. But this girl, this warm-voiced Nancy——

"Why, Mr. Wylie, there's no trick to understanding you," she said. "Anyone could follow that."

"No, not anyone," he said, shaking his head. "Not anyone."

Her brown eyes held a question which she didn't ask. "So that was the beginning of the city, was it?" she said.

"Yes, that was the beginning. The very bare beginning. The project went through several evolutionary phases, like most such things."

"What were they?"

"Well—" he paused thoughtfully—"mainly a change in the essential purpose of what I was trying to do. You see, I started in a purely imaginative, impractical way—dream city of the future, that sort of thing. But before I'd gone very far I threw that out. I had a new idea, probably very silly."

"Which was?"

"I decided to build the dream city of today, not of the future. So I eliminated all the fantasy—interplanetary rocket stations on the skyscraper roofs, that stuff." He smiled. "I had a lot of it, and I hated to let it go, but I did. As it stands, the city *could* be built, now this year, with the materials and machines we have at hand. I deliberately limited myself to immediate practicalities, and, as I say, the city *could* be built right away, not in 1980."

"Well, what's silly about that?"

"No." Stanton shook his head. "It was very silly."

"Why? I don't get it."

"Well, you see, Miss Mainwaring——" He paused, looking embarrassed. "You see, after I began to develop the thing, I had a strange notion that since the city *could* be built now——"

"Yes?"

"Somebody conceivably might build it," he added quickly. "I told you it was silly."

He appeared to be studying his hands, which were cupped around the highball glass. Nancy followed the line of his gaze and watched him twist the gold seal ring around his finger. *"Nil nisi bonum."* She said to herself, You know, Mr. Wylie, I wish I were in a position to order your city; I'd have you start on it next week.

"I must say, you seem to have found your own answer to the bomb," she remarked. "It's about the best one I've heard so far. When did you do all this work, incidentally?"

"I did most of the designing and paper work down at Oak Ridge, in my free time. Sort of a busman's holiday."

"Oh, was your wife there with you?"

"You wouldn't ask that if you knew her," Stanton said, smiling. "No, she never came to the reservation, and I'm sure if she had she would have cleared out as fast as she could. It was a pretty rugged spot in those days, and she isn't very good at roughing it. I didn't see much of my family while I was on the Project," he added. "There was a lot of red tape about passes to leave, and transportation was nearly impossible unless you were big brass."

Very casually Nancy inquired, "Was your wife doing any war work, Mr. Wylie? A.W.V.S. or anything like that?"

"I . . . I'm not quite sure," Stanton said. You know, Miss Mainwaring, that's a very provocative question, he told himself. Just what was Betsy doing while I was down at Oak Ridge? I would like to know the answer to that one. Or maybe I wouldn't.

Oh, oh, I take it all back, Mr. Wylie, Nancy thought, noticing the way his expression suddenly turned stony. I won't ask any more questions about your lady; at least, not unless you give me an opening.

"So you had the plans finished by the time you left Oak Ridge?" she asked quickly. "And then what?"

"Then I started on the model. I built most of it myself, still working evenings and week ends for about a year and a half. It was a lot of fun," he said. "I had a workshop over the garage, out in Westport." Amazing, he thought, that I was there only this morning and imagined it was home, and now everything is changed and it isn't home at all, and I'm riding across Ohio, and I'm not at all certain that I'll——

"Your son must have got a big kick out of that, didn't he? Did he help you?"

I only wish he had, Stanton thought, I only wish he had. I tried to get him interested, God knows I tried. But there was always something—school activities, and the parties on the week ends, always the parties on the week ends. Betsy, did you have to arrange all those parties for Jerry?

"Oh, yes, he helped a lot," Stanton said. "Yes, he was quite excited about it."

And this wife of yours, was she in on it, too? Did she help? Nancy nearly said, before she remembered that she had promised herself not to. Aloud: "Is it awfully complicated, full of gadgets? Moving sidewalks and so on?"

"No, no moving sidewalks—they wouldn't be necessary. The city is laid out so that no one needs to do much walking, unless he wants to. But all the pavements and stone floors have a composition surface—something like heavy linoleum, but much more durable—that reduces the fatigue of walking by at least a third, and also makes it an almost soundless operation. It's a very quiet city, I think the quietest that could be built," he added, and continued: "But the design is the important thing. It doesn't depend on gadgets. By the way, what is your definition of a gadget?"

"Oh—" Nancy's forehead wrinkled—"some tricky thing that usually doesn't work. Something slapped on top of something else for advertising appeal. Sounds wonderful and is actually a dismal failure when you try to use it. You know."

Stanton nodded, and said, "Well, by that definition, the city has no gadgets at all. There are some new things incorporated in the basic plan, but they're there because they belong and contribute to the convenience and enjoyment of the people. You see, that was the *real* idea, Miss Mainwaring—a city built for the people who would live in it, rather than the other way around. Now, cities have existed for thousands of years, and always will exist, if——"

"Yes?"

"If anything exists at all. I'm back at the bomb again, and let's assume it won't happen. Cities exist and have existed and will exist not only because of strategic economic location—the beginning reason for most of them—but because people have the hiving instinct. They want to rub elbows, herd together, have a common identity, more specific than nationalism or regionalism, and at the same time more expansive than the lodge or the chamber of commerce.

So a city isn't only a place where a few hundred thousands or a few millions are packed together by necessity, but a psychological device of identification."

"I think I'm going to need my notebook for this, Mr. Wylie," Nancy said. "And usually I remember my interviews without it."

"No, no, you won't, really, Miss Mainwaring. Probably I sound very foggy, and anyway it doesn't have much bearing on the case, except that a good many people have asked me why I planned the city as a concentrated, integrated unit, with a central group of big buildings, instead of spreading it out and ruralizing it. Part of the answer is that it *is* a *city*, not a group of suburbs, one of its functions being, as I say, to meet the psychological urge to crowd together. . . .

"However," he went on, after taking a swallow of his highball, "I think I've managed to eliminate most of the disadvantages of crowds and cities. Mine has no slums; no smoke; very little noise, as I mentioned; about the most efficient transportation system that I think could be built with present equipment, and no traffic problems, at least, not in any foreseeable future. Another thing: because of the design and the compactness of the city, I've been told by people who should know that the cost of essential services, general upkeep and administration would be a great deal lower than in any ordinary town with twice the population. So it really isn't as impractical as it may sound. Over a long enough period it would be self-liquidating, on the basis of comparative overhead expenses.

"Of course, that's just an aside, you understand. The essential purpose of the city is to provide a more attractive, gracious, enjoyable and perhaps inspiring environment for more people than the world ever has had before, on the theory that given optimum surroundings people perhaps would react to them and evolve a little faster in the right direction. Not," he added, "that I think a superior environment necessarily produces superior people, but maybe it's worth trying on a large scale, to see what would happen."

"It sounds wonderful, and I certainly hope you'll build it," Nancy said. "Will I have a chance to go over the model with you, Mr. Wylie?"

"Yes, I was going to suggest that. There's no point in my

trying to tell you the details now, because with the model in front of us you'll be able to see the whole thing. It's built in sections and comes apart, to show the underground arrangement of highways and tunnels and subways and so on. That's really the most important part of the whole design; that, and the way the skyscrapers and stores are grouped around a central recreation center. But let's wait until we have the model, shall we?"

"What's the best time, Mr. Wylie?"

"Well, the dinner's scheduled for seven, which probably means half past seven," Stanton said. "I'm supposed to have a press conference before dinner, from five-thirty to six, at the Stevens, so right after that, Miss Mainwaring, if that's convenient for you?"

"Don't worry about my convenience. After all, I'm here to get the story. I tell you what. Suppose I go to the press conference myself, and right afterward you can explain the model? That'll still give you time to change your clothes for the dinner."

"All right. Fine."

"By the way, what about your speech?" Nancy inquired. "Is it going to be mainly about the City, or something more general?"

Stanton shook his head. "I really don't know what I'm going to say," he replied. "I thought I had it all figured out this morning, but now I honestly don't know."

"Well! That leaves room for all kinds of interesting possibilities, doesn't it? . . . Oh, Lord!" she exclaimed, with a gesture toward the end of the car. "That man is here again, and he's really stiff. Look at him!"

It was the offensive bald-headed man they had seen in the diner, now very drunk indeed, and flushed to an alarming shade of crimson. For a minute or so he teetered unsteadily just inside the club-car door, blinking at the lights and wearing a loose, vacuous expression. Then he lurched forward, making for the nearest empty chair, and collapsed into it like a bag of sand. Down at the far end of the car the Filipino steward had just finished locking up the bar for the night, but Baldhead planted a stubby forefinger on the buzzer button beside his chair and held it there until the steward reluctantly approached.

"Please?" he said.

"Whisky and water," Baldhead demanded loudly and rudely.

"I'm very sorry, sir, but the bar is closed," the steward said in a placating manner.

"What's that?"

"The bar is closed, sir."

"Well, open 'er up! Wha's use having a bar not open?"

"I'm very sorry, sir, but it's after hours," the Filipino said. "I'm not allowed to serve anyone now. It is the rule of the train."

He started to retreat, but after an unsuccessful attempt at standing up, Baldhead shouted, "Hey, you, who told you to go? You get me that whisky."

"But, sir, I just explained, it is not permitted to serve you now. It is the rule of the train, sir."

The few people remaining in the club car set down their drinks and swiveled around in their chairs to witness this obtrusive byplay. A couple of them smiled or winked, while the others looked on indifferently.

Nancy and Stanton exchanged glances that were eloquent with distaste.

"I suppose it takes all kinds," she remarked. "But they ought to draw the line somewhere. Somewhere the other side of specimens like this one."

"Don't you talk to me like that, you yellow monkey," the man shouted again. He made another ponderous effort to get to his feet, and this time he finally made it. Swaying, with one hand braced against the back of the chair, he bawled, "What are you, anyway, a Jap?" He stared wildly around the car, as though seeking applause from fellow Occidentals. "Tha's what you are—you're a Jap!"

The steward unobtrusively had been edging back, trying to let the contest go by default. But now he stopped and stood still in the aisle, with a curious, strained expression on his dark face. Nor did he retreat when the man staggered toward him and growled, "Well, no dirty Jap talks that way to *me*, understand? You get that whisky, you yellow monkey, or—" he waved a huge pink fist at the steward—"or by God——"

And then, quite automatically, quite coldly, Stanton rose

from his chair and took three quick steps down the aisle. He halted directly in front of Baldhead, and in a firm, quiet voice which just carried to Nancy, he said, "If you don't sit down and keep your mouth shut, I'll put you out of this car."

The bald man couldn't quite focus his eyes, and he reared backward, peering at Stanton. His expression was slack-jawed, bewildered. "Wha's that?" he mumbled.

"You heard me."

"Only wan' get a drink. Why'nt you mind own business?"

"The bar's closed, as the steward told you. You won't get a drink."

"Won' get a drink, eh? Who you telling me I won' get a drink?" He squinted erratically at Stanton, then pointed a finger at him and announced, " 'Nother dirty Jap, tha's what you are. Jap. No dirty Jap talks like that to *me!* You get away, mind your own business."

"It is my business when you create a public disturbance," Stanton said. "Now, either sit down and keep quiet, or leave the car, one or the other."

Baldhead mumbled something of a threatening nature, took a lurching step toward Stanton and tried to push him aside by bumping him. With an easy gesture Stanton caught his elbow, swung him about with a pivoting movement, propelled him to the nearest chair, and then let gravity do the rest. Baldhead subsided with a final mumble, and a baleful glance from wildly roving, inflamed eyes. He was slobbering; trickles of saliva flowed in sticky little streams from the corners of his mouth. He made an impotent gesture of shaking his fist, struggled to stand up, fell back, muttering ominously, and promptly dropped off to sleep.

"I'm sorry," Stanton said to Nancy, when he returned to the table. "But I warned you. Remember? I told you, after a few drinks I'm apt to do foolish things. Why, what's the matter?"

Nancy's head was bent, and when she looked up her eyes were damp. She smiled ruefully at Stanton, shaking her head.

"Miss Mainwaring, what is it," Stanton asked in alarm. "Is something wrong?"

"It's nothing," she said finally, in a small, unsteady voice.

"It's just that every so often you remind me so strongly of . . . of someone. And just then—when you were telling off that boor—I could almost believe that you and he were— oh, let's skip it!"

"I'm afraid I don't understand."

"No, I wouldn't expect you to. That wasn't a foolish thing to do, Mr. Wylie," she went on briskly. "On the contrary I don't believe for a minute that the drinks had anything to do with it. I think you'd react the same way every time. Like your friend Bassett, and the barrel."

"It wasn't anything," Stanton said in some embarrassment. "I just don't like to see people being kicked around."

"No, neither do most people. But how many of them step out of the crowd and do something about it? You didn't see anyone else in the car making a move, did you? That's my point."

The smiling steward approached them. "Thank you, sir," he said to Stanton. "That was most nice of you."

"Don't mention it," Stanton said.

"It is sometimes difficult to avoid a scene," the boy said.

"With a bird like that one, it's impossible," said Stanton.

"And I do not like to be called a Jap that way. I was three years in Army. Pacific Theater." He leaned toward them, and in a lower voice said, "It is against the rules of the train, but if you and the lady would like another drink, I can bring it back to your compartment?"

Stanton glanced at Nancy. "How about it?" he asked.

"I could use another," she said. "Tell you what, let's just get the setups. I have a bottle of pretty good stuff in my suitcase. It's compartment G, one car back," she told the steward, and added to Stanton, "I always carry a little nip along on these trips, in case of snake bite."

"Very sensible," Stanton said, as they were leaving the car. "The snakes on these trains are a menace. I can't understand why the railroads don't do something about it. In fact, I think I'll write a letter to the Interstate Commerce Commission. Here, let me——"

They had arrived in the vestibule, with Nancy in the lead, and Stanton reached past her to open the door. As he did so the Century hit a long curve at full throttle, and the sudden impact flung Nancy against him. Stanton slipped his arm around her waist to steady her, and involuntarily her hands went up and rested on the lapels of his jacket. For a long moment they stood thus, in a semiembrace, neither of them making any effort to resist the pressure which was forcing their bodies so tightly together. Stanton moved his hand across her back in a small caress, and with his face very close to her fragrant brown hair, he murmured, "You know, Miss Mainwaring, I think you're very——"

"Don't say it, Mr. Wylie," Nancy said softly, "much as I'd like to hear it."

Gently she pushed away from him, slipping out of his encircling arm and thinking to herself, I feel just like a schoolgirl, tremulous and silly and excited, and all the rest of it. *And* guilty, she added as an afterthought. This is going to be quite a test of my character, to have this man sitting in my compartment with me. I would so very much like to—— Oh, cut it out, Nancy. Why make things any tougher than they have to be, you dope.

"Well, that was quite a bump, wasn't it?" she said brightly and casually, and to herself: Please, Mr. Wylie, don't look at me that way, please. You must know that I'm dying to throw myself at you—and can't. Please be a good Joe and don't give me any encouragement, please. "Shall we proceed?"

Stanton nodded silently. He seemed to be choking—part of a strange and powerful sensation of general turmoil. This is amazing, he kept saying to himself. This is amazing. I don't understand.

He was silent until they settled down with the drinks in the compartment. Then he turned to her, and said, "You know there's something very peculiar going on."

"Is there? I hadn't noticed. What would it be?"

"Well—" Stanton hesitated—"I've had the strangest feeling about you."

"You have? Such as?"

"Why, I don't quite know how to say it, but we only met a few hours ago."

"And?"

"All evening I've had this strange feeling that we've

89

known each other for years and years, and been very close. So close that I almost know what you're thinking without your saying a word. Do you see what I mean?"

"I think I do. I've had something of the same feeling myself. Rodgers and Hart put it into a very pretty song once. Remember 'Where or When'?"

"I remember the tune, but I don't know the words."

"Oh, you must. It's a minor classic."

"Can you sing it?"

"I can try. It goes:

> *"'It seems we stood and talked like this before.*
> *We looked at each other in the same way then,*
> *But I can't remember where or when.'"*

"You have a sweet voice," Stanton said. "Do you know the rest of it?"

> *"'The clothes you're wearing are the clothes you wore,*
> *The smile you are smiling you were smiling then,*
> *But I can't remember where or when.*
> *Some things that happened for the first time*
> *Seem to be happening again.*
> *And so it seems that we have met before,*
> *And laughed before, and loved before,*
> *But who knows where or when?'"* *

"Yes," said Nancy after a moment of reflection. "I feel the same way about you, Mr. Wylie. It's rather uncanny, too. I'm sure you've guessed—or gathered—that you put me very much in mind of my husband. There, that's out!" she added with relief. "I wanted to tell you before, but I have a mental block when it comes to talking about him. Anyway, I never met another man who seemed a bit like Ted—that was his name—and now you've come along and remind me of him so vividly that there were moments tonight when I could have closed my eyes and been very sure that he was with me again. I don't mean to make you sound like a ghost, Mr. Wylie," she went on. "I'm really paying you a great

* Copyright, 1937, by Chappell & Co., Inc.

compliment. As I said before, he was quite a wonderful man."

"I'm sure he was," Stanton agreed, not knowing quite what to say.

"And on top of all that," she continued, "it's absolutely fantastic that I'm going to this banquet of yours at the Stevens tomorrow night. Really, the weirdest coincidence I've ever heard of."

"What do you mean?"

"Well, you see, that's where I first met Ted—at a banquet at the Stevens. Yes, it's true," she said in answer to Stanton's incredulous expression. "It was in 1941, at the annual meeting of the Chicago Institute of Psychoanalysis. The office sent me out to cover it. My first out-of-town assignment, I remember."

"Oh, he was—? Was your husband a psychiatrist?"

"No, no. He was a G. P., just starting to practice in New York. He was more of a respiratory man than anything else, though, and he was interested in the psychosomatic factor in relation to tuberculosis. He called it the 'Magic Mountain' factor."

"Now, wait a minute!" Stanton protested. "I'm an architect, remember."

"Sorry, Mr. Wylie, I keep forgetting. More of this odd resemblance of yours to Ted, I suppose. Anyway, by the 'Magic Mountain' factor, he meant the unconscious resistance of some t.b. patients to getting well, because the treatment, by and large, is quite pleasant and some people would rather relax in a sanatorium than be cured and go back to the outer world. One of the Institute staff members gave a lecture on the subject during the meeting, which was why Ted happened to be there. And at the dinner they held, we both happened to sit at the same table. In fact, we were right next to each other."

"And one thing led to another?" Stanton said.

"Well, more or less." Nancy smiled reminiscently. "I remember, I was baffled by one of the speakers, he used such technical language. Finally he started talking about something called an encapsulated trauma, which made no sense at all to me. So here was this handsome, intelligent-looking man on my right, listening very seriously, and I tapped him on the arm and asked him prettily what the devil an encapsulated trauma might be."

"And of course he was able to tell you?"

"Yes, if he wanted to," Nancy said. "But he wasn't nearly so serious as he looked. He frowned a bit and then whispered that he thought it was some new kind of fountain pen. A little later they were talking about free-floating anxiety neurosis—I'm sure you're familiar with *that* term, aren't you, Mr. Wylie?"

"Of course. Use it all the time."

"And I asked Ted what that meant, and he said it sounded to him like a knee-action Buick, but he wasn't sure." She laughed. "We kept that up for an hour. It was fun." She paused for a moment, with a cloudy look of sadness in her eyes. "Ted and I always had fun, even when we were being most serious. And then, we had so many plans."

"Plans?"

"Yes, such exciting, lovely plans, about what Ted was going to do in medicine, and what we were going to do with our lives together." Her voice was faint and distant. "They would have kept us busy for at least a hundred years, and as it worked out we had only one year really to call our own."

"Your husband was killed in action?"

She nodded. "Yes, Germany. And with that, the conversation about Ted is finished," she said briskly. "Now suppose we reverse the field, Mr. Wylie. I've told you how much you remind me of Ted. What's on your side? Do I remind you of your wife perchance?"

Stanton gave a brief, humorless laugh. "On the strength of that, I think I'll pour myself another drink," he said. Nancy handed him the bottle, and watched him curiously while he mixed a highball. He lifted the glass, drank slowly, said nothing and stared straight ahead.

"Hello! Are you there, Mr. Wylie?" Nancy said.

"What? Oh, I'm sorry. No, you don't remind me of my wife, Miss Mainwaring. I was thinking that you are complete opposites—probably."

"Come now, that can't be. After all, we're both women. Sisters under the skin, et cetera."

"I hope not."

"What?"

"For your sake," he said. His voice was curt and hostile, and his expression made Nancy think of the dial of a broken clock, with hands stopped at six.

Then he shook his head, and the deep, gentle, softening lines spread across his face. "I didn't mean that. I'd like to take it back."

"All right. I'm not sure I know how to interpret it, anyway. You know, Mr. Wylie—" she paused—"I've already broken two of my own private rules tonight."

"Which were they?" he asked.

"Talking about Ted, for one. Getting so cozy with you, for another. And now I'm strongly tempted to break a third."

"What is that one?"

"I'm tempted to ask you about something that's none of my business."

"Well, go ahead," said Stanton. "I don't mind."

"I think you do, though. It's about your wife."

"Oh. Well . . . go on."

"Every single time her name has come into the conversation, you seemed to freeze up, somehow. I couldn't help noticing it, and I've been wondering what it meant. That's all. You don't need to tell me, if you don't want to."

"I wouldn't know how to tell you, Miss Mainwaring," Stanton said slowly. "It's difficult."

"I see. Well, let's let it pass. I think I'll have one nightcap with you, and then maybe I'd better think about a little sleep so I can be bright and efficient tomorrow."

"Miss Mainwaring——" Stanton began. He was interrupted by several taps on the closed door. Nancy and Stanton glanced at each other.

"It seems rather late for callers, doesn't it?" she said, and then called, "Who's there?"

"Train conductor" was the reply.

Stanton opened the door.

"Is this your compartment, sir?" the conductor inquired.

"No, it's mine," Nancy told him. "Why? What about it?"

The conductor pulled a watch from his pocket and held it in his hand.

"I'm sorry," he said, "but after one o'clock we don't like

. . . ah . . ." He coughed. "I'm afraid I'll have to ask you to go to your own space, sir."

"Well——" Stanton was taken aback. "We haven't been making any noise or disturbing anyone, have we?"

"No, sir, it isn't that. After one o'clock we don't permit ladies and gentlemen to remain together in compartments listed as single occupancy. I'm sorry, sir, but that's the rule of the train."

"How perfectly silly!" Nancy exclaimed.

"Well, miss, maybe so," said the conductor. "I don't make the rules, you know. Anyway, sir, when you finish your drink, if you don't mind?" He then vanished down the corridor. He pointedly refrained from closing the door of the compartment.

"It's a little like being back in boarding school," Stanton said. "I didn't realize they carried house detectives on these trains."

"Yes, they make you feel terribly wicked and surreptitious, don't they?" said Nancy. "He's a stuffy old party, isn't he?"

It seemed only a minute before the conductor reappeared. "If you please, now, sir?" he said.

"But we're having such a good time!" Nancy protested. "Besides, the door's open. You can chaperon us, if you like."

"Now, miss, I can't help what my orders are, can I?" the man said. "It's the rule of the train, and that's that."

Stanton drained his glass and stood up. "You're right, I'll get out," he told the conductor. "Anyway, I suppose we need some sleep," he added to Nancy. "Although I can't work up much enthusiasm for it. I'd rather stay here."

And sleep? Nancy asked herself. If it were anyone but you, Mr. Wylie, that's what you would mean. But you just mean what you say.

"I've had a wonderful evening with you, Miss Mainwaring," Stanton told her. "You're an awful lot of fun."

"I might say the same of you, Mr. Wylie. Another thing you have in common."

"In common?"

"With Ted."

"Oh, yes, Ted."

She started to stand up, and Stanton took her hands and

pulled her to her feet. He didn't release the hands, nor did she try to detach them.

"I hate leaving you," he said.

"Frankly, I hate letting you go."

"However, there's always the morning."

"Yes. Consolation prize."

She looked up at him, and he drew her closer. Then he swiftly kissed her forehead. Her eyes were shut. Stanton's big, gentle hands went to her face, cradled it, raised it, and he saw her lips shining and quivering. He bent toward her, and then, abruptly, she pushed away.

"Don't—oh, please don't," she said, in a strangled voice. "I can't, just can't. I want to, but I can't. Do you understand?"

He studied her face for a moment and then nodded, with a half-smile. "Yes, I'm afraid I do. Good night," he said. He stepped out quickly, and as he closed the door he imagined that he heard something like a sob from the compartment.

Before either of them slept there was light in the eastern sky, and the Century was skirting the Lake Erie shores, well into Ohio.

Chapter 6

STANTON dozed through the porter's warning calls in the morning and didn't come fully awake until the Century coasted into the station. He was aroused by the sound of luggage bumping along the corridor outside his compartment, and heard the voices of passengers who were lining up by the vestibule. His first coherent thought was to find Nancy Mainwaring before she left the train, and he shaved and dressed in such haste that he scraped his cheek with the razor and emerged from the compartment still buttoning his vest and feeling irritated and disheveled.

The last passengers were sorting their baggage on the platform as he loped back to Nancy's car, and when he reached her compartment it was empty, with the door standing bleakly open. He ran out to the platform, but there was no sign of her. He hurried to the waiting room of the station and then to the restaurant and finally came out on the taxi ramp. She wasn't there. At length he gave up, climbed into a cab and directed the driver to the Ambassador East. He was upbraiding himself as the cab bounced across the cobblestones and headed north. The day had started in the worst possible way, and the sights and sounds of the city did nothing to improve his spirits during the ride.

The trouble with Chicago, he thought, is that it can't stand sunlight. It was a vividly bright day, with a brisk wind nipping in from the lake; the sort of day which ought to have been an adornment to the city, like a new dress. Instead, the light merely seemed to accentuate the patina of filth which lay over the town, from the blackened piles of obscure refuse in the gutters to the greasy, soot-encrusted walls of the gaunt, archaic buildings. Of course, in the nature of the case, all cities were dirty—except, that is, for Stanton's own city, which had precipitrons at all smoke-producing points, and flushing systems built into the streets. New York was dirty, but it had a different kind of dirt which could be washed or swept away, whereas in Chicago the dirt was permanent and indelible, a kind of hallmark of the city.

And in New York, he reflected, no matter how dirty and noxious a neighborhood might be, you always could find a better one—or at least a different one—by walking a couple of blocks, or perhaps by only turning a corner. Whereas Chicago neighborhoods were interminable miles of filth piled on filth and ground into the skins and lives of the inhabitants. There was the spectacular exception of the proud stone fence along the lake front, but it was a façade which always made Stanton think of those cardboard and matchstick fronts which Potemkin erected against miserable Black Sea villages, to bemuse the Empress Catherine. Behind the glittering vistas of Michigan Avenue the whole city seemed to be waiting for another fire—or perhaps an atom bomb.

Stanton's taxi stopped for a light on Rush Street, in the midst of a jungle of dismal saloons, bleary and unwashed in the morning sunshine. He watched a girl on the corner gingerly testing a mound of garbage on a clogged drain before she stepped across the murky stream lapping against the curb. He wondered why Chicago women wore their skirts so short. It couldn't be the beauty of the knee, he decided. Not even Chicagoans could pretend that this joint was beautiful.

The light changed, and the taxi proceeded, spattering the girl's stockings halfway up her calves. She glared, and uttered an ugly obscenity. The taxi driver laughed, and said, "Tough babe, hey?"

Stanton didn't answer. He was thinking: Such a small thing, a girl's stockings being dirtied by a cab, and yet, multiply it by a million, and not only stockings but climbing stairs, nineteenth-century plumbing that doesn't work, crowding in subways, streetcars, elevators, all the bumping, knocking, shoving, bad temper, all the things that don't work as they should, the multiple abrasions and irritations of life in a badly built, badly arranged, planless big city. . . . Yes, even the girl's stockings. She was just starting out for the day, and no matter what she was or where she might be going for whatever errand, clean stockings were important. Now, with soiled stockings, she might return to her room and change, or get to her office or other destination with the spotted pair and be embarrassed and apologetic and for hours curse the taxi, inevitably embroiling others in this small personal whirlpool of protest. And it wouldn't stop there. The others would be infected by it, and it would become a spinning mass of separate angers finally whirled into a concentrated, chronic, concentric anger, solid and purposeful as the rotor of a gyroscope. No great overriding tyranny or injustice would forge the rotor, but the slow accretion of myriad small exasperations. . . . And in the City there would be none of these.

"Yes, sir, a real tough babe, hey?" the driver said. "They're real tough around here, ain't they? Yes, sir!"

Stanton said nothing. He looked at the festering gutters, the sooty buildings, the derelict streets, and thought of the proud white battlements, the airy cleanliness, of his own creation. But after a moment of reflection he took a somewhat more charitable view of the dirt; it was, after all, a by-product of Chicago's intimidating vitality, because if it did nothing else the city sweated energy through every one of its congested pores. It was the energy of money, the vast leverage of money, which was in Chicago's marrow from the abbatoirs and the Pit to the very money-smelling wind off Lake Michigan. Benét had it in a single couplet in *John Brown's Body*. Now, what was it? Oh, yes:

> *Enormous power, ugly to the fool,*
> *And beautiful as a well-handled tool.**

Yes, Stanton admitted to himself, even the ugliness creates a kind of beauty, if you want to look at it through dark glasses.

"Here y'ar," the driver said. "Ambassador East."

Rather to his surprise, he found that his mother already had arrived and was waiting for him in the lobby. The moment he entered she came bearing down like a Salem clipper under full sail—an illusion made graphic by the fact that her snowy white shirtwaist bellied out over a very full bosom, and that her high white-feather hat looked like a tops'l. Stanton noted with disapproval that she had dyed her hair to a bluish-gray tint since he had last seen her, that she seemed to be cluttered with even more costly jewelry than usual, and that she was carrying what appeared to be an antique quizzing glass. Altogether, the effect was quite formidable.

"Stanton, my dear, dear boy!" she greeted him, and gave him a resounding kiss. "How are you? Let me look at you." She peered at him through the quizzing glass. "Why, Stanton, you look exhausted! What have you been doing? Hasn't Betsy been taking care of you?"

"I'm fine, Mother dear," Stanton answered. "I didn't sleep very well last night, that's all. How are you and Arthur? How have you been, and everything?"

"Oh, Arthur was *so* disappointed to miss you! We hoped your train might get in early, and he was here with me. He waited as long as he could, and then he had to go to the office. He asked if you'd meet him for lunch at the Racquet Club—that's only a couple of blocks from here, you know—and would you call him sometime this morning?"

"Well, I'm sorry, Mother, but I'm afraid I can't have

* From *John Brown's Body*, published by Rinehart & Co., Inc. Copyright 1927, 1928, by Stephen Vincent Benét.

lunch with him, because I have another appointment. Kind of a business thing. I'll call him, of course."

"Oh, my, that's too bad. Well, if you can't you can't, I suppose. Now, I think we'd better go right in and have breakfast, because I told Johnson to come back for me in an hour. You see, I'm the speaker at a meeting of the Tax Abatement League at eleven. It's funny that we're both making speeches the same day, isn't it, Stan? Arthur thought that was *very* funny."

"Yes, it's very funny," Stanton said. "What is this Tax Abatement League, Mother?" he inquired, when they were seated in the dining room.

"What? Haven't you heard of it?"

"I don't believe so. Is it something new?"

"Well, yes, it's fairly new, and so far our influence is mostly around Chicago, but we're growing by leaps and bounds, and before long we'll have chapters all over the country."

"Well—just what are you doing, Mother? What's it all about? I gather you're trying to reduce income taxes, is that it?"

"That's part of it, of course. We intend to keep reminding the voters again and again and *again* how Truman mocked the will of the majority and tried to usurp the traditional fiscal powers of Congress by vetoing the Republican tax cuts."

Stanton smiled. "Is that part of your speech, Mother?" he said. "It sounds like it."

"What? Why, yes. Yes, it is. But that's only the bare start of our program, Stanton. We're offering a positive five-point plan for eliminating this insane waste of the taxpayers' money. Why, for one thing, we can *prove* that the Federal pay roll can be cut *at least* fifty per cent without impairing *any* of the essential functions of the government—just getting rid of the frills and froufrou."

"That's interesting," Stanton remarked. "What do you classify as frills and froufrou?"

"Oh, all this international boondoggling, for one thing. It was bad enough in the depression, but at least the money was being handed out *here,* while now we're just throwing away billions, bailing out one worthless foreign bankrupt after another. And then, all these refugees, and this agitation to allow immigration of all those surplus Europeans to come over here and stir up trouble, and——"

Now I know I'm in Chicago, Stanton thought. God, why did I have to get her started on this?

"We're taking a very *firm stand* on controlling undesirables of all kinds—Negroes, Jews and the foreign riffraff—who are simply flooding every decent community in the country."

"What do you mean by 'controlling,' Mother?" Stanton asked.

"I mean keeping them in their place, so that decent citizens won't be crowded right out of our own country, that's what! Why, the very *nicest* parts of Chicago are being ruined by these pushy Jews. And as for the Negroes—why, it's a scandal!"

"Mother——" Stanton began.

"But let's not talk any more about politics. My speech today is about taxes. You can listen to it, in case you want to. It'll be broadcast by WGN. How about yours, Stan? Will you be on the air?"

"No, I don't believe so, Mother. At least, they haven't said anything about it. Of course, it's only a small occasion, compared to your Tax League."

"Mm. That's a disappointment, though. I *so* wanted to hear my big boy make his speech."

"Well, Mother, you can come to the dinner, you know. Probably you'd find it pretty dull, but——"

"Oh, I just *can't* make it, Stan. I tried to plan on it, but I have *such* a full day with the League meeting, and this evening I have to entertain a group of our out-of-town members. There simply isn't a spare minute."

"No, I can see that. Well, Mother, I don't think you're missing anything."

"Ah, by the way, how much is this prize you're getting?"

"A thousand dollars."

"Really? Is that all? I thought it was five thousand. A thousand. That isn't very much, is it?"

"It isn't any fortune," Stanton said. "But the award is supposed to be the important thing, not the money."

"Yes, I suppose it's a great help to your business, isn't it?

How *is* your business, Stan? You must be doing pretty well, from what I hear."

"I'm doing well enough," he said dryly. "I turn down about four jobs for every one I accept."

"Why do you turn them down?" his mother demanded. "Can't you hire more people to help you? I know you can't do everything yourself, but it seems a shame to let things go."

"I don't let things go, Mother. The jobs I turn down are ones I wouldn't want to handle at all. Trivial stuff that doesn't mean anything."

His mother laughed. "You're still impractical, aren't you, Stan? Just like your father."

With an effort, Stanton suppressed a mingled feeling of anger and protest. "I suppose Arthur is very practical, isn't he?" he said.

"Why, of course he is. He has a lot of ideas for *you*, Stan —work you can do in Chicago. I really want you to talk to him, even if you can't have lunch. You know, with his connections, he could do a lot for you here."

"That's very kind, but I already have so much work——"

"There's been quite good publicity about this prize, you know, probably much more here than in New York. All the papers have carried articles about you and your model city. What do they call it?"

"It—just that. Just a model city."

"Oh, I thought they'd given it some special name. It's really very handsome, Stan." She reached across the table and patted his hand; her diamond and sapphire bracelet slapped against his finger tips. "Hard to believe that my little boy who used to play with toy trains and boats has grown up and plans model cities. It's a shame it can't be built somewhere, isn't it?"

"Yes, it is. Maybe Arthur could arrange it."

"What?"

"With all his connections, he probably could get me a contract to build the city, couldn't he?"

His mother surveyed him with the quizzing glass. "I hope you aren't trying to make fun of Arthur, Stanton," she said.

"Of course I'm not," Stanton replied. "I'm sorry if it sounded that way. It's only that—" he smiled—"whenever you talk about Arthur I always think of Aladdin, on the point of rubbing his lamp."

"Oh, I see. Well, you may not think much of Arthur, but in this town he comes quite close to *being* Aladdin."

There was a cold, prim note in her voice, and for some little time they were silent. Finally, Stanton said, "Oh, come on, Mother. I didn't mean to offend you about Arthur, honestly, and if I did, I apologize. Let's not brood about it. After all, today's a big day. We're both making speeches."

"Yes, we are, aren't we?" she said, brightening. "That reminds me, Johnson will be coming back with the car in just a few minutes, to take me to the meeting, and you haven't told me any of the news. You haven't said a word about the family."

"I haven't had much chance, have I, Mother? We've been talking about other things. We're all fine, and everyone sends his best, of course."

"How's that handsome grandson of mine?"

"Oh, Jerry's very well. Up to his ears in all sorts of activities—dancing schools, and parties, and concerts and so forth."

"Yes, I had a letter from Betsy a couple of weeks ago, and she said she'd enrolled him for a series at Carnegie Hall. I think that's just fine. He'll get so much out of it. She certainly is a wonderful mother to that boy, isn't she?"

"Yes," Stanton said, "she certainly is."

"I'm sorry she didn't come out with you, Stan. I more or less expected that she would. Nothing the matter, is there?"

"No, no, she's fine. It's just that . . . she had other things to do."

"Oh, yes. I know. She's told me about all her committees. She has *so* much energy, hasn't she?"

"Yes, she certainly has. Mother——"

"And yet, along with all her outside interests she manages to run a beautiful home, and be a wonderful mother, and a perfect wife. You're very lucky, Stan. I hope you appreciate that."

"Yes, indeed. I appreciate it a great deal."

"I get *so* distressed with all these divorces. Perfectly nice couples breaking up for no reason I can understand.

No home life you can count on any more. Why, only last week the Maddoxes—they're near neighbors of ours in Winnetka—suddenly decided to get divorced, and Liz is on her way to Reno. It came out of a clear sky, and they have two boys out of college and their daughter June at Sarah Lawrence. Now, what sense is there in that, I ask you? Bill Maddox does drink too much, but he's one of the most important men in the state, and what kind of life does Liz think she's going to have?"

"Mother——"

"It's a great consolation to your old mother to know that at least her little boy is happily married. I always say to people, when I hear about these divorces, 'If you'll come with me to Westport, Connecticut, I'll show you an ideal marriage—my son Stanton and his wife, Betsy.'"

"Mother, if you don't mind, I wish we'd change——"

"You know, when you and Betsy were married, your father was quite upset, because he thought you were too young, and the times were so uncertain, and I told him: 'They're in love, and I know it will last, and while it may not seem important to you now, he may never have another chance of marrying a girl like Betsy.' Of course, Stan, I don't mean Betsy didn't have a bargain in you, a very great bargain, but——"

"Mother——"

"You must admit, she's a wife in a million. Why, I ran into another old girl of yours a few days ago, a tall girl, the one you used to call the 'Princess.' Do you remember her?"

Stanton nodded.

"What *was* her name?"

"Corinne—Corinne Baxter, I think. No, Bartlett. That's it. Corinne Bartlett."

"Yes. Well, you were *quite* interested in her once, and when I met her the other day I thought to myself how lucky it was you married Betsy, because this girl is just—well, she married some shoe clerk or somebody named Branson, who works for Harvester, and really, you wouldn't recognize her. She's let herself go to pieces completely. I suppose it isn't all her fault, because her husband is just a salesman, and they probably live on fifty or sixty a week. But honestly, the contrast between that girl and Betsy!"

"Mother," Stanton said, "I wish you wouldn't keep bringing Betsy into the conversation all the time."

"What?" She stared at him incredulously. "What did you say?"

"I said I'd like to change the subject. I'd rather we didn't talk about Betsy any more."

"Whatever do you mean? I don't understand you. Why shouldn't we talk about Betsy?"

"Just because I'd rather not, Mother."

She raised the quizzing glass and peered at him. "Now, Stanton, don't tell me that you and Betsy have had a row. Have you?"

"No, Mother."

"Well, what *is* the matter with you, then? I've never seen you acting this way before. What's got into you? You've been just as strange as you could be, ever since you came in here."

"I'm sorry, Mother."

"Is something worrying you? Can't you tell me what it is? After all, I am your mother, and if anything is wrong I'm entitled to know about it, aren't I?"

Stanton hesitated. He was tempted, for a moment, to take her last statement at its face value, to blurt it all out, appeal to her, ask her to give him an answer. But then he looked at her, and he realized that it was hopelessly impossible. The answer would have to come from himself, somehow or other. Looking at his mother, with her bracelets and blued hair and triumphant hat, he had the perplexing sensation that he didn't really know her at all, that she was a stranger sitting at his table by mistake. From some dark, mysterious gulf the devastating feeling of isolation and loneliness he had experienced so many times of late rolled up like a huge, enveloping wave. He shook his head; a look of utter dejection was stamped on his face.

"Well, I don't know what to do about you, if you won't even tell me what the trouble is!" his mother exclaimed. "But if you've been quarreling with Betsy, as I presume you have, my advice to you is to patch things up before they get serious."

"Before they get serious," Stanton repeated in a dismal voice.

"Yes. Most of these quarrels are quite unnecessary. A little tact and mutual understanding can work wonders. And when you have a wife like Betsy——"

A headwaiter approached the table. "Your chauffeur is here, madame," he announced. "Shall I tell him to wait?"

Stanton's mother consulted a diamond wrist watch, cried "Heavens!" and tossed her napkin on the table. "No, I'll be right out," she said. "Stan, I'll have to run right along or I'll be late for the meeting. I'm sorry to dash this way."

"Its all right, Mother." He stood up, walked around the table and pulled back her chair. "It can't be helped. I'll walk out to the car with you. By the way," he added, "if it isn't too much trouble, do you think your chauffeur could drop my bag off at the Stevens and leave it at the desk?"

"Of course," she said. "He can do it after he drops me."

He followed in her wake while she made an impressive crossing of the lobby; she had the kind of presence which invariably commanded frenzied bowing and scraping by the flunkies. Outside, under the hotel canopy, she paused at the open door of the black limousine.

"Now, remember what I told you, Stan," she said. "Whatever this trouble is that you and Betsy are having, take my advice and straighten it out right away. And do try to cheer up. You'll really frighten the audience at that banquet tonight if you go on looking so gloomy."

"Yes, Mother."

"Well, the best of luck to you, Stan. We're all very proud of you, and I think your model city is *very* handsome."

Her tone was that of someone commending a child for a superior collection of butterflies.

"Thank you, Mother," Stanton said. I'm not going to wish *you* luck with your speech, he thought, because it seems to me that you're fomenting a lot of dangerous nonsense. "It's been nice seeing you, and I'm sorry it had to be so short."

"I'll be in New York in another three or four weeks," she told him, as the chauffeur helped her into the car. "I'll see you then."

"All right, Mother. That's fine. I'll look forward to hearing from you."

"Don't forget to call Arthur, will you?"

"No, Mother. Good-by."

He stood on the curb for a time, watching the limousine as it receded down the street. Then he went back into the hotel, picked up a newspaper at the desk and returned to the dining room to have another pot of coffee. But he couldn't concentrate on the paper, and after a few sips of the coffee he pushed the cup aside, paid his check and again left the hotel. He had no idea of where he was going, and after wandering aimlessly for twenty minutes or so in the vicinity of the hotel he came out on the lake front and sat down on a bench overlooking a muddy-looking beach. The wind was blowing harder now, whipping up a small, choppy surf, and the occasional strollers who passed along the beach were burrowing in their coats and turning up their collars. But Stanton scarcely noticed the weather. His mind was incapable of assimilating anything but that insistent, plaguing question: What am I going to do?

For now that he was alone, there was no escape from it, no diversion or defense. He made a brief, desperate attempt to hold his thoughts on the speech, but it wouldn't work; the question kept coming back, more and more urgently. Now, he said to himself, I must be rational and stop thinking in circles this way. What are the possible courses of action? First, I might try to ignore the whole thing, condone it, as Chester Hazen put it, but I know I can't do that. Perhaps I ought to call Betsy right now, on long distance, and demand an explanation. But there is no explanation. Well, then, should I see this lawyer, Woods, in New York tomorrow? Or should I rush out to Westport like the traditional outraged husband and have it out with Betsy? Ought I to stage some melodramatics with this man Paige? No, juvenile. I don't want to see him. Well, how about starting divorce proceedings immediately, without saying a word to Betsy, or seeing her? Ah, but then what? What about this other thing, this blackmail scheme, or whatever it is?

And aside from that, what about Jerry, what do we do about him? I suppose this is my chance to get the boy for myself—or more for myself, at any rate—but there's always the danger that if I try to do that I may lose him completely.

He stared out at the restless water and the uneasy sky and presently stood up.

"And I thought all this time that we were so happy," he said aloud, unmindful of the approach of a nursemaid and a small boy. "How big a fool can a man be?"

Then he noticed that the small boy was staring, and the nursemaid was watching him with an impudent smile.

"It's all right," Stanton muttered, turning away. "I'm just rehearsing for a radio program. A soap opera."

He resumed his directionless stroll, walking with head bent and shoulders stooped, eyes following the cracks in the pavement, hands plunged into his pockets. He followed the shore for a time, with the wind jabbing at his hat brim, then headed away from the lake and back toward the city. Stopping for the traffic on a bleak dusty corner, he realized for the first time that he was very cold—almost shivering, in fact. A few doors from where he stood a swaying pink neon sign proclaimed the attractions of the Cheerful Bar & Grill —Cocktail Lounge—Finest Wines & Liquors—Steaks, Chops—TELEVISION.

A pink neon arrow pointed downward, and Stanton followed it to a shallow flight of stairs which led below to the garish, murky basement barroom. A few shadowy figures were seated on stools at the bar; otherwise the place was empty. In the checkroom beside the entrance a thin, bored-looking girl with bleached hair and a wad of gum in her mouth dropped a magazine and stood up. "Check your hat, sir?"

"No, I don't think so," Stanton said. "I'll only be here a minute."

The girl smoothed her dress over her hips and shifted the gum around in her mouth.

"All gents that come in here check their hats," she said, with what seemed to him excessive surliness.

Stanton shrugged and surrendered his hat. "Since you insist," he said.

The girl handed him a check and tossed the hat onto a shelf. "I gotta live too, don't I, mister?" she said, picking up the magazine.

"I suppose so," Stanton replied, and stepped into the dubious cave beyond. He was halfway to the bar before he heard an indignant "Well, I like that!" from the check-room. He smiled faintly. The Cheerful, he said to himself. They must define their words differently in Chicago.

At the bar he ordered a double Scotch, neat, with a chaser of soda, and when it was served he asked the bartender where he might telephone.

"There's a booth over there in the corner, next to the men's room. And that'll be a dollar-ten," he said, shoving a check toward Stanton, who had not touched his drink.

"I'll be right back, I want to make a call."

"O.K., so it's still a dollar-ten," the bartender said. He was a squat, dark, simian fellow with tattooed forearms. "See the sign there?"

"Yes. 'Positively No Credit.' There's another one, too. 'We Trust in God, All Others Pay Cash.' That's very funny. You must have quite a sense of humor."

"Yeah."

Stanton brought out his wallet. He knew just where he had cached four fifty-dollar bills, and he immediately produced one of them and placed it on the check.

"That's the smallest I happen to have," he told the bartender. He picked up the whisky glass and swallowed half the liquor. "I'll make that call while you're getting my change."

"Hey, I didn't mean I didn't trust you, nothing like that. Don't get me wrong."

"I didn't get you wrong," Stanton said over his shoulder on his way to the telephone. "Nobody could do that."

A directory was hanging by a chain from the side of the booth, but the bulb over the telephone of course had burned out, and Stanton found his numbers by match light. He first canceled his luncheon with a prospective client, then dutifully called Arthur. Arthur's secretary reported that the great man was in an important conference, and Stanton disclaimed any desire to call him out of it, but he did spell his name twice, to make sure the secretary got it, and told her that he would try to reach Arthur later.

Then he dialed the number of the Time, Inc., office on Michigan Avenue and asked for Nancy Mainwaring.

"Mainwaring?" the switchboard operator repeated.

"She's from your New York office," Stanton said.

"Oh. Oh, yes. She was here for a while this morning, but I believe she left. Just a minute. . . . Yes, she went out about half an hour ago."

"Do you happen to know where I could reach her?"

"Just a minute, please. . . . No, sir, I don't. She didn't say where she was going, and they don't expect her back."

"I see, thank you."

"Do you want to leave a message in case she comes in?"

Yes, Stanton thought, tell her I think she's wonderful. Tell her I want to see her just as soon as I can. Tell her I've got to see her.

"No, thank you, I don't think so," Stanton said.

He walked back to the bar and gloomily finished his whisky. What now? he asked himself. The idea of being out in the streets, alone, was intolerable. What then? A movie? The Field Museum? Hire a car and drive along the lake? Go to the zoo? Or to the room in the Stevens which had been engaged for him? He still would be alone, and he began to perceive that the aloneness was the problem, not the locale. And it was not the kind of aloneness which would lift with Arthur at the Racquet Club, or with the client at the Blackstone, or with his mother at the meeting of her Tax Abatement League. But it might—he was certain that it would—dissipate if he could be with Nancy Mainwaring.

"Here you are, sir," the bartender said, in an unctuous voice. "Ten, twenty, thirty, forty, forty-five, six, seven, eight, eight-fifty, seventy-five, eighty-five, ninety. There you are sir. Want another, maybe?"

Stanton shook his head.

"How about one on the house, then? I'd like to square things, mister, because I could tell you was sore at me when you went to phone. I didn't mean nothing, honest, but I never seen you in here before and it's pretty early, and this time of day some guys come in and soak it up just to get straightened out from last night, and they've lost their wallet or something, and want a tab. Of course, I don't mean you're like one of those guys, but you gotta be careful, see what I mean? You gotta have a policy. Now how's about a little snort on the house?"

"Well, I'll have another of the same," Stanton said. "But I'll pay for it. Give me a new check."

"You mean you won't take one on the house?"

"No. I'd rather pay for it."

The bartender stared at him. "O.K., O.K., if that's the way you want it," he said, shrugging. "It's no difference to me—I'm not the boss here. I just didn't want you to be sore."

"Don't give it a thought," Stanton said. The checkroom girl suddenly materialized, carrying a tray of cigarettes.

"Cigars, cigarettes," she said, in a singsong voice.

"No thanks, I have some," Stanton told her.

"How about a nice souvenir, mister? Something to take home to the family? One of these dolls, maybe? They always make a hit."

"No, thank you. I really don't want anything."

"Why don't you ask the gent if he'd like his picture taken?" the bartender suggested, as he refilled Stanton's glass. "Corinne takes good pictures, don't you, Corinne?"

"They're all right, I guess. I don't get any complaints, anyway. How about it, mister? A nice picture to send to the folks? I can develop it in twenty minutes for you."

"No," Stanton said, shaking his head. "No pictures. But you've given me an idea."

Corinne. Corinne Bartlett. Now, what had his mother said her name was? Barstow? No, Branson, that was it. Corinne Branson. Not such a common name. He probably could find her in the book. He sipped his whisky and played with the thought of calling her. No doubt she had changed a good deal after all these years, but what of that? Stanton remembered her rather vaguely from a halcyon summer in Nantucket, during his pre-college days. Corinne had come out the preceding winter, and went with a considerably older crowd, but she had sailed with him, and twice he had taken her to the Saturday dances at the yacht club. They carried on a desultory correspondence after Stanton went back to school, and then during the Christmas party season in New York he kept running into her around town, and took her out several times. She was a tall, languid brunette who always was exquisitely dressed and had a much more restrained manner than most girls of her age and class; it was for this that she was nicknamed the "Princess." Girls were apt to refer to her as a snob, meaning that

110

they couldn't afford to dress as well as she did, and boys often dismissed her as a bad sport, meaning that she didn't enjoy being mauled in the back seats of automobiles, but it was this very aloof, untouchable quality about her which most attracted Stanton. He had heard rumors—which he never attempted to verify—that this was mere smoke screen, that she really was just like a good many others, only less obvious about it. But he had formed, and kept, a picture of someone elegant and maturely dignified. He found it hard to imagine Corinne living in the kind of bourgeois squalor his mother had described.

It's silly to call her, he told himself. She wouldn't remember me—why should she? But when he finished his drink, he thought again. He didn't want to spend any more time in the depressing atmosphere of the Cheerful, but the only alternative was the complete loneliness outside. Anything was better than that. It was worth a try. He paid his check and went back to the phone booth.

There were a good many Bransons listed in the book, but on the fifth call, to a near-North Side address, he recognized the sleepy, indolent voice which answered.

"Is this Mrs. Branson?"

"Yes," was the yawning reply. "Who's this?"

"Mrs. Corinne Branson?"

"That's right. Who is this?"

"Well, you may not remember me. I used to know you a long time ago, before you were married. This is Stanton Wylie, Corinne."

"Good Heavens!" There was a pause, and a slight rustling sound, as of someone sitting up in bed. "Why, of course I remember you, Stan! How could I forget? I even remembered your mother—think of that! I met her going into Field's the other day."

"Yes, she told me. I had breakfast with her this morning. . . . I hope I didn't wake you up?"

"No, I was just having a nap. I'm the lazy type, you know. And I had a rough night." Another yawn. " 'Scuse it, please. What brings you out here, Stan?"

"Oh . . . business."

"Didn't I read something about you in the paper? Some prize or something?"

"Yes." He coughed. "That's why I'm in Chicago. I'd like to see you, Corinne."

"That's a fine idea."

"I wondered if you could have lunch with me, or a couple of drinks anyway? Would that be all right?"

"Very good. I haven't a thing planned. It'll be fun."

"Do you want to meet me some place? Where would you like to go?"

"Mm . . . Well, to tell the truth, I haven't had my morning coffee yet, and I'm not good for anything until I do. Why don't you come up to the apartment? Where are you now?"

"I don't know, exactly. Fairly near the Ambassador."

"Oh. Well, that's not far. Jump in a cab and come over. I'll try to get organized. Then we'll decide where to go."

"All right, Corinne. I'll be there in a few minutes. It'll be good to see you."

"The place is called the Denham Arms—don't ask me why. Apartment 6 G. You can come right up."

The Denham Arms turned out to be exactly like a million other medium-sized apartment houses in second-rate neighborhoods across the nation; it was shabby, flimsy, and pretentious, and it tried to look a great deal better—or, at least, more expensive—than it actually was. The front of the building boasted a row of stone escutcheons, while the lobby seemed to be striving for a Spanish effect. Stanton noted that the construction of the place was so bad that even in the lobby sounds carried clearly from the first-floor apartments, and heavy odors of cooking and laundering swirled through the air. Both the noises and the odors were stronger when he stepped out of the self-service elevator on the sixth floor. It most certainly was a disheartening place to call home, he thought, as he pushed the buzzer of the Branson apartment.

Corinne called "Coming!" and after a minute or two he could hear her approaching footsteps. Then the door opened.

"Darling!" she greeted him. "Stan, this is so wonderful! I'm going to kiss you. Do you mind?"

Without waiting for an answer she wrapped her arms around him and kissed him on the mouth. It was a long, provocative kiss, not the kind given to a casual old friend, and at the end of ten seconds Stanton began to feel embarrassed. Still she clung to him. Her body was very warm, and she apparently was wearing nothing but a silk bathrobe.

Then she dropped her arms and broke away and cried, "There, how was that for a welcome? Come on in, Stan. I'm just out of the tub, and I look like the wrath of God, and the place is in a mess, but come in anyway. Gee, it's swell to see you!"

Stanton still was embarrassed, but he delivered the proper salutations with a degree of conviction and entered the boxlike foyer of the apartment. Corinne took his hand and led him through a short, dimly lighted hall, past a blazing bathroom where he glimpsed wet towels on the floor and heard the last of the water going out of the tub with a retching sound. In the living room he looked about swiftly, and saw that the room had not been cleaned after a party the night before. The ash trays were overflowing, dirty highball glasses and empty bottles and beer cans cluttered the tables, and the air was foul.

Corinne threw open a window and said, "I told you it was an awful mess, but it can't be helped. The group came around for a little celebration last night, and I didn't have time for cleaning this morning. I only have a part-time maid, two days a week. I get so sick of housework."

"Well, don't worry about it," Stanton said. "You can't be expected to be ready for callers at this hour." He was wondering why she had invited him here, with the apartment in this state, instead of meeting him outside.

"Callers are welcome any time—if they're like you. Most of the time it's just a guy collecting the gas bill. Sit down on the couch, Stan, and I'll be right with you."

She flicked the switch on a table radio and emptied some ash trays into the wastebasket. As she moved about, Stanton was able for the first time to get a good look at her, and he decided that while his mother's verdict about her might be extreme, there was no doubt that Corinne had changed a great deal for the worse. It was not a question of specific changes—she still was a handsome brunette, still had a presentable figure—but rather a general softening and coarsening, a subtle degeneration of some kind, a pervasive alteration of manner and attitude. He watched her closely while she moved around the room, trying to define what it was. Then it came to him: The Princess had turned into a slut.

Corinne said, "Excuse me a sec, Stan," and went into the kitchen. She came back carrying a cocktail tray with a jar full of martinis, two glasses and a saucer of olives and lemon peel.

"It's getting late, so I decided to finesse the coffee," she told him, placing the tray on a coffee table in front of the couch. She sat down so that she was directly beside him. "If I do say so, I mix a damned good martini, Stan. Here, try one."

"It's pretty early for martinis, isn't it?"

"Never too early for me," she said. "Go on, Stan, you'll like it. Cheers!"

"Well . . ." He took the cocktail and tasted it. "Cheers. Yes, very good, Corinne."

"I told you you'd like it." She emptied her glass in two gulps and immediately refilled it. "There, that's better."

She leaned back with a sigh and turned so that she was closer to him.

Stanton regarded his glass with a frown. "You must be hungry, aren't you?" he said. "Have you thought about where you'd like to have lunch?"

"Oh, let's not worry about that," she said, downing most of her second cocktail. "Let's have lots and lots of 'tinis and sit here and talk, and then we can bother with lunch, if we want it. Tell me about yourself, Stan. What have you been doing? You have a family, haven't you?"

Stanton nodded.

"Well, go on, give! Tell me about them."

"Why, I don't know, Corinne. I don't know that there's much to tell. I have a son who'll be going to prep school next year, and—" he shrugged—"that's about all. It's just another family."

"How about your wife?"

"What about her?"

"Well, good God! What's she like? Is she pretty and young and gay? Are you happy?"

"Yes, she's pretty, and young, and gay," he repeated.

"God, what a clam you've turned into!" Corinne exclaimed. "You need another 'tini. Six more, in fact."

"No, not yet, Corinne."

But she filled his glass anyway, slopping some of the cocktail over the rim of the glass. "Come on, Stan, drink up. I'm 'way ahead of you."

"I will, in a minute," he said.

"I know what let's do," Corinne announced. "Let's talk about old times. The hell with now! Let's talk about the good old days. Hold hands with me, Stan, and we'll get nostalgic together."

Stanton said nothing. He felt Corinne's hair on his cheek as she dropped her head on his shoulder, felt his hand being drawn toward her until she held it tightly just below her breast.

"Oh, Stan, I'm so-o-o comfortable," she sighed. "It reminds me of the old days, and all the wonderful times we had. Remember Nantucket, Stan? Remember the yacht-club dances, and the booming around in roadsters, and the way we used to crash the dances at the 'Sconset Casino? Remember the day we were swimming at Royal's, and there was a big shark scare, and it turned out to be an old inner tube?"

"Yes," Stanton said with a smile. "I also remember that when you walked along the beach in a bathing suit, everybody turned around to look at you."

"Well, I guess I could still do that, all right. . . . You used to have a divine yellow Chrysler, Stan. Remember?"

"Yes. It was my first car."

"It was all so wonderful," she said. "And now everything's so lousy, isn't it?" she demanded. "Isn't it all absolutely stinking lousy?" she said, with a peculiar ferocity. Suddenly she dropped his hand and swiveled around to face him. "Isn't it? Don't you agree with me?"

"Why, Corinne, I don't know. I don't know what you mean," he mumbled. She was holding her glass at a precarious angle, and some of the cocktail spilled on the couch. "What seems to be the trouble?"

She laughed—or at least Stanton presumed that the harsh sound was a laugh of some kind. "Everything," she said. "I live a crummy life, in a crummy flat." She waved despairingly at the living room. "I go to crummy places, wear crummy clothes, hang out with crummy people, do crummy things. I'm even married to a crummy guy. And everything used to be so wonderful."

"I'm sorry, Corinne," Stanton said feebly. "Things can't stay bad forever."

"Well, aren't you the little ray of sunshine!" she said venomously. Stanton perceived that she was in the stage of reveling in her miseries and resenting any implication that they might be less horrendous than she claimed.

She abruptly stood up, lurched into the coffee table, straightened, and started across the room with a wobbly gait. "Hold everything. Got to go to the can."

Stanton stared after her, caught in a mood of black depression. So he had come to *her*—had come *here*—to escape being alone. His first impulse was to grab his hat and rush out of the apartment while Corinne was in the bathroom. But something held him back. It might have been the repellent fascination of her decay. Perhaps he wanted to stay and discover how far the decay had spread, how deeply it had penetrated. Or it might have been the compassion which he also felt. She was sick, no doubt about it; something was terribly wrong.

The telephone perched on the leaf of a desk, just within the reach of his hand. He poked his finger into the dial and called the Randolph number of Time, Inc. No, no Miss Mainwaring, we haven't heard from her, we don't know where she is, we don't think she'll be back. There was an outside chance that she might have gone to the Stevens, and he called Information to get the number. Before he had an answer, however, he was interrupted by the sound of a toilet flushing, and a minute later he heard Corinne's voice.

"Why, Seabee!" she exclaimed. "Did Mother forget she'd put you in the closet? Oh—h, *poor* doggie!"

She came into the living room with a small black spaniel squirming in her arms.

"This is Seabee," she told Stanton. "Isn't she sweet? I call her Seabee because a Seabee gave her to me. That was during the war. Were you in the war, Stan?"

"Why, not exactly. I wasn't in uniform," he said, patting the spaniel. He was agreeably surprised to observe that

Corinne had apparently sobered. At least, she no longer had the wild, distrait look, and her voice was under control.

"I worked at Oak Ridge," he said. "In one of the atom-bomb plants."

"Oh, God, not really! How depressing! I get so fed up with all this stuff about atoms," she said. "Don't you? Let's not talk about *that*."

"All right. That suits me. What about your husband, Corinne? What does he do?"

"Jack? He works for Harvester—advertising department. He's had the same job for five years, and I don't think he'll ever be promoted." Her expression was contemptuous. "The old man was a director, but a lot of good *that* did. Jack's lazy, and dumb. He wants to be a writer."

"What does he write?"

"He calls it a novel."

"Have you read it?"

"Have I?" Her laughter was derisive. "I get it word by word and line by line. Aloud, if you please. 'Listen, Corinne,' he says. 'Just listen to this.' Then he reads it to me, and I want to throw up. I get so God-damned bored, putting on an act about how wonderful it is. If I don't, Sonny Boy gets terribly, terribly hurt, and won't eat his shredded wheat. Oh, Seabee! Seabee wants an olive, don't you, darling?"

The little spaniel was perched in a begging position, batting one black paw against Corinne's knee. She took an olive from the cocktail tray and gave it a toss. To Stanton's surprise, the dog jumped and caught the olive and swallowed it.

"That's something I've never seen before," he said. "She must go to a lot of cocktail parties."

"Oh, I take Seabee *everywhere*. Stan, how long are you going to be in Chicago?" she asked.

"Just today," he said. "I expect to fly back late tonight. It all depends on when I can get a plane."

"Oh, you don't mean it, Stan! You must be kidding!"

"Kidding?" he said in surprise. "What about?"

"About leaving tonight, of course. You just can't."

"But Corinne——" His expression was baffled. "I don't get it. Why do you care when I leave?"

"Tell you why. Corinne's all set for a good, old-fashioned, nonstop two-day binge."

"With . . . me?" he said incredulously.

"Sure. Who else?"

"Well——" He paused and looked at her, wondering if this rigmarole might be part of some obscure joke. But Corinne was grimly serious. "Your husband, for one," he finished.

Corinne snickered loudly. "Sonny Boy! That's funny. I can just see it! Anyway—I guess I forgot to tell you, didn't I?"

"Tell me what?"

"He's out of town. He's off on his annual ten-day trip around the country."

"Oh," Stanton said, "I see."

"It's the one time of the year when I can have fun without him griping about how much I drink, or who I go out with, or how late I stay out," she said. She moved closer to Stanton and put an arm around his shoulder and began caressing his neck.

Stanton was considering how poorly this declaration jibed with the earlier version of Corinne as the neglected and stifled wife of an untalented would-be author. Whatever sympathy he felt before had evaporated, but there was a certain residue of curiosity. He sat inertly, and waited.

"And when he packed his suitcase the other morning and went downstairs to get a cab, what a relief!" she went on. Her fingers were pinching the lobe of his left ear. "So here we are, starting a binge, the two of us. We'll do the town tonight, and then you'll stay with me, and tomorrow night we'll do the town again."

"Corinne——"

"No, don't argue. You've got to stay."

Stanton shook his head.

"I can't, Corinne. I'm here on business."

"Business! This is Saturday afternoon."

"I have to make a speech tonight at a banquet at the Stevens. That's the reason I came to Chicago."

"A speech! How thrilling! I'd love to hear you make a speech. I'll come to the banquet."

"Why, you wouldn't enjoy it at all," Stanton said uncomfortably. "It's a stuffy meeting, with a lot of technical discussions of architecture. You'd be bored to death."

"I don't care. I'm coming anyway."

He saw that this was an alcoholic *idée fixe* which would not respond to logical persuasion, and he tried to think of some other way to ward off her disastrous project. Oh, well, he reflected, she'll be so drunk by then that she won't remember anything about it, much less be able to get there.

"And right after your speech we'll get our binge started," Corinne declared with finality. "We'll have a warm-up binge this afternoon, and then we'll get our real party rolling tonight."

Stanton sighed patiently. "No. I really mean it, Corinne. I can't see you tonight. It's out of the question."

"Well, you're certainly a fine pal," she said bitterly. "Spoiling my fun. Ah, break down and be a sport, won't you, Stan? Please?"

"But I *can't*. I'm sorry, Corinne. Next time I'm in Chicago maybe we can go out."

"The hell with next time! It's this time, while Sonny Boy's away. Well—" she squinted at him, wearing a peculiar loose smile—"I know one way to make you change your mind."

"No, Corinne."

"Oh, yes. Yes I do. You come with me. I'll show you." She emptied her cocktail glass and heaved herself to her feet. "Come on."

"Where?" he asked guardedly.

"Bedroom."

"Why the bedroom, Corinne?"

" 'Cause you and Corinne are going to bed for a while, that's why. And if Corinne doesn't change your mind for you in bed, she'll be a——."

It was an obscenity he never before had heard a woman utter. He stared at her in silent embarrassment for a moment, but when he spoke he managed a somewhat flippant tone, as though passing it off as a joke. "Such language! I'm surprised at you, Corinne."

"Come on, Stan, quit stalling," she said. "Let's go to bed."

She reached out in the general direction of his near hand, missed it by a good foot and a half and nearly fell to the table.

"Whoops!" she cried, precariously bracing herself between the table and the couch. She started to sag toward the floor, and Stanton rescued her by placing his hands beneath her armpits and raising her to an approximately vertical position. Corinne came up with her hair dangling over her face, and before he could step away from her she twined her arms around him tightly and hung there with her head pressed against his chest.

"Come on, now," she murmured. "Why don't you carry me, Stan?"

"No," he said. He felt her arms loosen slightly, and by pressing firmly against her shoulders he was able to back away from her.

Corinne wiped the hair from her face and looked at him blankly. "What do you mean 'no'?" she said.

"Just that."

"You mean you won't sleep with me?" she demanded incredulously.

Stanton could tell that she again had suddenly snapped back to a comparative soberness. He nodded, and said, "That's right, Corinne. That's what I mean."

Corinne placed her left hand on her hip, and watched him through narrowing eyes. "And why not, may I ask?"

Stanton shrugged and shook his head. "Because——" he began. He wanted to say, Because I think you're a mess, and I don't want to have anything to do with you except say good-by and get out. But he noted her expression and the way her face was coloring with anger, and decided on the course of prudence. He had no desire to sample the variety of hell fury which a scorned Corinne might produce. So he merely said, "Because of a lot of things."

"That's no answer."

"I'm sorry for that," he said, with another shrug. "There probably isn't any answer."

"I suppose you're bored with the idea, is that it?" she said, still watching him with a concentrated, catlike look. Stanton said nothing. "I suppose you think I'm not good enough, is that it?" she went on, taking a short step toward him. "Maybe you think I'm too old for you, is that it? Well, guess again, old boy. Baby knows her stuff."

"Corinne, will you stop it, please?" Stanton said sharply.

"Why should I?" she said sulkily.

"Because I'm leaving now, and I may never see you again. I shouldn't have called you this morning, I suppose, but, at least, I'd like to say good-by decently. That's all."

"If you really want to say good-by decently, you can do it in bed," she said.

Stanton glanced once at her face, and once at the living room. Then he shrugged in a tired way.

"Good-by, Corinne," he said. He turned and started toward the corridor leading to the foyer, momentarily anticipating a barrage of cocktail glasses from behind. But there was none.

He reached the far end of the room and was about to turn into the corridor when she called to him. He paused.

"Yes?" he said, looking back over his shoulder. She was standing in the same place, in the same position.

"I want to ask you something."

"Well?" He waited.

"Why *did* you call me this morning, Stan?"

"I told you before, I wanted to look up an old friend."

"Nothing else?"

"Corinne, what are you driving at? I called you as an old friend I hadn't seen for years. It's a perfectly natural thing to do, isn't it?"

Corinne didn't answer. She looked down at the floor for a time, and finally seated herself on the arm of the couch.

"Do you have a cigarette?" she said.

Stanton stood where he was. "You have some right beside you, on the table," he said. "I don't mean to be rude, but I must be leaving."

"No, wait—I'll tell you why I asked that, Stan."

"All right, tell me."

She had a cigarette between her fingers, and carefully lighted it. Then she puffed out a cloud of smoke. "You see, Stan, in the old days you were about the only boy I went out with who never made a pass at me, and I was too repressed to make a pass at you. I always wondered why you didn't because I always wanted you to."

She paused, waiting for him to make some reply, but he said nothing.

"When you called this morning, I thought to myself, 'How nice, now we can get together, after all this time.' But you didn't seem responsive, and I wondered what the trouble was. I thought maybe you were shy. I tried to make it easier for you, but still no dice." Another pause, another puff of smoke. "So it looks as though I've become so unattractive that you just won't have anything to do with me. Is that it?"

Stanton smiled a little, extracting a certain amusement from the palpable dishonesty of everything Corinne was saying. He wondered idly what her motive was, and decided that she was simply playing for time. Well, there was one thing he wanted to discover before he departed.

"Now I want to ask you something," he said.

"Go ahead."

"Do you go in for this sort of thing very often?"

"I don't have many opportunities, do I? That's what's so depressing about you leaving me today."

"And it doesn't bother you at all?"

"Bother me? In what way?"

"I mean, about your husband? Don't you care anything about him?"

Corinne yawned. "What's that got to do with the price of fish? Sonny Boy's out of town, and if I want to have myself a time, what he doesn't know won't hurt him."

"That's not what I mean," Stanton said. He frowned at her in a perplexed way. "Don't you have any feeling of loyalty toward him? Don't you have any conscience about what you do, whether he's away from home or not?"

Corinne laughed. "Conscience! You must be getting noble in your old age, Stan. My God!" she exclaimed. "Don't tell me you wouldn't sleep with me because of *him!*"

"That would be part of it," he said.

"My God, why?" Corinne demanded. She stood up and moved toward him. "If I don't mind, why should you?"

"I won't try to answer that one," Stanton said. "It would take too long, and anyway I don't think you'd understand."

"And you still won't go to bed with me?"

"No. I'm going now. You've told me part of what I want to know. Thanks a lot."

She stared at him, shaking her head. "I just don't get it," she said. "I just don't get it."

She followed him to the door, shook hands with him coolly and now seemed to be in a hurry to get rid of him. Gratefully, Stanton stepped out into the hallway. Corinne held the door and called, "By the way, Stan——"

"Yes?"

"What does *your* wife do when you're away on trips? You might look into it sometime."

Then she snapped the door shut. Stanton heard her quick footsteps retreating, and, after a moment, through the thin walls of the apartment came the faint clicking of the telephone dial. He moved heavily to the elevator, but after waiting a couple of minutes he left it and took the stairs down to the lobby. Outside the Denham Arms he stood on the pavement for a little time looking up and down the street and occasionally shaking his head, rather like a big hunting dog trying to locate a scent. Then he pulled at his hatbrim, set his face against the rising wind and started walking.

Chapter 7

THE chairman was a tall, bony, stoop-shouldered man with an Adam's apple protruding like a piece of bent stovepipe between the wings of his starched collar. Gold-rimmed *pince-nez* dangled on a narrow black ribbon from his lapel, and the braided black cord of a hearing device stretched from the collar of his dinner jacket to the black button embedded in the hairy depths of his right ear. He had a thin, reedy, querulous voice, and a nervous mannerism of pulling at his chin when he talked. His hand already was reaching for his chin when he entered the vestibule of the banquet room. "I've talked to the others," he said to Nancy Mainwaring. "We don't know what to do."

Nancy lighted a cigarette, although she had just snuffed her last one less than half smoked.

"We couldn't hold up the dinner any longer, you know. There are two hundred and sixty out there. We couldn't keep them waiting any longer." He tugged at his chin, then fiddled with the *pince-nez*. "Nothing like this has happened before. We don't know what to do. We're quite upset."

"I don't blame you, Mr. Davis."

"What's that?"

"I say, I don't blame you," Nancy repeated in a louder voice, while the chairman cupped a hand over his ear. "I'm worried about him too. I can't imagine what happened to him."

"You're *quite* positive he planned to meet you here before the press conference?"

Nancy nodded, and said, "Definitely, Mr. Davis. We arranged it last night. He was going to show me the model, after he finished with the newspaper people."

"Yes . . . ah . . ." He looked up at the wall clock over the desk where Nancy was sitting. "It's after eight, and we really don't know what we ought to do. You . . . Miss . . . ah . . ."

"Mainwaring."

"Of course. I beg your pardon. I was about to ask if you knew any other place where he might be?"

Nancy shook her head. "I'm afraid not, Mr. Davis," she said. "I called his mother in Winnetka a little while ago, and she hadn't heard from him since morning. Then I tried the Harvard Club on the chance he might have gone there, but he hadn't. I can't think of anything else."

"Did he seem to be all right, when you were with him?" the chairman asked, rubbing his chin. "There wasn't anything the matter with him, was there?"

"Why——" Nancy considered. "No, I don't believe so. I had the impression that he was rather disturbed about something, but he wasn't ill, as far as I know."

"I see. I see. Of course, he might have had an accident."

"Yes, I've been thinking about that."

"I suppose we ought to call the hospitals, find out whether they've admitted anyone of his description today."

"I suppose so," Nancy said uneasily. "To tell the truth, I was on the point of doing that myself, but . . . I don't know. I kept waiting another fifteen minutes, thinking he'd arrive."

"Yes, the committee felt the same way about it," said the chairman. "One of my colleagues wanted to notify the police some time ago, but I think that's the last step, don't you? We don't want any unnecessary publicity, and no doubt there's some perfectly simple explanation."

"Yes, I'm sure there must be," Nancy said. But, frankly, I'm terrified, she added to herself. *Please,* Mr. Wylie——

"Still, it might be as well to check with the hospitals."

Nancy nodded, and said, "I'll do it, Mr. Davis. I can call right here."

"Oh, no, you don't need to. I'll get one of our people. Why don't you go on in and have your dinner? There's a place for you at the press table."

Nancy smiled faintly and shook her head. "I really couldn't eat a thing, Mr. Davis. I'm afraid this business is getting to be too much for my nerves."

The chairman gave a brief, whinnying laugh. "I haven't much appetite myself," he said. "Well, if you care to make those calls, Miss Mainwaring, I'll excuse myself for a minute and let the committee know what we're doing. They may feel that some announcement is in order."

He moved to the leather-covered door leading to the banquet room and partly opened it; the vestibule filled with the modulated hum of polite talk from the two hundred and sixty diners, punctuated here and there by the rattle of silverware and crockery. "I want to thank you for being so helpful, Miss Mainwaring," he said with an angular bow. "We appreciate it a great deal."

"It's nothing at all, Mr. Davis," Nancy replied. "Just so we find Mr. Wylie—and soon."

"Amen to that," said the chairman. He waved a long, claw-like hand and disappeared through the door. Alone in the vestibule, Nancy ground out her cigarette, then immediately lighted another one. Her fingers were shaking while she held the match, and by the time she had come to the HOSPITALS listing in the telephone book she was biting her lip and fighting an irrational sense of panic. Dear God, she said to herself, while she dialed the first number, please let him be all right. Please!

It seemed to take hours to make the connection—actually it was only a few seconds—and then an interminable time—perhaps a minute—before she talked to the admitting clerk. She was halfway through her description of Stanton Wylie when she heard his voice.

"Hello, Miss Mainwaring."

Nancy dropped the phone as if it had suddenly turned red-hot, and jumped up from the desk. "Stanton!"

"Here I am—the fatted calf. Or is it the black sheep?"

He was standing in the entrance of the vestibule, leaning wearily against the wall. He held a rain-soaked felt hat in his hand, and beads of rain still glistened on the lapels of his tweed suit. He was smiling, in an odd way—smiling without a smile—and the lines in his face were so deep they might have been graved by a sculptor. Nancy was startled by the resemblance. He looks like Lincoln, she said to herself, in one of the old Brady photographs.

Aloud, she said, "Oh, Stanton!"

"Yes, the ghost arrives at the feast. I missed you, Miss Mainwaring."

"Nancy, for short."

"And I've called you here, and called your office, and there, and everywhere. I missed you. Desperately."

"I missed you, too, Stanton," Nancy said. "Don't think you have any corner on the Bell System, though. If I weren't so glad to see you, I'd be sore as the devil. I've been so afraid. Where have you been? What have you been doing? Why are you late? Oh, Stanton——"

He had moved toward her, and Nancy toward him, and their arms were around each other, locked around each other, and the wet felt hat was rolling into a corner, and he pressed his forehead against hers and lifted her face and searched for her mouth. But Nancy shook her head and slipped away from him.

"Not here, Stanton dear," she said, shaking her head. "Of all places, not here."

"What's the matter?" he said. He looked puzzled and perhaps a little wounded.

"It's just the way the coincidence has worked out. Remember, I told you how I met my husband? The meeting at the Stevens?"

"Yes."

"Well——" she took a deep breath and nodded in the direction of the door to the banquet room—"it was right in there, the same room where you're making your speech. You see?"

"Oh." He stared glumly at the door. "I seem to keep running into your husband, every time we——"

"Don't talk that way, Stanton," Nancy interrupted. "Please?"

"I'm sorry. You're wrong about one thing, though."

"What?"

"The speech. There isn't going to be any speech."

"What are you talking about?" she demanded sharply.

"I mean, I'm not going to make the speech. I only came here to get you, and apologize to the committee. I suppose I ought to do that."

"Do you realize a couple of hundred people are in there, waiting to hear from you?"

Stanton shrugged, and stooped to pick up his hat. "I can't help that. They're getting their dinners, aren't they? There are other speakers on the program."

"Are you out of your mind?"

"Maybe." He smiled. "Very likely."

"There's nothing funny about this, Stanton. What's come over you? Won't you tell me what the trouble is?"

"There's no trouble, Nancy. I just decided not to make the speech, that's all."

"Yes, you keep saying that. I want to know why. Where have you been all this time?"

"Out walking."

"Walking!"

"Yes. I walked all the way across Chicago, and all the way back again."

"I gather you stopped in at a few saloons along the way, didn't you?"

"Well, here and there. When I got cold. But that was nothing."

"It's the only answer that makes sense. Are you drunk?"

"Of course not. No, I was walking, and while I walked I was thinking. And when I finished thinking, I decided not to make the speech."

"Stanton, you're not making any sense!" Nancy cried.

She was angry, and frightened, and impatient all at once. "Stop acting!"

He looked at her in reproachful surprise. "Why, Nancy, I'm not acting," he said. "I may not make any sense, but I'm not acting. I mean what I've been saying."

She studied his face, slowly shaking her head. "Have you forgotten the City, Stanton?" she asked. "Don't you want to build it? The speech might help, you know."

"I thought about that, too," he said. "Somehow I don't care any more."

"Do you mean that, Stanton?"

He didn't answer for a moment. Finally he nodded, and in a small, miserable voice he said, "Yes, I'm afraid I do."

Just then she had no anger left; she wanted to put her arms around him, and stroke his hair, and comfort him. But she stood where she was, and the tone of her voice in itself was a rebuke when she said, "So all you were telling me yesterday about the City was moonshine and make-believe, is that it, Stanton?"

He looked away. "I . . . don't know. I know only that I need *you*, Nancy. That was the end result of my thinking. I just want to be alone with you."

"If that's true, why did you take so long getting here? Good God, Stanton, I almost went into hysterics, waiting for you!"

"You did?"

"Yes, of course I did. I imagined you being run down by taxis, and all sorts of horrible things. I——"

"I know, it was inexcusable," he said. "I simply lost my sense of time. I'm sorry. And now let's go. Let's get out of here."

Nancy faced him and said slowly, "We'll go after you've made your speech. Not before."

"Nancy—I can't. I just can't."

"You mean, you think you don't want to."

He didn't answer, and after a few seconds she shrugged and turned to the desk. "I suppose there's nothing more to say, then. You go along, if you feel that way, and I'll let the committee know. They were about to send out a police alarm."

"Nancy——"

"Oh," she went on, "here are some telegrams that came for you. Probably from well-wishers. Go on, read them," she said. She sat down at the desk. "I have to make a call."

"Nancy——" he began, but she waved for silence, holding the phone, and he opened the telegrams. The first was from his assistant, Jake Bundy, and it read:

THE NAG CAME AT EIGHT TO ONE AND I BET YOU WILL BREAK THE TRACK RECORD OUT THERE. BEST. JAKE.

The second was from his secretary:

I AM PRAYING FOR YOU TONIGHT MR WYLIE. HELEN.

Nancy watched him obliquely, pretending not to. She noticed the way his face softened when he read the first two wires, and the way it hardened as he looked at the third.

WE KNOW IT WILL BE WONDERFUL AND WISH WE WERE WITH YOU. MUCH LOVE. BETSY AND JERRY.

He read it and tore it across and across again. Then he rolled the pieces into a ball and dropped them into the basket beside the desk. "Why not sign it 'Betsy and Billy'?" he muttered. "Why drag Jerry into it?" The other telegrams he put into his pocket. He looked down at Nancy's brown, brown hair, with the white splash at the temple. Her right hand rested on the edge of the desk, fingers tapping nervously, and he heard her say:

"Yes, Circle 5-4100, New York. That's right. No . . . No, charge it to Room 1083, Mainwaring . . . Yes, Mainwaring."

"Nancy, what are you doing?"

"I'm calling the office."

"New York?"

"Yes."

"Why? What for?"

She covered the receiver with the palm of her hand and said, "Since you aren't going to make the speech, it probably kills the story. I don't know what they'll decide, but I have to let them know. . . . Yes? How long? . . . All right, I'm on extension 18." She put down the phone. "The circuits are busy."

"Does it make any difference?" he said. "Can't you send a wire and let it go at that? The story doesn't matter now."

Nancy lighted another cigarette and stood up and looked at him with a challenging expression in her eyes.

"You're beginning to annoy me, Mr. Wylie," she said. "The story *does* matter—to me, at least. You forget——"

"No, Nancy——"

"You seem to forget that I'm a member of the working press, Mr. Wylie, and that means getting the story assigned to you. I'm here to write a close-up about *you*. That's why I'm in Chicago—there are pleasanter places, I think. Bermuda, for one."

Her hands were clenched, and she hated herself for the unfairness of what she was saying. But she kept on with it. "You forget that I gave up my vacation to do this close-up about you, and you also forget——"

"Nancy!"

"You forget that the only reason we met was the assignment, the story. . . . Oh, Stanton, Stanton, darling!"

Because it was he who now sat behind the desk, and she stood in front of him, facing him, looking down at him. Nancy could not bear looking down at him that way, with his fingers in his hair and his hands covering his face. She placed her hands on his shoulders, and leaned across the desk. "Stanton."

"Yes?" He raised his head slowly, and his big hands reached for her wrists and closed around them. "Nancy—"

Just then the vestibule door swung open, and the room filled with the sound of the banquet. It was the chairman again, followed by two committee members.

"Why, it's Mr. Wylie!" he exclaimed, in his high, excited voice. "Gentlemen, Mr. Wylie has arrived! Would one of you let the others know? We had just decided that it was time to call the police about you, Mr. Wylie. You've given all of us quite a scare—including this young lady here."

"I know," Stanton said. "I owe everyone an apology."

"Well, better late than never, as the saying goes. We were fearful that you had had an accident." He installed the *pince-nez* on the bridge of his nose and inspected Stanton. "Are you all right?"

"Quite, thank you. I was . . . unavoidably delayed. I couldn't help it."

"Ah, yes, those things will happen, won't they? We're all very pleased to see you, late or not. Dear me!" he added, apparently noticing Stanton's clothes for the first time. "You haven't changed yet, have you?"

"No, I just got here."

"Yes, I see," the chairman said, rubbing his chin. "It's rather unfortunate, though, because they've nearly finished dinner, and I don't want to hold up the program. What do you think, Mr. Fisher?" he added, turning to the committeeman. "Should we postpone things for a bit, until Mr. Wylie changes?"

"As a matter of fact, Mr. Davis——" Stanton began.

"Oh, Mr. Davis, I don't think it makes any difference, do you?" Nancy broke in. "It's the speech that's important, no his suit. Why break up your schedule because of a dinn jacket?"

"That's true, that's very true." The chairman smiled benignly at Nancy. "This young lady has a good head on her shoulders. Well, how do you feel about it, Mr. Wylie? Would you be uncomfortable going on just as you are?"

Stanton hesitated. He glanced at Nancy and for a second held her steady gaze. She nodded, slowly, and finally he said, "No, it won't bother me at all."

Nancy gave an involuntary gasp of relief, and the chairman looked at her in mild surprise. "Then I think we might as well go in," he said to Stanton. "I tell you what I'll do, old man." He patted his shoulder with fine *camaraderie*, and guided him toward the door. "I'll say something about your suit in my introduction. Something humorous. And we'll see you a little later, Miss Mainwaring?"

"Yes," Nancy said. "Make it good, Mr. Wylie."

"I wonder," he said, as he disappeared through the door.

The longer Nancy pondered this cryptic exit line, the less she liked it. By itself the statement might have meant nothing more than an honest doubt, but the tone of his voice had been odd, and his face had worn the same remote, withdrawn expression which she had found so disturbing on the train. During the conclusion of the dinner she kept looking at him from her seat at the press table on the side of the room, and by the time the waiters were clearing away the demitasse cups and the cloudy frappé glasses she had become almost as uneasy as she was in the vestibule before Stanton made his appearance.

The committee's table was placed on a low stage projecting from the wall opposite the vestibule, and the line-up of elderly gentlemen in their dinner jackets made Nancy think of an old-fashioned minstrel show. Stanton had the seat of honor, next to the chairman, and in his tweeds he seemed to be at least twice as large as any of the others. Directly in front of him, on a second table somewhat lower than the committee's, the white model of his city gleamed like a wedding cake beneath the rays of concealed spotlights on the ceiling. Even in miniature, and even viewed at a distance across the smoky room, it was a dramatic, proud and altogether gorgeous creation. The clean, soaring lines seemed to express something which could be felt, but not defined—something like the emotional appeal of a great painting, and as impossible to analyze. It might have been the translation —in bits of wood, wire and plaster—of the kind of dream which could come to a man while watching the stars on a clear, windy night. Or—if it were frozen music—it might have been the climax of some noble anthem. Whatever it was, it seemed to say: This man can do, and for this, much of man may be forgiven.

Nancy didn't like the way Stanton stared at the model, with the deep, frowning lines of his face. She didn't like the way he sat in his chair, motionless, with his hands folded in front of him on the table. She didn't like his abstracted manner when he responded to the questions of the committeemen. She noticed that a couple of them were glancing at him doubtfully and whispering together. The longer she observed him, the stronger grew her sense of foreboding.

Presently the waiters cleared the last tables, and the gavel rapped from the stage. There was a general shifting, and heaving, and turning of chairs. Cigars were lighted, and conversations hushed. The lights dimmed in the room, until the shining model beneath the spots was left as a hypnotic island of brilliance. The chairman rapped again, and adjusted the microphone standing on the table.

"I hope you enjoyed the dinner." The words roared through the room, and he fiddled with the microphone, tapping it with a fingernail. "I hope you enjoyed the dinner," he repeated. "You had filet mignon, you know, and I understand we lost forty-five cents on every serving. We arranged the menu some time ago, before we realized that the price of a good piece of beef would go nearly as high as the price of a good house."

The audience responded with the usual courtesy laughter of audiences on such occasions, but the chairman held a hand aloft and waved it as though to subdue an ungovernable outburst of mirth. Then he continued: "It is a great pleasure to greet all our old friends, and welcome the many new ones who are with us this evening. For all of us, I know, the year has been filled with progress and failures."

He proceeded to inventory these intangibles, gradually working around to a discussion of the state of the building industry, and the future role of private capital in large construction projects *vs.* Federal subsidies. He yielded presently to the Secretary of the Association, who read minutes and reviewed, at generous length, the current and future projects of the group. The Secretary was followed by the Treasurer, who rendered a gratifying financial summary, and then a committeeman offered extended remarks covering labor unions, income taxes, municipal building codes, and the importance of doing something about low-cost housing. The air thickened with smoke, epidemics of coughing seized the audience at diminishing intervals, and by the time the committeeman finished there was a rising hum of talk from the tables at the far end of the room.

The chairman once more applied his gavel, and announced: "I believe that concludes the necessary business of the meeting—business before pleasure, you know—and now we come to the high spot of the evening. Before introducing our principal speaker, and the winner of our 1947 award, I would like to say a few words about the very exceptional—and as you can see for yourselves, very beautiful —model city here before me." He paused, pointing toward the table under the spotlights. "Our competition this year was remarkable in many ways. In the first place, the judges considered the entries of more than four thousand contestants—last year, you may recall, there were about three thousand—and this set an all-time record. Furthermore, I think it is safe to say that, on the whole, the entries established a surprisingly high standard of excellence and originality. As you can imagine, therefore, the judges' task was by no means an easy one, until Mr. Wylie entered the contest and sent us his model city, accompanied, of course, by a prospectus and a set of plans." The chairman stopped to pour a glass of water from a heavy glass carafe. "Mr. Wylie's entry came in late—he will forgive me, I know, if I remind him that he himself came in late for this meeting—and after we had studied it carefully I think there was little doubt left in our minds about the eventual decision. All of us felt that Mr. Wylie's creation was a unique expression of a great and original talent. . . ."

The chairman went on in this vein for several minutes, and Nancy's attention wandered. ". . . bold vision, vast imagination, combined with a sense of practicality which is rare indeed when one considers the ambitious scope of the projected city," she heard him saying. "It is, therefore, a matter of pride and gratification for me to give the Association's 1947 Award to Mr. Stanton Wylie. Ladies and gentlemen, Mr. Wylie."

Nancy joined in the vigorous applause which went up from the tables as Stanton rose and shook hands with the chairman. Photographers were kneeling in front of the stage, and flash bulbs popped in Stanton's face.

"First, the Association's gold medal," the chairman said, producing a square black jeweler's box.

"Next, the scroll of honor . . ." He handed Stanton a diplomalike roll of parchment tied with blue ribbon.

"And, last but not least, the . . . ah . . . honorarium." Here he took an envelope from his pocketbook. "Heartiest congratulations, Mr. Wylie, and our very best wishes to you, both in life and in your career."

"Thank you very much, Mr. Davis," Stanton said. There was more applause, and more flash bulbs went off.

"And now, as the radio announcers say, I'm going to turn

the microphone over to our distinguished guest," the chairman said. "You probably have noticed that Mr. Wylie is in mufti, so to speak, and the reason for that is that he was delayed this evening. He wouldn't tell me what he was doing, but I strongly suspect that he was out looking around for a good site where he could start building his city." He again waved a hand, as though he had just perpetrated some epic of humor. "Ladies and gentlemen, Mr. Wylie."

Stanton moved over to the microphone and raised it an inch or two. Then he stood still and waited, looking out over the audience, the way Chester Hazen had instructed him. He looked back and forth across the clumps of faces at the tables, and discovered that the old lawyer had been more than right. Everyone was watching him with growing expectancy, and the room was nearly silent.

"Mr. Chairman, members of the Committee, ladies and gentlemen——" he began. He spoke quietly, and it seemed to Nancy that his voice was unnaturally husky. "I seem to have a very poor memory for jokes, and I'm afraid I won't be able to start off with the conventional after-dinner story. However, I'll try to make up for that by being brief.

"Mr. Davis, your chairman, just remarked that I might have been late this evening because I was out looking for a likely place to build my model city. In a somewhat backhanded way, he was fairly close to the truth. Actually, I've spent a good many hours walking across Chicago. I walked from the North Side all the way to Stagg Field at the University and then back again, and I assure you it was a thoroughly dismal and depressing experience. Stagg Field, you remember, was where they built the first atomic pile, and where the bomb first crossed the line from theory to reality and began to take shape."

Stanton paused, facing an audience already uncomfortably puzzled. It was his manner, more than his words, which accounted for this, because he certainly did not look, sound, or behave like the conventional after-dinner speaker—with or without the funny story—at the formal annual banquet of a distinguished professional society. In the dimness of the room—all the light seemed to be sucked toward the table where the model city gleamed so brightly beneath the spots—Nancy sat in her chair at the press table and alternately puffed a cigarette, and tied intricate knots in the limp napkin she was squeezing and rolling between her palms.

"I don't mean to offend the sensibilities of the native Chicagoans who may be here," Stanton continued. "But I must confess that by the time I reached Stagg Field this afternoon, I decided that the only decent thing to do to Chicago was to blow it up and start building my city on the ruins. First, of course, evacuating the Chicagoans."

Some highly uncertain laughter greeted this remark, but for the most part the audience maintained a nervous silence. The committee, however, was becoming visibly agitated.

"I don't want you to misunderstand me," Stanton added. "I have no specific grudge against Chicago. I'd probably feel the same way after walking across most of the cities in the country, because I'm sure I'd find just what I found today. It impressed me as a kind of vast torture chamber from which no one could escape. There were no racks or thumbscrews, granted, but I think in the long run there are worse things, and today I saw many of them—unbelievable ugliness, for one, ugliness so colossal and so extended that it must have been deliberately planned; complete degradation everywhere in the midst of ugliness; cheapness, meanness, vulgarity, cruelty, a kind of slimy vileness spreading out like oil dropped on water; poisonous stenches in the air, a lunatic symphony of noise, and everywhere filth. In short, a monument built by greed, and maintained by sloth."

He stopped, but only long enough to draw a breath. "But by the time I finished walking back from Stagg Field, I realized that nothing would be accomplished by blowing it up and building my city on the ruins, because I had forgotten one thing. I had forgotten that the evacuated Chicagoans would move back in."

The audience gasped, and a minor tumult broke out at the committee's table. The chairman stood up, put a hand on Stanton's arm, and said something in an urgent, pleading manner. Stanton shook his head.

"Bear with me," he said. "I'll try to explain what I mean, and I promise that I'll be quick about it." He pointed at the model, and went on: "I've been asked a good many times how I happened to get started on this project. As some of you may know, I worked at Oak Ridge during the war, and

I had a small part—a very small part—in the development of the atom bomb. Frankly, I've always felt guilty about it, and to some extent, I suppose, the model represented an attempt on my part to give some kind of answer to the bomb. I suppose I wanted to say—or perhaps kid myself into believing—that we are still capable of creating more than we destroy, and that the tremendous energies which went into the bomb under the pressure of war might conceivably be mobilized in peace for a diametrically opposite purpose: that is, to demonstrate that we might be as ingenious in cultivating the arts of living, not for an elite, but for everyone, as we are in advancing the arts of killing—and dying."

He kept his eyes on the model, and continued: "Admittedly, the city could be no more than a symbol, since the arts of living can only be pursued by people, not by stone walls. And yet, in looking at the average city, as I looked at Chicago this afternoon, I thought of the enormous total of physical and emotional energy which is subtracted from the population by the planlessness and ugliness, the needless congestion, the smoke, the noise, the antiquated transportation, the shoving and herding, the resulting bad temper and bad manners, and all the rest of it. Of course, there is no precise measure of the effect of such things, but it still can be studied. You can see it written on the faces of the passing crowd in the late afternoon, and you can hear it in their snarling voices on the subways. And you can go farther, if you like, and watch it at work in their homes and their lives —tired, angry, frustrated, disappointed lives, for the most part, no matter how long you talk about the American standard of living, free enterprise, or whatever popular slogan you fancy. Empty, sterile lives, with no past and no future, creating nothing, fearing everything, quaking at the earliest frost and bending to the mildest breeze. Lives endlessly devoted to the pursuit of escaping life, dedicated to the pursuit of the ostentatious and mendacious; lives geared to comic strips and soap operas, free-dish double features, bingo games in what is quaintly called the Church, saloons, dance marathons, prizefights; lives feasting on the brutality and pornography of the stories in the lowest-common-denominator press; lives glorying in ignorance, crudeness, and cruelty, and resenting and mistrusting anything better.

Worst of all lives that subscribe to a shameful hypocrisy."

He paused, and took a sip or two of water. Except for the rasping of a match and the sound of a chair being shifted around, the room was quiet. The committeemen were all leaning forward, watching him.

"Of course, as I say, there is no precise measure," Stanton went on, in a somewhat calmer voice. "It's anyone's guess to what extent the moral and intellectual debasement of people can be ascribed to their physical surroundings. My own opinion is that it must be very great, and I'm not referring to the extremes of Tobacco Road or Nazi prison camps, but to the ordinary environment of the city masses. At any rate, that was one important element in my over-all philosophy when I planned the model. I attempted to project a city where the usual ugliness, inconvenience, and soul-racking grind would be eliminated. In addition, I tried to conceive of a plan which might have some inspirational value, but this was secondary to the main attempt."

He stopped for a moment, and watched the firefly points of cigars and cigarettes winking in the smoky gloom.

"You may wonder what I expected to accomplish by all this in the long run. Certainly it wasn't just a case of art for art's sake. I must confess, I was naïve enough to believe that in the course of time, people living in an ideal city might possibly become a bit more ideal themselves. I don't mean that I expected overnight to have a Velásquez in every art studio, a Pasteur at the head of the health department, a Jefferson for mayor and a Pitt on the board of aldermen, while a Voltaire wrote the most popular newspaper column and a Hogarth did the cartoons. . . . I won't go on with it; you can supply your own candidates right down the line. No, nothing like that, I assure you. But I did have a simple—in fact, simple-minded—idea that perhaps, eventually, people in such a city might look out on wider horizons, and raise their sights to some slightly higher ambition than huckstering their way through life with a new car every year and a record of taking every mean advantage they could to . . . well, end with a bigger tombstone.

"The idea was that people might gradually develop a sense of values a little more satisfying than the value of the dollar. They might find that the pursuit of happiness isn't synonymous with the pursuit of money. They might distinguish more clearly between education and learning, between statesmanship and politics, between thought and prejudice, between a living faith and a quarter in the Sunday collection box, between applauding a Fourth of July orator who talks about liberty and displays a singular apathy the rest of the year. They might play with the meaning of that weary old word 'tolerance' and in time discover they had been too tolerant of a good many things incompatible with their lip service to the dream of our republic.

"I'll stop. You can fill the rest of the list according to your own notions. . . . The only point was that we had all the machinery at hand for the full life, and nothing was done with it. When I planned my city, I thought I might be doing something to bridge the gap by releasing a lot of energy that was wasted on the mechanics of living in outmoded cities. I thought that energy might—if given freedom—perhaps rise like gas in a balloon and lift the people tied to it."

He paused, shook his head, and sipped more water.

"That was why I planned the city," he said. "It was long ago, and as I confessed before, I was very naïve. Perhaps I'd been living in an ivory tower, or perhaps I was so wrapped up in my own work that I never saw what was going on around me. Lately, however, I've been learning the facts of life the hard way, and it seems laughable, now, that I once not only believed these fine theories, but even was mad enough to try to put them into practice with this——" He waved toward the model with an oddly contemptuous gesture of dismissal. "But no longer. My education has progressed to a point where I can see the absurdity and futility of my delusions, and I now realize clearly where they would end. While I walked across Chicago this afternoon I watched the faces of the people along the way, and I began to understand that it is all very well to move the hogs out of the wallow, but they still will be hogs, and they will bring their filth with them. Put them here——" he motioned again toward the model—"and, like the hogs they are, they immediately will try to turn it into another wallow. The idea of living in anything else, in any other way, would frighten them. It would make them feel even smaller than they are, even more insecure. Their twisted little egos would cry out in revolt, and they would rush about, snorting and trampling and smashing, strewing their filth and smearing their obscenities over everything in a frantic effort to debase it and get back to the wallow. In the end, of course, they would destroy it, no doubt using their newest gadget for quick results."

There was a grim smile on his face as his hand tightened around the neck of an empty water carafe. He lifted it from the table and held it at arm's length in the glare of the spotlights, above the model. Then he turned it upside down.

"You'll all recognize it, I'm sure," he said. "The familiar mushroom trademark . . ." He studied the inverted carafe and added: "One should do the job nicely, I think."

Suddenly he opened his hand. The heavy carafe dropped squarely to the center of the model city and struck with a splintering, cracking sound. Then it bounced aside.

"But if one isn't enough, there's always another."

He ignored the confused shouting from the audience; ignored the committeemen and the chairman reaching out to stop him. He even ignored the cry he heard from the press table at the side of the room: "Don't, Stanton, don't!"

Quickly he reached for another carafe. This one was nearly full of water, and this time he didn't drop it; he raised it overhead and threw it down as hard as he could. This time there was the crunching of wood and the sound of shattering glass. Stanton glanced once at the wreckage of the model city, and said, "That does it."

Brushing aside the committeemen, he walked quickly around the banquet table and jumped down from the stage. Swiftly he threaded his way across the room, with the startled dinner guests backing out of his path as though to avoid a dangerous animal. He went directly to the press table, stopped in front of Nancy Mainwaring, seized her hands and said, "Come on, we're leaving."

Chapter **8**

Where are we bound, incidentally?"

"Oh, I don't know," Stanton said. "Anywhere."

"That isn't much help to the driver, is it?" Nancy replied. "He's already gone around the block twice, waiting for you to decide."

"Well, you suggest something. I can't seem to think."

The taxi turned right on Michigan and commenced its third circuit of the Stevens.

"There used to be a place called the Parakeet that was fairly nice. At least, you could breathe in it," Nancy said. "Driver, is the Parakeet still running?"

"Yes, ma'am. It's on Walton."

"Let's go there, then. Does that suit you, Stanton?"

He nodded. "Just as long as it isn't another one of the places where you and your husband used to hang out."

"Is that necessary, Stanton?"

"No. . . . I suppose not. But I am working up quite a case of jealousy."

"Hm. I suppose you're going to tell me that that accounts for the exhibition you put on at the banquet. A fit of jealous rage, was that it?"

He smiled a little. "Not quite, Nancy. Go on, you might as well get it off your chest. Tell me I made a fool of myself. Tell me I'm a disgrace. Tell me I'll never be able to look my friends in the eye again."

"You can't laugh it off, Stan."

"I know."

"Since you built the model, I guess you had a right to smash it if you felt you had to. But——"

"But what?"

"Oh, I don't know. I haven't had time to sort out my thoughts, if any. Except that I've rarely heard such arrogance in one short speech."

"Arrogance!" he exclaimed.

"That's the only word for it."

"For what? I don't see what you mean."

"Don't you think it's rather arrogant to set yourself up as an arbiter of the entire human race? Isn't it arrogant to be handing down such devastating verdicts, as though you were an Old Testament prophet? Oh, I admit, it was very dramatic and very effective, but, I repeat, it was arrogant."

Stanton was genuinely shocked. "I swear I didn't intend it that way, Nancy. That wasn't the idea at all."

141

"Very likely it wasn't. But that's the way it came out. Well," she added, as the taxi came to a stop, "here we are at the dear old Parakeet."

A doorman wearing a shako and a greatcoat with gilt frogs and epaulets handed them out of the cab, and inside the club a pair of glossy, villainous-looking Levantines condescended to lower a green velvet rope and admit them.

"Heavens, it's all been changed," Nancy said, as they followed one of the Levantines into the throbbing interior. "It used to be a little place—*intime*. Now look at it!"

Stanton rejected a table on the floor in favor of a quieter location farther back. The captain seated them and took their order, then hovered until Stanton suddenly realized what was expected of him. He brought out his wallet and silently handed the man a folded bill, which he pocketed without acknowledgment.

"Nice fellow," he remarked. "He just wants to make us feel at home."

"That's what you get, with all this chi-chi," Nancy said, looking around the flashy room. "I'm sorry, Stan, it wasn't a bit like this, the last time I was here. A third as big, and twice as pleasant. No dice game. Think of that."

"What?"

"Haven't you noticed that practically every joint in Chicago has one of those dice boards, where you can roll for drinks? If they don't have it next to the bar, you're in tony surroundings. Probably means roulette upstairs."

"Oh. . . . Well, I can live through the evening without roulette."

"Yes, I'd say you'd had enough excitement for one day."

"I suppose it was pretty awful, wasn't it?" Stanton said. "The old boys on the committee probably wish they'd never heard my name."

"I don't know. You may have caused a few cases of apoplexy, but when they think it over they'll probably decide that you're a mad genius, and let it go at that. Anyway, it's partly my responsibility. I egged you on into making the speech."

"I'm rather glad you did, in a way. I feel better, now that I've got it out of my system."

Nancy lighted a cigarette and leaned back in her chair.
142

She looked at Stanton for several moments, and said, "I think it's about time you told me what the trouble is, don't you? After all, I seem to be involved in it myself."

Stanton shrugged. "The speech——"

"I don't mean the speech," Nancy interrupted. "I mean the reason for all this."

"Why, I . . . when I got up there and started talking, I just had to say what I thought, that was all."

"Now, Stanton, you don't expect me to believe that that speech was the one you planned to make when you came out here."

He smiled faintly and shook his head. "Hardly. I had a nice, conventional, soothing little talk in mind. Full of fine phrases about service and ideals. You know the kind."

"Yes, and I want to know what accounted for your—shall we say radical?—revision. I admit that a long walk across this town might do strange things to you, but there certainly must have been more than that."

He nodded.

"Well, what happened? Please tell me."

"Are you really interested?"

"That's a silly question, Stan, and you know it."

He looked at her with a gentle smile and reached for her hand. "You don't know what you do for me," he said. "It's so good to be with you again."

Nancy held his hand between both of hers and smiled back at him with a sunny warmth in her brown eyes. "I'm not a bit ashamed to admit," she said, "that for me, it's been one of the longest days I can remember."

This soft and tranquil moment was violently terminated by a brassy fanfare from the orchestra. There was a sunburst of harsh light from the canopy over the dance floor, and a bouncy master of ceremonies hopped out from the shadows behind the bandstand and did a jigging walk to front and center while the silver honeycomb of a microphone descended from the ceiling on a black cable. He went through the business of shaking hands with himself and bowing to the applause.

"Welcome to the Parakeet—the *new* Parakeet," he shouted, displaying teeth which looked the size of piano keys. "I'm glad to see all you lovely people out there enjoying yourselves, but me, I got bad news tonight. Yes, I'm down in the dumps. On the way over here I ran into an old friend of mine who's an acrobat in vaudeville. He got engaged to a lady contortionist in the circus, and tonight he told me the bad news." Pause. "They broke it off."

"Oh, really," Nancy murmured, "this is too much. I'm sorry."

Stanton moved his chair closer to hers and held her hand more tightly, and found that there was nothing to say.

After an exhausting monologue the master of ceremonies leeringly introduced the Parakeet Pretties—a line of six languid-looking bordello alumnae who waved hips, breasts and *maracas* approximately in time to "Come to the Mardi-Gras," with a frenzied climax of tossing the *maracas* to the cash customers and retreating with volcanic bumps. Then there was a comedian who gave "impersonations" of Maurice Chevalier, Wallace Beery, Charles Boyer and Zazu Pitts, in that order. Next came the "song stylings of lovely Adele so-and-so," a trite bleached blonde in a black dress shining with sequins who sang "My Bill," "Ain't Misbehavin'," and "If This Isn't Love" in a treacly voice from a bath of blue light. Finally the Parakeet Pretties reappeared for the concluding number, and the lights mercifully faded.

"I wouldn't have believed it, if I hadn't seen it," said Nancy. "It reminds me of the night-club scene in *Pal Joey*. Did you see it?"

"Yes, twice," Stanton answered. "It was great."

"Yes—and what a score! Remember 'Bewitched' and 'I Could Write a Book'?"

Stanton nodded, and said, "Maybe the orchestra would play them, if we asked."

"No. Not now. First, tell me what goes on."

"Well——" Stanton hesitated. He signaled a waiter for another round of highballs, fumbled with a package of cigarettes, looked at Nancy, then away from her, then toward her again, nervously tapping a plate with his heavy seal ring.

"Go on, Stan."

"Well, it's an awfully old story," he said with an effort. "You've heard it a thousand times, and it's very dull except for the people mixed up in it.

"In a nutshell," he continued, "it comes down to the fact

that I have far too much in common with a man named Paige. Billy Paige."

"The actor?"

"Yes. Do you know him?"

"No. I've heard about him, and I've seen him on the stage. In fact, I saw this current play of his awhile ago."

"Oh. Well, very likely my wife was somewhere in the audience, admiring her hero," Stanton said wryly. "You see, she's the thing I have in common with Mr. Paige. I told you it was an old, tawdry story."

Nancy regarded him silently for a time. Then she said, "Of course, I knew something was troubling you, almost as soon as we met, and I gathered that it had to do with your wife. But I didn't think—— How long have you known this, Stan?"

He spread his hands apart in a baffled gesture. "You know, it's the damnedest thing, but I've discovered that you can't always measure time by the clock or the calendar. It seems to me I've had this business on my mind for twenty years, but it's only been a little more than a day. It's incredible. I heard about it only yesterday afternoon, just before I went to the train. It . . . it came out in a peculiar way. I suppose I might as well tell you about it," he said. He went on to describe his morning meeting with Chester Hazen, and the later denouement in his office. In retrospect, the encounter seemed even more unreal than it had when it took place. "It was the way it all happened, apart from what he told me," he finished. "It hit me between the eyes."

"I should think so," Nancy said gravely. "I'm amazed you got on the train at all."

"To tell the truth, I don't remember anything about getting on the train. There's a big empty space there, when nothing seemed to happen."

"Hiatus."

"Yes. It's a lucky thing I did make the train, because if I hadn't met you I don't know what I would have done. You really saved me. It sounds corny, but I mean that."

"I'm glad I helped, Stan. I didn't do anything."

"Yes, you did. You were there. You were warm, and friendly, and sympathetic, and—just generally wonderful. You were someone I could hold onto."

"Thank you," she told him. She stroked the back of his hand for a moment. "I'm beginning to understand some things that puzzled me about you, but there's more, isn't there? What did happen today, Stan?"

"Nothing specific. A lot of muddled thinking about the whole mess, getting more depressed and more confused the longer I thought. Things seemed to keep piling up on me all day . . . starting with the breakfast I had with my mother. That was the first mistake."

"Was it? Why?"

"Oh, Mother's always been inordinately impressed by Betsy's social position and the amount of money her family has, so I kept hearing about what a wonderful wife she is, and how I ought to appreciate her, and so on and so forth. I tried to talk to Mother, but it didn't work. She's very smart about money," he added bitterly. "And not much else, I'm afraid. Anyway, the breakfast was pretty ghastly."

"Mm. And then what?"

"I wandered around in circles, still trying to think things out and getting nowhere. Then I got cold and went into a bar and had a couple of whiskies, and tried to call you at your office. I never needed anyone in my life so much as I needed you just then."

"I wish I'd known, Stan. I'd have come like a shot."

"I know you would. Anyway, the idea of being alone was more than I could face, and that led up to the second big mistake." He paused and shook his head. "A real lulu. You see, at breakfast my mother happened to mention a girl I used to know years and years ago, and just to have someone to talk to, I called her up. At that point I didn't need any more lessons in how wrong I could be in judging people, but she certainly gave me one. It seems that her husband was out of town on business, and——"

His account of the Corinne episode was extensively censored, but Nancy could fill in the gaps for herself.

"The worst of it was that, after all, Corinne and Betsy had just about the same background," he went on. "They moved around with the same people, turned up in the same places and went to approximately the same schools, and the rest of it. I don't know. I began to think that, except for having more money and being better preserved, Betsy probably was exactly like Corinne, and had been all along, and I never realized it."

Nancy watched him frowning at his highball glass while he talked. Poor Stanton! she thought. Poor, poor Stanton! What am I going to do about you?

"When you take something on faith for as long as I have, and then all at once you find it isn't there and never has been there, it leaves a vacuum," he was saying. "I guess I lost my orientation. I felt as though I was stumbling around in some dark forest, without a compass, with no idea of where I came from, or where I was heading. It seemed to me everything was disintegrating. I'd look at the people on the street, and wonder why they were there—why anything was there, for that matter. I kept wondering what held it all together, if you know what I mean."

"Yes. And did you find the answer?"

"I believe so. I decided it was an illusion. Faith in something that never existed. That's all there is to tell, Nancy. Except that I don't know what possessed me to go all the way to Stagg Field. It's a hell of a long walk."

"Stan, what was your marriage like, before this happened? Were you happy?"

He gave a sardonic laugh and finished his drink. "I was even able to extract some amusement from that little joke I'd been playing on myself. Yes, I thought I was happy. I thought she was, too. Lately it seemed to me we were having too many quarrels about nothing in particular, but compared with what I'd seen of a lot of other marriages I thought ours was pretty good. Funny, what?"

"Isn't there a chance you may be wrong about all this, Stan? I mean, couldn't there be a mistake somewhere?"

Stanton shook his head. "If it had come from anyone but Chester Hazen, that might be a possibility. I thought about it. But no. It isn't just what he told me. It's all sorts of odds and ends I never paid any attention to before, but as soon as I started looking at them they fell right into place. My memory has been working overtime the last twenty-four hours," he said grimly. "All the time we were talking on the train last evening I kept remembering things. Like that line you quoted from *Private Lives*—it started me thinking about the first time Betsy met Paige, out at Westport."

She nodded, reflecting that his expression now was almost as tortured and desolate as it had been then.

"Stan, tell me about her, will you? What's she like?"

"Corinne asked me the same thing this morning; and I wasn't able to tell her anything at all," he said with a shrug. "Betsy—what's she like?" he repeated. "Yesterday morning I suppose I could have given you some kind of a description, but not now. I just don't know."

However, with Nancy's urging he did bring himself after a few minutes to talk about Betsy. His words were halting at first, but as he went on he spoke more fluently. Nancy listened to him in silence, and by the time he finished her face had a puzzled frown. "Oh, yes," she said. "How old is she, Stan?"

"Betsy? She's about my age; a little younger. Why? Why do you ask that?"

"I——" She paused. "You talk about her in such a strange way, Stan. If I'd been overhearing you from the next table, I would have assumed you were describing a child."

"A child!"

"Yes. A very lovely child." She paused again. "You're quite mad about her, aren't you?"

Stanton looked at her in astonishment. "What?" he exclaimed. "Mad about her, like—a—a——"

"Never mind," Nancy said, with an odd little smile. She looked at him thoughtfully, and asked, "What are you going to do about it, Stan? Have you decided?"

"No," he said morosely, "I haven't decided a thing. I've been asking myself the same question all day long, and I've been hoping that you might give me the answer."

"That *I* might? You mean, you're putting it up to me?"

"Yes, that's just what I mean," he said. "I haven't been able to get anywhere by myself, and I . . . I don't know, Nancy." His hands tightened around hers. "I have this feeling about you, somehow. This afternoon, while I was walking and wondering about everything, I had the feeling that you were the only person in the world I could come to, and talk to, and—trust."

"Bless you, Stanton."

"So, you see, I hoped that you——"

Well, Mainwaring, Nancy said to herself, this really does put it up to you, doesn't it? Are you going to be honest enough to face the fact that what you want most is to console him, in any and every way you can—and do it? What's to stop you? There's no barrier. There's not even a question of right and wrong—much. He's here, and he wants you, and you want him, so where do we go from there? Ah, yes. He'd like you to answer his question, and maybe he can give you the answer to your own. If you'll let him. Or let yourself let him.

Suddenly she laughed, and said, "When *Life* told me to do the Stanton Wylie close-up they handed me quite an assignment, didn't they?"

He glanced at her in surprise for a moment, and then joined in her laughter. "They did at that, didn't they? Well, let's forget it. I—would you like to dance?"

"Yes, of course." She stood up, smoothing her hair with one hand and her skirt with the other. "What's your style, Stan? Arthur Murray, Fred Astaire or Don Pallini?"

"Oh, an elusive blend of all three. I'll give you fair warning. The last girl I danced with said it was like trying to pull a car out of a mudhole. I forget her name."

"Why, was she leading?" Nancy inquired.

They stepped onto the floor and embraced lightly. The orchestra started playing "Sweet Lorraine," and after a few turns Nancy said, "Stan, you're a big faker! You aren't bad. Not a jitterbug, but very smooth and pleasant. I like it."

"I wish Betsy could hear you say that. She's always complaining——"

"I thought we were going to try to forget about that for a while. Or can't we?"

"Yes. I'm sorry. Let's see about that request now, shall we? What'll we ask for?"

" 'I Could Write a Book' is my candidate."

Stanton maneuvered her across the floor to the bandstand and paused beside the piano. "Do you happen to know ' I Could Write a Book'?" he asked.

The pianist launched a vicious attack on the keyboard and barely glanced up. "That's an oldie, isn't it?"

"It's not so old," Stanton said. "We'd like to hear it."

"I dunno. . . . Hey, any of you guys remember 'I Could

Write a Book'?" he said out of the corner of his mouth, addressing the brass section. One of the men nodded, tightening the reed of his saxophone, and the pianist said, "Okay, coming right up."

"Thanks a lot," Stanton said. He held Nancy closer, pressing his cheek against her hair, feeling an electric shock of pleasure at the warm congruence of their bodies, and the way her elastic flesh moved and yielded against his. Suddenly he felt buoyant, relaxed and confident, filled with an uncommon sense of well-being. He struck out more boldly than before, and, as he whirled her around, Nancy's fingers slipped between his and squeezed them, while her other hand gently tugged at the hairs on the back of his neck.

"My, such energy!" she said, looking up at him with a bright smile. "Oh, here's our song, Stan. They're actually playing it straight, not lousing it up with fancy stuff."

"Yes. . . ." A lone trumpet was carrying the melodic line against a subdued accompaniment by the strings and piano, and Stanton listened to the clean, simple notes spinning out of the horn like knots on a silver thread. In a small voice, Nancy sang:

> " 'If they asked me,
> I could write a book
> About the way you walk and whisper, and look.
> I could write a sonnet
> On how we met,
> So the world would never forget.
> And the simple secret of the plot,
> Is just to tell them that I love you a lot.
> And the world discovers, as my book ends,
> How to make two lovers of friends.' " *

Now the trumpet faded, and three violins picked up the tune and repeated it. Stanton and Nancy swayed together in time to the music, scarcely moving from a spot at the corner of the floor. Enormously moved and almost childishly elated, Stanton caressed her shoulder and drew her toward him even more closely. He bent his head until his cheek rested against her hair; he could see the jet of startling white shining in the smooth, deep-brown mass.

"Nancy—?"

"Yes, Stan?"

"Do you want to know something?"

"What?"

"I think I must be falling in love with you."

He felt her body give a tiny, involuntary jerk and heard the sudden intake of her breath. "No, dear," she murmured.

"I'm sure I must be."

"I'm sure you aren't. . . . It's nice to hear."

She looked up at him with a wan little smile which accentuated the slight tilt of her mouth, but there was sadness in her eyes, and after a second she shook her head and looked away. Her hand moved across the back of his neck.

"Then how do you account for this feeling I have about you, Nancy? This sense of intimacy, and warmth, and—well, everything. You said you felt some of it yourself."

"Yes, Stan."

"It isn't just rebound from the . . . the other thing. It isn't so simple as that."

"No, dear. I know that. It's something else."

"Well, then?"

"Let's not try to label it, Stan. Let's just let it be there—as long as we can have it."

"I was thinking——"

"Yes?"

"The strange way we've talked to each other tonight, and last night, too."

"Strange, dear?"

"Yes. . . . As though—as though we were married."

"Oh, Stan! Stan, darling!" She said it with a sob. Then with a heedless, impulsive gesture she threw both her arms around his neck, lifted her face to his and kissed him on the mouth.

"There," she breathed. "There, Stan, dear. Now let's sit down, shall we? They're starting to play a samba, and I'm just not up to it."

They were oblivious of the amused stares which followed them as they went to their table. Stanton was holding Nancy's chair when someone touched his arm. He heard a bored, nasal, excessively upper-class voice saying, "Well, if it isn't my old chum, Stan Wylie!"

Stanton recognized the voice, long as it had been since he had heard it. He turned slowly, and his expression was stony. "Hello, Fairchild." He spoke in a flat voice, and deliberately kept his hands at his sides, ignoring the other man's outstretched right. Nancy glanced curiously at the stranger. He was about as tall as Stanton, but heavier, and his gray flannel suit fitted too sleekly. He had wavy, graying hair and a bland, supercilious face. She noticed that he was holding a black cane with a rubber tip, and then she saw that his foot was encased in a heavy, misshapen orthopedic boot.

"This is Mr. Fairchild," Stanton announced perfunctorily. "Miss Mainwaring."

Mr. Fairchild nodded slightly, and made some indistinguishable sound of acknowledgment. "I saw you on the floor," he said to Stanton. "Turned into quite a dancer, haven't you?"

Stanton didn't reply.

"I hear you've become quite an architect, too," he went on. "Doing well, no doubt?"

"Yes," Stanton said. "How are your jokes, Fairchild? Know any new ones?"

Mr. Fairchild gave a brief snort which might have been interpreted as a laugh. "Oh, come now, Stanton! You're not brooding about *that*, are you?"

"Try it yourself sometime, Fairchild."

"Well . . . what a cordial reception. Still married, Stan?"

Stanton nodded. "Still Betsy? Or——" He glanced at Nancy. An insolent glance.

"Why don't you get back to your own table?" Stanton said. "No one invited you over here."

Mr. Fairchild shrugged lightly. "I just wondered," he said. "I saw you two on the floor, and——"

"Clear out, Fairchild. Go on."

"Of course," said Mr. Fairchild. "Do you need to be quite so boorish, Stan? Why don't you brush up on your manners a bit? Read Emily Post, or something." He turned and took a couple of limping steps. "So nice to have met you,

Miss . . . uh . . ." he said over his shoulder. "I really don't understand how you put up with him."

Stanton watched Mr. Fairchild as he stumped around the dance floor to a table on the far side of the room. There was angry color in his face when he sat down close beside Nancy. "Sorry," he muttered. "That certainly was a fine climax to our—oh, hell!"

"Please don't, Stan," Nancy said. "Take it easy, won't you? What's it all about?"

Stanton didn't answer immediately. He waited until the choking rage died in his throat, and his hands loosened their grip on his highball glass.

"Sorry, Nancy," he said presently. "I haven't seen him for years. He was in my class at Harvard. Clay Fairchild—you've heard of him?"

"Mm—steel, or something?"

"No, you're thinking of Fairless. No, the Fairchilds control most of the Lakes shipping west of Cleveland. They're pre-Mother O'Leary Chicagoans, and—oh, you know. Clay's famous as the greatest practical joker in the United States. Winchell talks about him."

"Oh, *that* one. He has a club foot."

"Yes. That's why I didn't slug him. I've always wanted to."

"That sounds rather out of character, Stan."

"Does it?" Stanton smiled. "I'm not so sure."

"He knew your wife, I take it?"

"You can call her that, if you want to. I don't."

"Stan, please!"

"All right, I'm sorry again." The rage had been quenched in his throat, but there still was a dull glow of anger in his belly, and his hands were still tense, his eyes too narrow and too bright. "Yes, he knew Betsy," he said curtly. "Who didn't?"

"Stan!"

"Well, yes, I'm being a damn fool. He knew her—that had nothing to do with it, though. He was the prize funny boy of the class—snakes in your bed, air out of tires, ink squirting on your shirt from a lapel button, that sort of thing. No one ever did anything, because of his foot. He used it like a foxhole." Stanton paused. "His mother had a

153

house in Boston, on River Street, across from the Lincolnshire Hotel—do you know the Lincolnshire?"

"Just the Statler," Nancy said.

"And he gave a party, the night before Commencement . . . an awfully hot night. All the windows were open, and most of us were in the garden in back. . . . Betsy came with me, and Clay kept hovering around, making a play for Betsy. . . . A lot of funny stuff went on, as usual. But he saved the big joke for me—the Zonite."

"The *Zonite!*"

"Yes, Zonite, you know. I'll tell you what happened. It's not pretty—do you want to hear what happened?"

She nodded.

"Well, as I said, it was hot as hell, and Betsy and I were sitting on a couch in the living room, because there was more breeze there, admiring a Chinese rug on the floor, and a butler came along and asked what we'd like to drink. We said we'd like ice water, and a couple of minutes later who do you think came back with the ice water?"

Nancy nodded again.

"Yes, Fairchild. Betsy got the ice water, and I got the Zonite—in a tall glass, with a lot of ice on top to kill the smell. It looked like water, and I was thirsty, and I swallowed a mouthful before I knew what it was. Then——"

"Then?"

"Then I was sicker than—I don't know what. When it hits your stomach juices the stuff boils up and expands about a thousand times its own volume. I remember doubling up, falling off the couch, and being on my hands and knees, and trying to crawl away from the Chinese rug before I let go. I was out cold for two or three hours."

"And your—where was Betsy?"

"Oh, she stayed. She waited. Yes, indeed. She was very, very kind, and so understanding. Apparently she believed what Clay said—that I'd had too much to drink."

"I suppose the club foot is the answer."

"No. I told you, he just used that as an excuse for getting away with as much murder as he could, because he knew no one would be likely to beat him up. He's simply a natural-born stinker."

"Without the club foot he might not be, though. Stan!

Don't look so offended!" Nancy burst out laughing. "I'm not trying to defend the man!"

"Well, why make up excuses for him?"

"I'm not making up excuses. Oh, Stan dear, I'm sorry. I suppose it's my journalistic training. I have an unfortunate habit of always trying to find another answer than the obvious one, because when you turn people and things around a little and look at them from the side or the rear they practically never are what they seem to be on the front. You must know that."

" 'To know all is to forgive all'—is that it? I think if you'd had a swig of Zonite you'd be a little less charitable."

"I'll save that for some particularly morbid occasion. . . ." She reached for his hand, and said, "Don't be angry, Stan. We have such a little minute to ourselves, and it's running out so fast."

He stared at her. "What do you mean?"

"I mean the time, darling. Do you know what time it is?"

"Why, it must be midnight."

"It's half-past two, Stan, and this girl has to be in the office tomorrow morning. No, *this* morning."

"The *office!* You mean, you're still planning to write the close-up about *me?*"

"Certainly I am. Why not?"

"Well, after that speech, I should think——"

Nancy smiled. "In the first place, the speech probably makes it a better piece. I expect you'll be a national celebrity before the week's out, what with the publicity about smashing the model of a city that everyone in the world wants to live in. . . ." Her smile broadened, and her glance was taunting and provocative. "Stan, tell me the truth. Are you sure you didn't do that on purpose, because you knew it would have publicity value? After all, Salvador Dali did pretty well when he smashed his own exhibits in a department-store window on Fifth Avenue. And when the world's greatest writer—that's Saroyan—turned down the Pulitzer Prize, he——"

"No, wait a minute! You know perfectly well——"

"I'm only teasing, Stan." She patted his hand. "No, I'm certain they'll want the piece. If they don't, that's all the more reason for Nancy being on deck. If they kill the

Wylie piece, don't you see, we'll have to run something else, and that involves all sorts of last-minute rushing around, the coffee-benzedrine routine, and I'll be needed. At least, I hope I'll be needed."

"All right. Suppose you were sick? Suppose you broke a leg, or something? You couldn't go to the office. The magazine wouldn't suspend publication, would it?"

"No, *Life* goes on, one way or another, and they haven't had any blank pages so far. Of course, if I'm out of commission, there are others. But the subtle point is that I'm *not* sick, and I *haven't* broken my leg, and that makes all the difference. Even for you, Stan, even to make our little minute a little longer, I couldn't throw the story. I couldn't. . . . No, Nancy has to put herself on a plane to New York. Right away."

"New York," he repeated. It was an exhausting prospect. New York.

"Yes. . . ." She gripped his hand. "You're awfully tired, aren't you, Stan?"

He nodded.

"What are you going to do?"

"Coming with you, of course."

"I hoped you would."

"You knew I would. Kiss me?"

"Yes." Her oblique eyes with the slow, sleepy, creamy-brown lids were closed, but her lips were like the wings of homing pigeons. She kissed him with the winglike lips parted, her teeth grinding against his, her tongue darting to the corners of his mouth and searching the tiny banks of warm, wet flesh beyond, below, beside, above, and——

"Oh!" She pushed away, shaking. "No, Stan, no."

"I love you."

"Do you? Yes—for our little minute I love you. I . . . let us . . . I . . . We must go, Stan. Must, must, must."

She fastened her arms around him like steel hoops. Then: "Stan, do you love me? Tell me again you love me."

Ten minutes later they were in a taxicab carrying them in morose silence from the Parakeet to the Stevens. The vacant lobbies of the hotel droned with vacuum cleaners and waxing machines, and a gray bent man with a pail was scavenging cigar butts from the sand-filled urns along the concourse. Stanton paid his bill and retrieved the luggage while Nancy called the airport. Then they were in another taxi speeding along endless flat streets between endless rows of black houses, flagged block by block by a neon BAR. . . .

It was an old DC-2, flying a milk route with stops everywhere between Chicago and New York. The ceiling lights were off, and the hostess conducted them through the rustling blue gloom to the double seat at the head of the line, behind the pilots' compartment. She spread a blanket over their knees; there was the fiddling with the locks until the seats went back to a reclining position. Stanton heard the dull cough of the port engine, the nervous revving, the starboard engine coughing. . . . The rev . . . The quick drag down the runway and the sense of having your frame pulled away from you leaving your stomach and everything else on the ground while a skeleton flew on . . . The fading lights . . . The markers on the runway . . .

And before the plane cleared the field Stanton was sound asleep, with his head resting on Nancy Mainwaring's shoulder. She pulled the blanket up around him and kissed him gently on the forehead before she, too, went to sleep somewhere over Indiana.

Chapter **9**

THE plane was late getting into LaGuardia, and it was mid-morning by the time they finished an uneasy breakfast in a restaurant across the street from the Airlines Terminal. Nancy searched the *Times* in vain for mention of Stan's speech. He watched her in desperation while she finished her coffee and picked up her gloves and her purse.

"I suppose there's nothing I can say that would make you change your mind, is there, Nancy?"

"No, dear. I'm sorry, but it can't be helped. Don't make it any harder for me, Stan. I'll have one cigarette with you, and then I must go."

He lighted a match for her and held it in a hand that was not altogether steady. "It's such a crazy muddle," he said gloomily. "I meet you because of this article, and now the damned thing takes you away from me."

"I know, dear."

"I—could I go to the office with you, and just wait?"

Nancy smiled at him and shook her head. "I wouldn't be able to get a bit of work done with you there, Stan. Besides, if the morals committee found out about it there'd be hell to pay."

"Morals committee?"

"An unofficial organization of spies, snoops and gossips, self-appointed custodians of other people's behavior. You know. Every big office has one. The girls would have *such* fun if they knew that you and I . . ." She left the sentence unfinished, but to herself she said, If they knew that you and I what?

"Yes. . . . I guess that wasn't a very good idea. I just can't face leaving you. I don't want to go through another day like yesterday."

"But . . . aren't you going home?"

"Home! Home for what? That's the last place. No, I'll stay in town and wait for you. What time will you be through?"

"I don't know. Probably around six. . . . Then you haven't decided anything, Stan?"

He shook his head. "Nothing. Nothing at all. I suppose I'll call that lawyer. Not that I want to."

"But you have to face it, Stan, one way or another."

"I know. I know," he muttered. "I'll have it out with Betsy sooner or later, but I need more time . . . to straighten out my own thoughts. Maybe the lawyer . . ."

Nancy took a last puff of her cigarette and ground it out in the ashtray. "Well, I must be off now, dear. I'll meet you in the lobby of the building a little after six, if you're really staying in town."

"I'll be there."

"And, Stan, try to hold onto yourself, will you?"

"Yes."

"No, really. Promise me you won't do anything foolish. I'll be worrying about you all day. Promise?"

"All right, I promise." The only trouble is that I'm not sure what's foolish and what isn't, he was thinking. They left the restaurant and went out to a Forty-second Street strange in its Sunday morning emptiness. The day was fair, with a cool, stimulating breeze, a day for a fast drive across country with the top down, through the flaming October woods to an ocean finished with summer softness and looking hard and purposeful, with chromium glints on the crests of the breakers, and the spindrift flying in puffs of white mist; then a venerable country inn somewhere at dusk, and a warm, strong drink—perhaps a hot buttered rum—on a cobbler's bench before a stone fireplace flanked by old copper; room to stretch out legs, and time to do no more than feel peaceful and settle the desperate problem of charcoal-broiled whole live lobster with drawn butter and potato chips *vs.* charcoal-broiled top sirloin with French-fried onions. . . .

He found himself holding the door of a taxi at the cabstand by the Grand Central entrance.

"Six, then, Stan dear, Time & Life lobby."

"Yes." They kissed lightly and swiftly, and he closed the door. The taxi went into gear with a sound like an antique coffee grinder and moved along Forty-second Street toward Madison. He saw her face in the rear window, saw her wave. . . . Then he was alone with the city.

He gazed up at the vacant, glittering windows in the stony hedge of skyscrapers, lonely and hostile, with their empty offices and locked bronze doors. Above them a tiny, soundless yellow airplane was completing the "s" in "Pepsi-Cola" while the "P" raggedly crumbled in the upper wind. Beneath his feet the curbstone trembled with the vibration of a passing train. A red cross-town bus boomed across the Lexington Avenue intersection. A group of taxi drivers were arguing outside the Commodore, and in the showroom at the corner of the Chrysler Building the virginal automobiles revolved on a slow turntable like cruets in a Lazy Susan. People strolled idly, idly paused at windows, idly went on. The curbstone trembled again. . . . A man dropped his newspaper into a wire basket and stood with his feet apart, lighting a pipe. When it was drawing satisfactorily he spat into the basket and walked away.

Stanton could read the headline on the discarded paper: TRUMAN ANNOUNCES NEW PLAN TO EASE FAMINE.

He temporized and procrastinated. For some reason he remembered a confused day of boyhood, his first day away from home, when his mother delivered him at the rustic headquarters of a summer camp and left him there, and he cried in front of the hearty, impatient camp director when the dust settled behind the heavy old Pierce-Arrow limousine driving down the sandy road. Within a week, of course, he was engrossed in raucous exploits and happy as the other pagans, but in the beginning, for the first few days, he was a stranger among strangers, and he felt like—well, like Stanton Wylie standing on the curbstone of Forty-second Street that Sunday morning with strangers passing and the rumble of trains shaking the concrete beneath him. The little yellow plane rounded out a fat "a" in the "Cola" and darted away while the "Pepsi" was disintegrating in the fine autumn air of the Bronx.

Stanton remembered that he needed a shave, and after discovering that no barbershops were open in the vicinity he dropped into one of the Liggetts in Grand Central and purchased a razor, a box of blades, a washcloth and a tube of cream. This equipment he carried to the men's room, where he engaged a twenty-five cent shower and washbasin compartment, and proceeded to bathe and shave.

He felt a little better after this, and compelled himself to go to a phone booth. He fumbled in his pockets, searching for the slip of paper which Chester Hazen had given him, but before he found it his fingers brought out another paper, folded in a perfect square, from his vest. He looked at it incredulously—the note which Nancy had sent to him on the train: "Dear Mr. Wylie: If you feel strong enough to begin the ordeal, I'm holding down a table in the club car and thought you might like to join me here. . . . Nancy Mainwaring, *Life* magazine." The note was barely a day and a half old, but Stanton stared at it as though it were a rare document of antiquity. Then he again folded it and returned it to the same breast pocket.

He found the lawyer's number after a bit, and dialed it reluctantly. There was something irrevocable about this step, something which would plunge him into dreaded realities, and he feared it. A woman's voice answered the phone.

"Is Mr. Woods there?"

"Who's calling, please?"

Stanton told her, and the woman said, "Oh, yes, Mr. Wylie. This is Mrs. Woods. He was expecting your call, I know. I'm terribly sorry, but he was called down to Washington yesterday afternoon, and I don't expect him back until late tonight. He asked me to apologize, and said to tell you that he can be reached all day tomorrow at his office. Do you have that number?"

"Yes."

"Then you'll call him tomorrow?"

"Yes. . . . I believe so. Good-by."

He hung up the phone and left the booth with a decided sense of relief, relief which he knew was childish, because he knew that what Nancy had said was true: "But you have to face it, Stan, one way or another." Nevertheless, it was there. For a while longer, nothing would have to be done.

Out on the street again he stood on the curb and wondered where to go. For a moment he thought of walking over to the Harvard Club, but he gave up that idea when he recalled that it was Sunday morning. The Harvard Club would not be merely dim and religious as usual; it would be positively sepulchral. Then he had another idea, and hailed a cab.

"Where to, Mac?" the driver demanded rudely.

"Twenty-one West Fifty-second."

"Huh? You mean the Twenty-One Club?"

"That's right."

The driver swiveled around and squinted at him. "Why, they ain't open Sundays, Mac," he said pityingly. "They ain't never open Sundays."

Stanton was both bored and irritated. "I didn't ask you whether they were open," he said sharply. "I told you where I want to go. If you don't want to take me, I'll get another cab."

The driver, subsided, muttering, and they drove on. When they arrived at the address he again swiveled around and said, "See—I told you. They ain't open." He left the meter running, obviously expecting another destination, but

Stanton was in no mood to proceed farther with him. He paid his fare, adding a minimum tip, and climbed out of the cab. No doubt it was an irrational gesture, but he had no intention of being patronized as a yokel who didn't know one end of Fifty-second Street from the other.

Then he laughed at himself. What an infantile reaction to a completely trivial incident! He smiled as he stood on the pavement in front of the celebrated iron gate of "21"; gate which was the nemesis of so many aspiring egos lured thither from far, unlikely corners of the republic by Duncan Hines and the Broadway columnists. He still was smiling when he became aware of the shuffling approach of a wraithlike figure, ill clad and unshaved, who moved in a cloud of whisky vapors.

"Mister——"

Stanton regarded the creature impassively.

"Don't get sore, mister," the scarecrow pleaded. "I don't want you to get sore."

"Nobody's sore," Stanton said. "What do you want?"

There was the familiar tale of the lost railroad ticket, the job waiting in Philadelphia and no money to get to it, the empty stomach these many hours, the frantic need for a cup of coffee, and the ardent promises of early repayment. The scarecrow recited all this as mechanically as a radio announcer reading from a script, and with about as much conviction.

"Why don't you just say you want a drink, and let it go at that?" Stanton demanded. "Why go through all this?"

The creature snuffled and mumbled, and allowed that that was a sensible approach, but some folks unaccountably refused to give handouts for liquor. He conceded that, if pressed, he *could* handle a snort just to settle his stomach, because his stomach was giving him a powerful lot of trouble lately. Stanton fished in his trousers for a quarter. Then he looked at the shambling old wreck before him and thought, What the hell. He brought out his wallet. Somebody might as well have a good day. And in this case it could be purchased so easily, so cheaply. He reflected that all the righteous folk then kneeling in churches and cathedrals from Trinity to St. John's would regard it as a deplorable gesture; on the other hand——

"Here, maybe this will help," he said. "Go on, have a good time. Be a man of distinction. And," he added, "good luck to you on that job in Philadelphia!"

The scarecrow peered at the bill. For a moment he looked as though the money was the key to riches beggaring those of Fort Knox. But he turned the bill over, snapped it between his fingers and confronted Stanton with a snarling face and a snarling voice.

"Oh, a wise guy, huh?" he muttered between yellow, broken teeth. "Want to get me picked up for passing bad grass, huh?" He ripped the bill in half and threw the crumpled pieces into the gutter. "I did time for that once, you——"

He shuffled away, yelling obscenities, leaving Stanton to contemplate the remnants of a ten-dollar bill in the gutter and to wonder if the Corn Exchange Bank had decided to take up counterfeiting as a sideline. That was where he had got the bill—or, rather, Miss Rice had got it for him, when he sent her over to the bank to cash a check. . . . He shook his head. It was so strange, this automatic disbelief of generosity, this spiteful, self-seeking—oh, hell! He had brought it on himself, he decided. He stooped and retrieved the scraps from the gutter, thinking that he could put the bill together again with Scotch tape and redeem it. Like Humpty Dumpty. Why didn't I give him the quarter?

But the incident was salutary, because it had the curious effect of breaking through the stalemate of his own inanition. He watched the old bum roving aimlessly down the street, headed nowhere, and some essential switch in his brain suddenly closed. He would have to face it, one way or another, and the time might as well be now. He again consulted the slip of paper which Chester Hazen had given him, and started walking toward Sixth Avenue.

Chapter **10**

THE building was a rusty old brownstone walk-up on a mean street in the cheap-jack neighborhood bordering the theatrical district in the West Forties—street of parking lots, dim little basement restaurants, and pianos counting the measures of Chopin *Études* in the parlors of obscure studios. Through an open window Stanton glimpsed a girl in leotards practicing ballet turns in front of a mirror. Somewhere in the vicinity a soprano was doing scales and cracking on high C with an agonizing persistence.

In the dusty hallway he found MCKENNA printed in pencil on a smudged card, and he pressed the button beside it. There was an interval before the door lock started clicking, an interval in which Stanton fought down the impulse to turn and bolt.

The apartment was at the rear of the ground floor, and as he approached a face peered at him through a door held open a suspicious two inches.

"Yes?"

"I'm looking for Miss McKenna," Stanton said. "Is this her apartment?"

"Yeah."

The door opened a few inches farther, and Stanton looked at the girl in surprise. She was very young, very fresh-faced and bright-eyed. She was dressed to go out, wearing a little toy hat with a toy veil.

"Are you Miss McKenna?" he asked.

The girl shook her head. "No, Dreamboat's inside. You want to see her?"

"I'd like to speak to her."

"Hey, Dreamy," the girl called. "There's a guy here wants to see you." From the apartment came the answer: "Tell him I'm not buying anything."

"She says she's not buying anything," the girl repeated.

"I'm not selling anything," Stanton said.

"He says he's not selling anything," the girl relayed.

164

Something was said which he didn't understand, and then, after a moment, another figure appeared at the door.

"Yes? What do you want, mister?"

Stanton of course had formed an unconscious picture of what Dreamboat probably would be like, and the picture was not too inaccurate. At least, he felt as though he might have recognized her if he had seen her without knowing who she was. Dreamboat's age was indeterminate—the early thirties, most likely; certainly the age of her face was beginning to make questionable the validity of her bright, brittle-looking blonde hair. She had a slender, compact body, still retaining the hardness acquired during years of professional dancing, and a sharp, alert, wary little face which did not readily smile. She had an air of tense watchfulness, combined with a kind of instinctive hostility. Altogether, an uncomfortable sort of person.

Like the girl, she was dressed up and ready to go out.

"Miss McKenna, my name is Wylie, Stanton Wylie," he announced. "From Westport, Connecticut."

If there was any reactive expression on her face, he couldn't detect it.

"I wondered if I might have a little talk with you?"

"What about, mister?"

"A private matter that concerns both of us."

There might have been the merest flicker of something, but it was so quickly gone that he couldn't be sure.

"I can't talk to you now," she said. "I'm just leaving."

"Well, later, then? When you come back?"

"I may be out all day."

"I thought we might be able to reach some agreement, if we talked things over," Stanton persisted.

She gave him a long, appraising look. "How do I know you're on the level? How do I know who you are?"

"I'll be glad to show you my identification," Stanton said. "And I'd really appreciate a chance to talk to you. I'm anxious to work out a settlement—" he paused to let the word sink in—"as soon as possible. I'd like to do it right now."

She gave him another long scrutiny, then nodded briefly and said, "O.K., I guess so. You don't mind going by yourself, do you, Flo?" she added to the girl. "I couldn't go with you, anyway."

165

"All right, Dreamy."

"Let me know how it turns out, huh?"

"Sure. I'll stop around later."

"Good luck, kid."

The fresh-faced young girl brushed past him with a muttered "Excuse me, mister," and Stanton faced Dreamboat McKenna in the frame of the open door. She motioned him across the threshold and closed the door behind him; he heard the latch snap shut.

Then she turned and looked at him. "Well?"

"I wanted to talk to you about your husband, my wife and yourself," Stanton said. "Here's my driver's license, if you care to look at it."

She took the paper, turned it over, and handed it back without comment. Standing there in the square, shabby room, with her body as taut as stretched rubber, and her keen eyes still giving him that calculating look of appraisal, she reminded him of a fighter in the first round of a bout, studying an opponent before moving in to attack.

"Go on," she said.

"I understand that you are planning to divorce your husband in New York, naming my wife as co-respondent, and that you may also take—other action as well."

"You know a lot, don't you, mister? Where'd you pick that up?"

"Is it true?"

"Could be. Say, what are you, anyway—a lawyer?"

"No, nothing like that. I came here because I——"

"I'll tell you why," Dreamboat broke in. "You came because your wife's got herself into a jam and you want to fish her out of it before some of the mud gets plastered on you; that's the score on that one."

"It isn't quite that. I——"

"Mister, you're wasting your time. Mine, too."

"Miss McKenna," he pleaded, "all I'm trying to do is to save a completely innocent person."

"Innocent!" Dreamboat exclaimed with derision. "That's a laugh, all right. Mister, if you think she's innocent, just go and ask my lawyer for the stuff he's got on them."

Stanton shook his head. "I'm not talking about my wife, Miss McKenna. I'm talking about my son."

"What?"

"My son. Didn't you know I had a son?"

For the first time since he entered the room, she shifted her gaze from his face, and her tense, hostile expression underwent a peculiar change. A frown puckered the corners of her pale, gray-green eyes, and her lips tightened to a thin straight line. It might have been a look of annoyance, or surprise, or perhaps of both. Stanton found it impossible to read her face.

"No, I didn't know it," she said. "So what?"

"Now that you do, does it make any difference to you?"

"How do you mean, 'make any difference'?"

"Well, I mean——" He paused. "Miss McKenna, I wonder if we could sit down and discuss this thing calmly?"

She shrugged, and said, "Sure, I guess so. It doesn't cost anything." She indicated a day bed against the wall behind Stanton, and for herself chose one of the three chairs in the room. She moved it slightly so that her back was toward the light coming through a pair of skimpily curtained windows which looked out on a vista of fire escapes, clotheslines, and a weary old maple tree with leafless branches.

"Oh, say, mister," she said, "could you spare a cigarette? I ran out this morning."

"Yes, certainly."

"You don't have to get up," she said. "Just toss it over."

But habit alone brought Stanton to his feet. He presented the cigarettes with a courteous gesture and courteously held a match for her. When it was lighted, she gave him a quick, puzzled glance, as though she couldn't understand why he, of all people, would be showing her this unaccustomed consideration; that he automatically would do the same for anyone from a duchess to a scrubwoman was something which wouldn't occur to her at all.

"Thanks," she said, drawing deeply on the cigarette. "That's better; I haven't had one since breakfast."

Stanton returned to the day bed and sat down. He waited for a few seconds, studying Dreamboat while she smoked the cigarette with an almost primitive enjoyment. The light fell strongly on the left side of her face, and he could see that beneath a thick coating of powder her complexion was rough and pitted.

Suddenly she raised her hand and covered her cheek. Her eyes again were fixed on him relentlessly, and her expression again was hostile. He had studied her face too long, and now he was embarrassed.

"You were talking about your kid," she said. "What about it?"

He looked down at the worn figured carpet which extended a bare inch under the bed. The edges of the carpet were scuffed, and there were a couple of old stains, a few charred, oblong brown spots. Burns.

"I . . . the boy's thirteen," he said, still looking at the carpet. "I came to see you on his account. He's my son, and I love him. I want to save him. That's why I'm here. That's the only reason, believe me."

Dreamboat took another long puff, and said nothing.

"It's not as if he were a little baby any longer. He's a big boy now. He goes to school and reads the papers, and—everything. He's growing up. He has no part of the mess, and if he finds out he'll be—well—you can imagine what it might do to him."

"Why didn't your wife think about that when she started fooling around with Billy?"

Stanton simultaneously shrugged and spread his hands.

"I don't know. I have no idea what she thought, or whether she thought at all. I haven't spoken to her since I discovered what's been going on."

"Just how did you get your dope, mister?"

"Why, by accident," Stanton said. "A friend of mine, a lawyer, heard something by chance, and took the trouble to investigate, and then told me you were planning this—action. I have no idea how he found out the details."

"That story smells like strictly from fish."

"I'm sorry, Miss McKenna. That's the way it happened. Why would I make it up?"

"That's what I'm wondering. If your wife——" She stopped short.

"What?" Stanton demanded. "If my wife what?"

"Nothing. Skip it. Wrong number."

"All right. Since we're playing 'How Much Do You Know?' with each other, Miss McKenna, I'd like to ask how *you* found out so much about their relationship?"

Dreamboat gave a harsh laugh. "I guess you don't know much about show business, do you, mister?"

"No," Stanton replied, and added to himself: Thank God for that. "What's that got to do with it?"

"In show business, an actor has about as much private life as a . . . a dummy in Macy's window. Everybody knows everything about you as soon as it happens, and half the time six months in advance. Besides, Billy lives in a hotel."

"Yes, but what—?"

"Other people live there, too. They see things, and hear things, and talk, don't they?"

"Yes," Stanton conceded. It was becoming even more sordid than he had imagined—more sordid, and more trivial, more inexcusably cheap. "I see."

"But I didn't have to wait for the word to get around," Dreamboat continued. "I'd of heard all about it, don't worry. But Billy saved me the trouble. He told me."

"*He* . . . he told you?"

"Sure. Quite some time ago."

Between dry lips Stanton muttered, "Why?"

Dreamboat laughed—laughter like breaking glass.

"Billy's a funny guy, the cheap son of a bitch. I guess he's got one of those things—what do you call them?—complexes. Yeah, a complex, that's it." She appeared to be quite pleased with herself for the successful gestation of the word. "He's the kind of a guy, if he knocks over some tramp from Brooklyn who's working in the line, that's like drinking a cup of coffee—not worth talking about. But if he knocks over some real high-class tramp from Newport, or Westport, or one of those places, then he's got to talk about·it, see what I mean? He's got to tell *me* about it, to show how he's coming up in the world. Get it?"

Stanton winced. His stomach arbitrarily performed some unpleasant convolutions.

"What's the matter, mister?"

Stanton shook his head. He was unable to speak, fighting the up-welling sickness. The thing was monstrous, degrading, incredible; it lacked even the minor saving grace of the illusion of romance, the *grande passion* which might account even for mean things perpetrated in mean ways. It was nothing. And it was nothing in such public, indecent fashion.

"I'm all right," he said, finding his voice at last. Absurdly, he remembered a magazine article he had read about the bodily manifestations of mental turmoil, remembered vivid diagrams of hearts and stomachs reacting to anger and frustration, and decided that he agreed completely with the thesis. Oh, yes, it was about psychosomatic medicine, and it had run in *Life*. And then . . . then he remembered that Nancy Mainwaring had met her husband because he was interested in the psychosomatic factor in tuberculosis. . . . It seemed very distant, the banquet room at the Stevens.

"What are you doing about your wife?" Dreamboat asked. "Say, do you have another cigarette?"

Stanton nodded, and repeated the ceremony of rising from the day bed, walking over to her chair, giving her the cigarette and lighting it for her. And Dreamboat repeated the puzzled glance of someone unable to understand why he did it. She even smiled a little smile.

"You're a funny guy," she said. "I don't figure you."

He sat down, and said nothing.

"What about your wife?"

He shook his head wearily. "I don't know," he said. "I can't decide anything about her until I settle the question of what's to be done with Jeremy—my son."

"I see. What's your proposition, mister?"

"Well, I presume you intend to divorce Paige anyway?"

"You're damned right I do."

"Then I'd like to persuade you to do it in Reno instead of here, to avoid the publicity."

"Why should I?"

"Naturally, I'd expect to make it worth your while."

"What do you think it would take, mister?"

"I have no idea. That's for you to say, isn't it?"

"And if I say nothing, what happens then?"

"Then—" Stanton paused—"I suppose I take my son as far away as possible and keep him away until the thing blows over, on the off chance that I can keep him from finding out the truth. Then I suppose I move permanently to a different part of the country, and try to invent some story or other." He shrugged hopelessly. "But it wouldn't work. Sooner or later it would be bound to catch up with him. After all, Paige is well known, and my wife is prominent."

"I know all about how prominent she is, mister. Billy made a big production of it."

Stanton glanced at her curiously. "I didn't realize you ever saw him. I understood you were estranged."

"I see him, all right," she said bitterly. "I see him at the stage door, nights he gets paid, when I try to get some of the dough he owes me for support."

"Can't your lawyer do something about that?"

"Billy knows more ways of getting around lawyers than you ever dreamed of, mister. It's tough enough trying to collect money from an actor even when he wants to pay, and Billy's the slowest guy with a buck in New York. But I get it out of him—sometimes. Once he wouldn't cough up and I waited until he left the theater and started yelling 'Stop thief' out on the sidewalk, and a whole gang of people was chasing him down the street. Gee, that was funny! He came through, all right."

"Yes, I can see. . . ." He looked at her, reflecting that with a natural toughness and no encumbering scruples, she would be a fairly terrifying adversary.

"Well, Miss McKenna——" he said. The sudden, stabbing ring of the doorbell interrupted him.

Dreamboat jumped up as quickly as a frightened cat and opened the door the merest crack. She peered out furtively for a moment, then laughed and pushed the button to release the outside door. "It's my friend Clancy, from the station house," she said. "He's a detective."

Clancy materialized a couple of seconds later, a husky, gray-haired man of about forty, with a quiet voice and a polite manner. "I hope I'm not disturbing you, miss," he said. "I've been out looking around for those bums, and I thought I'd stop by and ask if you'd seen anything of them, the last day or two?"

"No, I haven't," Dreamboat replied. "Come on in, why don't you? Sit down and I'll get you a beer."

"Well, I could use a beer, at that, miss," he said. "Thank you kindly. I've been walking all over the neighborhood the last few hours."

He stepped into the room, and nodded at Stanton.

"This is Mr. Wylie," Dreamboat announced.

"How do," said Clancy.

"I'm pleased to meet you," Stanton said.

"Miss McKenna's been bothered a number of times lately by a bunch of bums that hang around the saloon on the corner," he explained, when Dreamboat went out to get the beer. "Real nasty customers, too. We've had quite a few complaints from other women as well, but it's hard to catch these fellas doing anything we can book them for. I've got my eye on them, though," he added. "We'll get them."

This was Stanton's first contact on the social level with a detective, and he was inquisitive. "I suppose, with your job, you develop a different attitude toward people, don't you?" he asked. "That is, different from mine, say."

"People? What do I know about people?" the detective said. "All I get to meet is a lot of animals." He stared gloomily out at the macabre tree beyond the windows. "It's a terrible city," he went on. "Full of terrible things happening, and terrible people, you wouldn't believe it. Do you like deep-sea fishing?" he asked unexpectedly.

"Why, I haven't done much of it," Stanton replied.

"It's my hobby," Clancy said. "The reason I asked you that, if you were a deep-sea fisherman you'd know about all the horrible-looking things that live 'way down in the ocean. You wouldn't believe such creatures were down there, until you caught them by mistake. I've often thought, it's the same way with the city—all the horrible creatures, deep down where you don't see them, but there nevertheless. Yes, and doing horrible things in the darkness. In a way, the job makes me sort of a deep-sea fisherman of the city, if you see what I mean?"

Stanton merely nodded, too amazed by this morbid analogy, and its source, to make any reply.

"Well, it's too fine a Sunday for such thoughts," the detective said. "I'll sit down and take it easy."

Dreamboat re-entered, carrying a can of beer and a tumbler. "I only have one can on ice," she said. "Sorry."

"Split it with you?" Clancy suggested to Stanton.

He shook his head. "No, thanks, I really don't want any."

"What's new, Clancy?" Dreamboat asked. "Got any good stories today? Listening to Clancy's better than listening to the radio, any time," she added to Stanton.

"Yes, I think it would be," he said.

"Just the usual," Clancy said. "Good beer, thank you, miss. No, the usual. Oh, I did have a funny one the other night. We have a new rookie in the station, just been on a week. So the other night this woman calls up about eleven-thirty, all excited, and says there's a crazy man without any clothes on, hiding in the bushes in the back yard. I go over with the rookie to investigate, and he's getting more and more excited, ready to nab a dangerous maniac, see? He's asking me to let him handle it alone, so he can be a hero." He paused and chuckled, and sipped his beer. "So I told him, sure, handle it alone, sonny, but I bet you a dollar it isn't any maniac, and you won't be any hero. I won the bet."

"But what was it?" Stanton asked. "What happened?"

"Why, we get calls like that all the time," Clancy said. "Some guy skedaddled out of a bedroom window and down a fire escape into the back yard because somebody's husband came home ahead of time, without letting her know. She threw his clothes out the window after him, but they didn't hit in the same spot. The rookie helped him find some of the stuff. Oh, well, when I was a rookie I used to get excited about those things, too."

Dreamboat cast a curious glance toward Stanton. "You certainly have the funniest things happen to you," she said to Clancy. "Tell about the time you raided that—you know —that house. I never get tired of hearing that one."

The detective shook his head and finished his beer. "Not today, miss," he said. "I'd better be getting back on the job now. Thank you kindly, again, and I'll be in touch with you." He nodded pleasantly to Stanton and went out.

"He said you'd been having some kind of trouble," Stanton remarked.

Dreamboat nodded. "Yeah. Some wise guys down the block. . . . This is a lousy neighborhood, anyway."

He looked at her for a few seconds, then said, "Would you care for another cigarette, Miss McKenna?"

"All right. Thanks."

And when he had lighted it for her, he inquired, "Have you thought about my suggestion?"

"Yeah, I've thought about it," she answered. "You want to make a deal, mister, and it boils down to this: I'm supposed to be a good little girl and go off to Reno and get a nice, quiet divorce for nonsupport or mental cruelty—God knows I don't have to dig up grounds!—so nobody's fingers get burned around here. That's the deal."

"I told you, I'd expect to make it worth your while."

"I know. I've been figuring that angle, don't worry, mister. But I don't figure that you *could* make it worth my while."

"I'm no millionaire, Miss McKenna. But I . . . one way or another this is very important to me."

"So I'm a good girl and get my divorce in Reno and everything's just swell for the whole lot of you," she went on. "Especially Billy. Yes, especially our handsome lady-killer with the black hair, and the voice that makes me want to toss my lunch. Sure, Billy Paige, the guy with the critics raving and the audience yelling and the movie studios sending him hot offers three times a week. . . . Sure. Billy Paige, the cheap bastard who'd put his own mother on the streets if he thought he could pimp a buck a week out of her. Oh, sure. I go to Reno like the little lady, and Billy stays here and gives the girls the grin, the face, the hair and the voice. Yeah. I'm going to put the bastard in the jug. I should think you'd want to, too."

Stanton watched her face. Her eyes were bright, indignant, and she was working up to a fine rage. But somehow he didn't quite believe it, and he wondered. . . .

"I've told you," he said. "I'm only trying to save my son. The price is up to you, and I'll meet it if I can. My son," he repeated. "Would you consider ten thousand, plus Reno expenses?"

She laughed. "Come again, mister."

He waited a little, and then said, "All right, Miss McKenna, suppose you quote a price—for my son. That's what it amounts to."

Dreamboat looked away. Her face again wore a mixed, indecipherable expression. "I'm not trying to hurt your kid," she said. "Or you either, mister."

"In that case, wouldn't you be content with some other form of revenge?" he said. "If you divorced Paige in the usual way, you could stick him for heavy alimony, and I gather he isn't fond of parting with his money."

"You can say that again, mister!"

"But you can't collect alimony from him if he's in jail."

"No," she said slowly. "But if he's in jail he can't be any fancy-pants actor, either, with bobby-soxers asking for his autograph. He can't do any boasting about how he's sleeping in high society these days. . . . Look, mister, ever since I've been married to the bastard *I've* done the creeping, and crawling, and scratching, and forgiving and excusing. Jesus! When I think of what I've taken from the guy."

"Yes, I can understand your feelings very well."

"That's what you think, mister! You can't understand any part of it, because you don't know anything about what I've gone through. Listen, I was a pretty good specialty dancer when I married him, he was only a chorus boy."

Stanton sat back and nodded through Dreamboat's long recital of the indignities she had suffered. His nods became perfunctory after a time, because the story soon turned out to be usual, even predictable. There were the tribulations and disappointments of the young, unknown dancing team; the frantic search for engagements; the living in verminous boardinghouses and the harassment by malevolent landladies; the constant eating out of tin cans, and the frequent starving; the endless, screaming battles over money, ending in physical combat; the shameless backsliding by Paige, leeching on her and every other woman he could ensnare; the frightful humiliations he had inflicted. Like the time they were stranded in San Francisco, and he forced her to accept—for a lousy twenty-five bucks—a job dancing naked on a table at a stag dinner. Like the time in Chicago he had promised her boudoir services to a cheap night-club operator, in exchange for a couple of weeks' work in his lousy show. Finally, the cut-rate abortion he insisted on her having in St. Louis, an abortion which produced a severe infection, rendered her permanently sterile and ended her dancing career forever.

"I should think you would have divorced him long ago," Stanton said. "Why did you put up with him?"

"God knows," Dreamboat answered. "I was in love with the bastard, I guess, and I kept hoping things would change. And there were times when it was all O.K. He liked me, in his own two-timing way, the only way he knows anything about. I figured that the real trouble was that we were broke all the time, and because of that we were fighting all the time. So finally, when I couldn't take it any more, I told him I was leaving him, and we worked out a deal."

"A deal?" Stanton repeated incredulously. After Dreamboat's catalog of horrors, the idea of working out a deal with a king cobra seemed more plausible than one with Mr. Paige. "What kind of a deal?"

"It was like this. He agreed with me, about the dough part of it, see? So instead of getting a divorce, the deal was that we'd separate and leave each other alone until one or the other of us landed something good. Then we'd get together and try again, when we had enough to go on without tangling over every nickel. It didn't make any difference who got the break. If I got it, that was O.K., and if he got it, O.K. too. See?"

Stanton nodded.

"That was three years ago. I can't say I exactly like the way I've had to get along, mister, but we'll skip that. You wouldn't get it, anyway."

"What?"

Dreamboat looked at him with resentful eyes. "I know guys like you," she said. "I can tell by looking at your face you've never been hungry once in your life. I can tell by the way you talk you went to college, and everything, and probably you can spell every word in the dictionary. I can tell by the way you act you never were afraid of anything, and never had to do anything you didn't want to. You'd say I was a tramp," she finished bitterly. "And according to your ideas, you'd be right."

"Please, Miss McKenna——" For the first time since she had started talking about herself, he felt genuinely distressed. The rest of it had been so bizarre that it scarcely affected him. But this did.

"Yeah, according to your ideas," she went on. "But try it once, mister, without what you've got and always had, just try it. And see what happens to those ideas of yours. You'll find out. You want to know something? Those ideas of yours are like a Cadillac automobile or a yacht or an apartment on Park Avenue—you get them because you've got dough, and that's all. And without the dough they go down the pipe. And when they do, you have to do like other people you used to call tramps, except they aren't tramps any more because you're right there with them. You're a tramp, too. Yourself. And you don't like it."

Stanton started to say something to the effect that standards of behavior were not inevitably in direct ratio to the size of a bank balance, but he thought better of it. As long as he was identified as a product of the sheltered life, nothing he could say would make any impression on her. Besides, he no longer was any too certain that his own ideas of behavior were reliable.

"Anyway, I sweated it out," Dreamboat went on. "I kept thinking that for once in his life Paige was on the level with me. He told me he was all for making a fresh start as soon as he could, and he sounded like he meant it."

She paused. "Then at last comes the break," she continued. "He gets this show, it's a big hit, and overnight he's the big glamour boy of Broadway. Everything's lined up for a ten-strike, so I say to myself, Kiddo, this is it, here's what we've been waiting for. I'm all set to go out and order furniture for our new apartment we'll be having. I even think maybe we could adopt a kid, if any adoption agency was crazy enough to . . . Yeah, I had a lot of ideas. Only, they weren't the same ideas as Mr. Billy Paige has got. No, sir. Mr. Paige has forgotten all that about us getting together again. Mr. Paige is now in the chips for the first time in his life, and I don't look so good to him any more. Mr. Paige is now getting a play from people that wouldn't let him in the same room with them before, and he thinks I wouldn't know how to act right with people like that. Most of all, Mr. Paige doesn't want me around because no matter how many airs he puts on, I know all about him, see? I remind him of the way it used to be, and that's the last thing he wants to be thinking about.

"At first he plays it smart," she went on. "He says let's wait awhile so he can pay off his tabs, and maybe he'll have to go to Hollywood, so he don't want to get any apartment here until he finds out. I go along with this song and dance, like a dope, but we're getting nowhere fast. I know he's got a run-of-the-show contract, and the show's sure to run through next spring at least, so this Hollywood gag is a lot of baloney. Also, he's posing for liquor ads and guesting on radio shows, and he's got all the dough anybody needs. So at last I wake up and realize I'm being a sucker, and we have a showdown, and he tells me I got about as much chance to go back living with him as a dead cat, and why don't I try some playboy? And then he throws it at me about this swell dame in Westport who's running into town to see him every other day or so——"

"I'd rather not hear the details, Miss McKenna," he interrupted.

"O.K., mister," she said. "Anyway, that's the payoff."

Stanton looked at her and shook his head. "I still can't understand why he told you so much," he said. "After all, he was talking against himself, wasn't he? Telling you that, I mean?"

Dreamboat laughed. "I said before you couldn't understand it, because you never lived with the bastard. First place, he's a ham; he's got to overplay every scene he gets, on or off the stage. He can't do it any other way. And he's a guy who thinks he's such hot stuff with the dames, he thinks he can give them the brush any way he likes and they'll always come back for more. Like me, for instance. He kicked me in the teeth all the time we were living together, and I was always there for another one. No matter what he did to me, he figured I'd still be hanging around, waiting for him any way I could have him. He'd never believe any woman could ever get over him, no matter how he treated her, and least of all me. . . . Well, he can think *that* one over in the jug. Got another cigarette, mister?"

After he had lighted it for her he walked over to the window and gazed out at the abject-looking tree and the forlorn back yard, trying to decide why he almost—but not quite—believed the story. He had no doubt that it was true in general outline, and he didn't doubt the truth of many particulars, but still, still, there was a question. Before Friday he would have dismissed such a story as medodramatic poppycock, but since then his threshold of credence had been lowered to sea level. Anything might happen, anywhere, any time, with anybody; that he now realized. Façades made no difference, either, as he now understood. He once had accepted Billy Paige as a friend—or, at any rate, guest—in his own home, because he was well-mannered, amusing and presentable, and Betsy liked him. Yet Dreamboat's private version of Paige was thoroughly believable, even inevitable. He thought of Corinne's façade—at least, the one he remembered—and the reality behind it. And Betsy's façade: that lovely mask with the shining hair and the violet eyes . . . that adroit slim goddess in so many postures.

Still, he had the lingering doubt. Somehow, somewhere, there was a flaw in Dreamboat's story, an insincerity, a false note. He didn't know what it was. Perhaps the way she told it, saying it as though she had rehearsed it and throwing away the lines, the casualness of her descriptions, the easy taking-for-granted of the calamities Paige had inflicted. There was something wrong with it, somewhere.

And apart from that, specific questions were beginning to take shape in his mind. For one, if Dreamboat and her lawyer had gathered evidence to prove adultery, evidence enough to support criminal charges, it seemed to him that they would have known about Jeremy. But she had said she didn't know, and he believed her. Why? At length he turned away from the window and said, "We seem to be back where we started, don't we, Miss McKenna?"

"Yeah. I guess so."

"I did have one idea which you may not have considered," he went on. "To a man in Paige's position, publicity of any kind is better than none at all. If you go ahead with your plan to press charges, it certainly will mean a great deal of publicity. In the long run you might find that you had done him more good than harm. You might defeat yourself. . . . By the way," he added, "do you know whether he has any thought of marrying my wife eventually?"

Dreamboat was visibly startled. "Why, no," she said quickly. "Why do you ask that?"

"It's a possibility, isn't it?" Stanton said. "Let's just suppose for a minute that it's in the cards. Let's say you start New York proceedings and even send both of them to jail. There'd be a terrific uproar about it—bound to be. And suppose at the psychological moment they make some dramatic announcement of undying devotion and so on, and say they're going to be married as soon as they can. If anything like that happened, I think you'd find public opinion running pretty strongly against you and *for* them. Do you see what I mean?"

"It's an angle," Dreamboat admitted.

"They might even be built up as the hero and heroine of one of the great romances of all time. Like the Prince of Wales and Mrs. Simpson."

He smiled at her faintly. "At any rate, I'd think about the chances of the whole thing backfiring, because it could, very easily. You might set out to ruin Paige, and end by doing just the opposite. If he were anything but an actor it wouldn't work that way, but in the theater . . ." He paused for a minute, then in a quiet voice added: "Aside from that, I suppose I can only plead with you once again not to ruin my son's future. I'm not exaggerating; I think it would have a lifelong effect on him. You said yourself you didn't want to hurt him."

Dreamboat stirred uneasily. She looked away from him. "Well, I don't, mister. I told you that."

"All right. Then the choice is between a theoretical revenge on Paige which may not hurt him at all, but which certainly will hurt my son, and the other suggestion. You know, you haven't told me yet what would make it worth your while."

"I don't know," she said. "I'll have to think about it. I'll talk to my lawyer and see what he thinks."

Stanton sighed deeply. "Perhaps it's asking too much, Miss McKenna," he said. "But isn't there some way that we could settle the matter right now? I . . . this whole thing has been a shock and a strain. I have a lot of important decisions to make, and I can't make any of them until I know what I can count on with you. Do you understand? It's been a nightmare, ever since I heard about this, and the idea of having the nightmare go on and on——"

"I can't decide anything without my lawyer, mister."

"After all, he's *your* representative, Miss McKenna. He has to follow your instructions."

"No," she said decisively. "I'd have to talk to him first."

"Well, is there any way of reaching him? Couldn't you call him?"

"It's Sunday, mister."

"I know that, but couldn't you try?"

The urgency in his voice startled her. She looked up at him and for a time studied the lines of weariness and desperation on his face. At last she nodded. "Sure, I guess I could try," she said. "I guess there's no harm in trying. We'll have to go out to a pay station," she added. "I don't have a phone here."

"Miss McKenna, I—well, thank you."

When they were leaving the apartment house, Stanton automatically offered her his arm, and, after a moment of surprise and confusion, Dreamboat accepted it. Her rather sallow skin suddenly turned quite pink.

"Doesn't it make you feel funny, walking along with me this way?" she said, with her hand resting on his sleeve. "Like we were old pals, instead of—you know."

"Why, no," Stanton replied. "Not at all."

"You're a funny guy," Dreamboat said. "I thought you'd try to pull some rough stuff and start yelling at me or something, in the apartment. But you know—" she glanced at him brightly—"you treated me swell. I like you, mister."

"I'm glad of that," Stanton said with considerable embarrassment. "Ah, by the way," he added, trying to change the conversation, "what about your young friend, the one who was leaving when I came in this morning? Does she live with you?"

"Oh, you mean Flo. No, she doesn't live with me. She just stopped by, on her way to see the priest."

"Priest?"

"Yeah. The kid's having a tough time. She wants to get married, but her mother won't let her, and she went to the priest to ask him to talk to the old lady."

"Well, is she under age, or what?"

"No, she's old enough. But this guy she wants to marry, he's in a funny sort of business. He's a——"

"Yes?"

"No, I don't want to talk about it, mister. It's a pretty dirty business, I guess, and, oh, I don't know. It's such a swell day," she added irrelevantly. "I can call from the drugstore, down there. He might be home."

They proceeded for a few minutes in silence. Then, as

181

they were approaching the end of the long block, her fingers tightened on his arm, and her steps lagged. "Let's go across the street," she said suddenly.

"What? The drugstore's on this side, isn't it?"

"That tavern there," Dreamboat said. "See those fellas that just came out?"

Stanton saw the tavern, and saw three or four nondescript men lounging about the entrance; heard some loud, uncouth talk emanating from them.

"They're the fellas that Clancy's looking for," she said. "The ones that got fresh with me. . . ." She tugged at his sleeve. "I don't want any more trouble with them."

He looked down at her worried face, and shook his head. "You won't have any trouble."

"You don't know these fellas—they're cokey, or something. They're mean."

"I am *not* going to cross the street, Miss McKenna. Not for them. This is my street, too."

"Please, mister."

"No," Stanton said. "We stay on this side."

She stared at him with a puzzled, wondering expression. Then she again took his arm and stood closer to him than she had before. They walked by a parking lot and were approaching the tavern when one of the loungers looked around and nudged the others. "Hey, here's the girl friend," he called. "Here comes Dreamboat."

He was a short, bandy-legged fellow wearing a leather jacket and a pair of discolored old G. I. trousers. He stepped out to the middle of the pavement and performed a mock bow. There was an ugly smirk on his unshaven face, and his mean little eyes had the coppery appearance of drunkenness. The others stood along the wall, snickering at him.

"Let's get out of this," Dreamboat pleaded in a low voice. "Can't we, mister? I'm scared of these guys."

Stanton shook his head, and continued on his way. "Just don't pay any attention to them," he said.

This admonition, however, was easier to give than to observe. As they drew nearer, the man in the leather jacket commenced shuffling from side to side directly in their path. He winked at his companions, and with a most offensive tone and manner said, "How's about that date we was going to have, Dreamboat? What do you say we go into the back room right now?"

"Naw, you ain't got a chance, Frankie," said one of the onlookers. "Dreamboat's out of your class. She just raised her prices last week."

"Up to what—two bits?" said the man in the leather jacket. This jest produced loud guffaws, and the man swaggered toward Dreamboat and thrust out a hand. "What's your hurry, baby?" he demanded. "Stick around awhile."

He made a quick grab at her wrist, but Stanton was quicker. He suddenly side-stepped so that he stood in front of Dreamboat, facing the man. "Keep your hands off the lady," he said firmly. "And get out of my way."

The creature known as Frankie looked at Stanton as though he hadn't seen him before. His reddish pig eyes went from his face to his necktie and then to his suit.

"Well, look at who's talking!" he said. "Look at Dreamboat's new boy friend, willya? He's the guy that owns the sidewalk, how d'ya like that?" He glanced over his shoulder at the men leaning against the wall. "We got to get off the sidewalk, boys, so this —— has plenty of room."

There were snickers, and a low muttering. Stanton perceived some movement out of the corner of his eyes; then he felt Dreamboat's fist pounding his shoulder, felt her hand yanking his sleeve. He heard her loud whisper: "Beat it!"

Stanton shook his head. "Will you get out of our way?" he demanded. He spoke flatly.

"Sure," said the snarling mouth. The man stepped backward toward the curb. Then he repeated his parody of bowing. "Sure, you own the sidewalk; you can have it."

Suddenly he lowered his head and dove toward Stanton like a football tackle. Stanton braced himself and closed his hand—the one with the heavy gold ring. There was a split second before the butting head between the outthrust crab arms could strike, and Stanton made a brief spatial calculation. He pivoted back on one foot and swung up from hip level. By right, and calculation, the uppercut should have stopped a charging bull, but it didn't. It didn't connect. It couldn't, because almost as soon as Stanton started his calculated swing, he was jostled off balance from behind, and a tripping foot threw him down.

183

He landed on the pavement, on knees and elbows and barked knuckles, and the spider in the leather jacket was punching his ears and neck. He heard Dreamboat yelling, caught a glimpse of her beating at one of the men with her handbag. He rolled away from the punches, jumped up and made a confused counterattack, on the uncertain edge of the curb. One of his swings grazed a face.

"Look out, he's got a blackjack!" he heard Dreamboat shouting. "Duck, mister!"

Stanton ducked and whirled simultaneously, and as he did so he felt and heard the crunch of his cheekbone when the blackjack struck. All at once the world became a vague, fuzzy, uncertain place of shifting colors and wavering lines. From a tremendous distance he listened to the approaching scream of a police-car siren and watched the green car swoop to the curb and stop in front of the tavern. He wondered lazily why so many people were running and shouting down toward the corner . . . wondered why Dreamboat was climbing out of the gutter, why one of her stockings was all bloody and torn below the knee. Lazily, very lazily, he sat down and watched the policemen helping Dreamboat to her feet, talking to her. Then he saw her pointing at him and there was the detective, Mr. Clancy, coming over.

It wasn't exactly a black-out; more like a buzzing fog. He knew that he tried to stand, precariously balanced for a second and was caught by the detective. Next it seemed to him that he was sitting in the police car, and one man was waving a bottle of something under his nose, while another held a very cold towel against his forehead. He saw Dreamboat and Clancy in conversation and he thought he heard the detective say something about it being lucky the blackjack hadn't landed farther up. Then the whole street seemed to fill up with people, swarming from nowhere, gathering like hungry fish after bait, and . . .

That was Stanton's last coherent thought for a time. He didn't black out—not quite. A reddish gray haze closed in over everything.

He came to himself slowly, in dim, unfamiliar surroundings. He was lying on a cot in a small room which led into a kitchen, and Dreamboat was sitting on a stool next to him, wrapping some ice cubes in a cloth. He watched her without speaking, and it was several moments before she noticed that his eyes were open.

"Hello," she said. "Feeling better now, mister?"

"Well——" One side of his face was throbbing hotly, and there was an uncomfortable sensation of pressure around his eyes. But the gray haze had cleared away. "Where am I?"

"My apartment."

"Funny. I don't remember. How did I get here?"

"They drove you around in the police car, and a couple of the boys helped you in. You were walking." She removed one wet cloth from his forehead and applied the fresh one with the ice. "The cops wanted to send you to Bellevue in an ambulance, but I didn't think you'd want that. I was there once myself, and it's no fun. So I thought if you came here and rested you'd be O.K. Do you want a doctor?"

"No, I don't think so. That was very nice of you, Miss McKenna. You're very kind."

"Kind, nothing. After you got beaten up on my account, what else can I do?"

"Did they catch those men?"

Dreamboat nodded. "Yeah, all of them. And boy, did the cops give *them* some pointers on how to beat up people. Right on the street. You should have seen those guys when the wagon got there."

"Didn't I see you fall down? Were you hurt?"

She shrugged, and said, "Aw, I ripped a pair of nylons and took a little skin off one leg. Nothing like you, mister. I told you those were mean guys. They'd just as soon kill you, for the hell of it." She looked at him thoughtfully. "What I don't get is why you didn't beat it, when they started picking on me? I know how to handle guys like that better than you do."

"Why, I couldn't let them talk to you that way," Stanton replied. "I was the one who insisted on staying on that side of the street, and after all, you were walking with me."

"Yeah, but getting into a fight with those bums on *my* account, when you'd just met me, and we're—" she shook her head and looked at him with a baffled expression—"not friends, or anything."

"There was nothing else to do," Stanton said.

"That's what I don't get, the way you say that. You could of beat it, easy."

"I don't think so, Miss McKenna. In fact, I know I couldn't."

"You certainly are a funny guy, mister," she said. "I guess I never met anybody like you before. I'm not used to having guys stick up for me, that way." She paused, and added: "You want to know what I think?"

"What?"

"That wife of yours, she must be an awful dope, being married to you and falling for a guy like Paige. I don't get it."

"Oh . . . that." Stanton thought for a second, and said, "I'd forgotten, for a while. I don't suppose you had a chance to call that lawyer, did you?"

"No, mister. . . ." Dreamboat turned slightly on the stool and looked toward the kitchen, so that he couldn't see her face very clearly. "As a matter of fact, I decided I . . ."

"Yes?"

She shook her head. "Nothing. I'll tell you later, mister."

From the adjacent living room came the shrilling of the doorbell.

"That'll be Clancy," Dreamboat said with relief. "He told me he'd come back to get a statement. He said he'd like to talk to you, too, if you were feeling all right. How about it?"

"Why, yes." Stanton took the improvised ice bag from his forehead and gave it to Dreamboat. Then he jacked himself up on his elbows and swung his legs over the edge of the cot. When he first reached the standing position there was a detectable increase in the throbbing of his face or the feeling of pressure behind his eyes. But after one step both his cheek and his eyes seemed to explode with pain, and he was overcome with dizziness. He sat down heavily, his face as white as paper, and then slowly sank back on the cot.

The doorbell sounded a second time. Dreamboat quickly replaced the ice bag, and patted his arm. "Don't try to get up," she told him. "Take it easy awhile. You can talk to Clancy some other time."

Ordinarily he would have protested, but a protest now would be a dull gesture, and he had no ambition for false heroics. So he lay quite still, and closed his eyes, and let the welcome band of coldness on his forehead do its work. Dreamboat softly left the room and closed the door.

He wanted to sleep, and he nearly did—but not quite. The walls of the apartment were thin, and the door was a flimsy scrap of wood which fitted the frame only at the top. Sound traveled through it like water through a sieve. For a few minutes Stanton heard the conversation in the living room, without listening to it. But presently the words spoken beyond the door began to penetrate, and he realized that Dreamboat wasn't talking to the detective.

". . . told you not to come busting in here like this, you damn fool, anytime day or night." It was Dreamboat's voice, hushed and furious. A reply, muffled or whispered, indistinct. "Yes, in *there*, out cold. . . . Why didn't you tell me about the kid? You know I don't like that stuff. Oh, yeah, sure . . ." No, it certainly was not Clancy, whoever else it might be.

Then he heard the voice answering Dreamboat, and he recognized it. It was unmistakable as a trademark. He placed the ice bag on the stool, and slowly rose to his feet and forced them to carry him to the door. He twisted the porcelain knob a few times, then tugged at it. The door, finally, flew open with a jerk. Stanton leaned against the jamb.

For a long minute they looked at each other silently. Then Billy Paige lighted a cigarette. "Hello, there, Wylie," he said. "I heard you were in there. Quite a surprise, meeting you here."

He flashed one of his famous ivory smiles, and Stanton was forced to admit to himself that Paige had something.

"I'm surprised you're not out in Westport, taking care of Betsy."

Paige laughed carelessly. He passed a hand over his shining black hair, and made some artistic adjustments of the points of his pocket handkerchief. "Couldn't make it today, old man," he said coolly. "Benefit show, you know. I did talk to her on the phone, though, and she was quite upset because you weren't home."

"That's very gratifying," Stanton said.

"Sorry about this . . . er . . . misunderstanding, you know."

"What misunderstanding?" Stanton said. "Everything's perfectly clear."

"Oh. . . ." Paige glanced at him swiftly. "Dreamboat tells me you were blackjacked by somebody, out on the street. Too bad. I suppose it's lucky for me, though, isn't it? I suppose if it wasn't for that you'd be making noises like an outraged husband and threatening all kinds of things."

"Billy, get the hell out of here," Dreamboat spoke unexpectedly. "Go on, scram!"

Stanton glanced from Paige to Dreamboat and then back to Paige again, and suddenly he knew the answers to those indefinite questions. Of course, it was ludicrously simple.

"Go on, get out!" Dreamboat repeated.

Paige shrugged unconcernedly and picked up his hat. "See you, Wylie," he said on his way out. "Give my regards to your wife, will you?"

Stanton stood where he was and said nothing. He looked steadily at Dreamboat, and suddenly she shook her head and turned to the window. Her back was toward Stanton, and her shoulders seemed to be quivering.

"There wasn't any lawyer to call, then, was there, Miss McKenna?" Stanton said at last.

Dreamboat didn't answer for a minute, and when she did her voice was shaky. "Yeah, there was a lawyer—Billy's lawyer. I only saw him once or twice. They didn't tell me about your kid. Honest, I didn't know about your kid."

"I believe you," Stanton said.

"You ought to be lying down, mister," Dreamboat said. She was leaning forward against the windowpanes, which were beginning to turn the blue of late afternoon.

"Then it was all made-up—that story you told me," Stanton said musingly. "You never had any idea of divorcing Paige at all, did you?"

Dreamboat shook her head.

"You—I must admit, I'm curious—have you pulled off this sort of thing before?"

"Yeah," Dreamboat said. "But never where there's a kid, mister. I told Billy I never wanted to have anything to do with it, when there was a kid."

"Yes. . . . Do you mind telling me what happened—usually?"

Dreamboat shrugged. "Nothing much happened, mister. Billy always picked some married dame with dough of her own, and when the right time came I moved in with my act, and right after me came a lawyer. Then I'd let the dame persuade me not to start trouble, and Billy would move on to the next one. Don't worry, mister," she added. "He'll never see your wife again."

Stanton experienced a kind of uncanny fascination at the mechanical, emotionless way that Dreamboat spoke. She might have been describing a picnic, or a visit to the Central Park zoo. He reflected that life must at least be beautifully simple for people like her; in fact, its only problem would be getting results.

"You are married to him, though, and living with him?" he said.

"Oh, sure, we're together most of the time. That was true, what I told you about us separating and planning to get together again. . . . Funny, we were going to let your wife buy us a house."

"And . . . it never bothered you, having Paige carrying on these affairs with other women?"

"Not much," Dreamboat replied. "I figured he'd be doing it anyway, so what the hell, I might as well cash in and have something to show for it."

She slowly turned away from the window and faced him. "There's one other thing that's true, too, mister," she said. "When you told me about your kid, and after what happened with those guys on the street and everything, I decided to call the deal off, and I was going to tell you. Honest."

Stanton didn't answer.

"That's God's truth," she said. "I'd like you to believe it."

"All right," Stanton said. "I believe it."

"So you can forget the whole business," Dreamboat said. "But I'm going to fix it so one person doesn't forget."

Stanton's eyebrows phrased the question.

"That wife of yours," Dreamboat said. "I'm going to scare the living hell out of her."

Chapter 11

Sᴛᴀɴᴛᴏɴ was resting against the tulip-shaped marble information desk in the empty lobby of the Time & Life Building when Nancy Mainwaring stepped out of the elevator a few minutes after six. On the way down she had been talking shop with a pair of *Time* researchers and a gaunt, uncombed *Time* writer who was put together like a steel girder and carried a paper-bound volume with a French title in the pocket of his tweed jacket. They repeated the usual Sunday evening chatter about the unreasonableness of spending a fine autumn week end in the office to accommodate a capricious publishing schedule. The *Time* writer towered aloof, in the corner of the elevator, but they all were weary, and after an elaborate yawn he said something about going across the street for a drink, and would they care to join him? It was pure *noblesse oblige,* since he wanted to be alone with Voltaire or Racine or whoever it was in the paper book, and think brooding, distant thoughts over a glass of sour white wine with a romantic candle flickering to its grave in a smoky *cave* on Forty-eighth Street.

The researchers nodded thirstily, and for a second Nancy thought it might be fun to bring Stanton into the group, just for a quick one. Then she saw him leaning against the marble tulip and excused herself abruptly. Her heels clicked across the stone floor and made quickening echoes through the lobby. Simply looking at him made her excited.

He stretched out his arms as she hurried up to him and was on the point of embracing her when she suddenly caught sight of the side of his face. She stopped where she was. "Oh, Stan!" she breathed. "Darling, what *have* you done to yourself? That bruise on your cheek . . . your hands. You've skinned all your knuckles!"

Stanton grinned at her. "I know I look disreputable," he said. "Do you think you can put up with me?"

"I can try . . . but what did happen?"

"Well——" She moved closer, and he put his arms

around her. Nancy rubbed her face against his rough tweed shoulder, then quickly kissed him on the chin. She was aware of the amused, inquisitive glances from people coming out of the elevators, but they didn't bother her at all.

"I missed you so much," she told him softly. "I just sat at my desk and thought about you, and wondered what you were doing. And such clock-watching as I've never done before! Did you think about me?"

"As often as I had a chance," Stanton said with a smile. "I've had quite a day."

"Not like yesterday?" she said, discreetly detaching herself from his arms. "Don't tell me that."

"No . . . no, this was different. It's a long story, and it had better keep awhile. I'm still feeling a little shaky," he said. "Let's go some place where we can sit down, shall we?"

Her brown eyes searched his face anxiously. "You do look battered, Stan—as if you'd been in a fight."

"That was part of it."

"Oh, Stan! Come on, we'll go to my apartment. It's only a few blocks—over on Madison. I don't feel in the mood for any more public drinking."

"I was hoping you'd suggest that," Stanton said.

They walked hand in hand out to the cabstand on Forty-eighth Street, and on the way Nancy said, "It may surprise you to hear that I had several conversations with your wife today, Stan."

"What!"

"Yes. She called the office, thinking you might be there, and the switchboard put her on my line, since I'm the big Wylie authority now."

He smiled, by no means agreeably. "Boy, if she only knew where I really was this afternoon!" he said. "What did she want?"

"Why, she wanted to find you, of course. She called—I guess it was four times—getting more and more upset. In fact, she was quite frantic the last time. I spoke to her just a minute before I went down to meet you."

"So she was upset, was she?" he said. "What about?"

"Oh, wanting to know where you were, and so forth."

"Um. I suppose she was afraid she'd miss her precious cocktail party. Here's a taxi."

He helped her inside, and when she had given the driver the address he said, "What else?"

"I—oh, yes, she'd heard all about the speech, somehow. I think your mother called her this morning from Chicago. She was upset about that, among other things."

"Good. I'm glad to hear it."

Nancy glanced at him with a small, reserved smile and opened her handbag.

"By the way," she said, "I have something here I thought you'd be interested in seeing."

She handed him a folded sheet of yellow paper—teletype paper. Stanton opened it and read down the lines of capital letters:

MAINWARING,
NY OFFICE

RE YOUR QUERY PRESS REACTION TO STANTON WYLIE SPEECH, ALL PAPERS HERE CARRIED STORIES IN FRONT NEWS SECTION THIS AM, AND HAVE AIRMAILED CLIPS. TRIBUNE STORY ON PAGE THREE WITH TWO COLUMN PHOTO WYLIE DROPPING SOMETHING ON MODEL. STORY HEADLINED: BLOW UP CHICAGO! N.Y. ARCHITECT URGES A-BOMB TREATMENT FOR CITY THE LEAD GOES THUS: QUOTE CHICAGO LAST NIGHT SURVIVED ITS BIGGEST THREAT SINCE THE FIRE WHEN A FOREIGNER (SIC) FROM NEW YORK TOLD THE ANNUAL DINNER MEETING ETC ETC. UNQUOTE. YOU CAN GUESS THE REST. VERY FUNNY MAYBE. SUN STORY HAD NO PIX, HEADLINE: QUOTE. PRIZE-WINNING ARCHITECT DESTROYS OWN MODEL CITY AT BANQUET—MEETING IN CONFUSION. UNQUOTE LEAD: QUOTE. THE ORDINARY DECORUM OF THE BANQUET OF THE ETC ETC WAS SHATTERED LAST NIGHT WHEN STANTON WYLIE OF NEW YORK, WINNER OF THE ASSOCIATION'S AWARD FOR THE GREATEST ETC ETC MADE AN UNORTHODOX SPEECH WHICH CULMINATED IN THE DESTRUCTION ETC. UNQUOTE. YOU KNOW THE REST OF THAT ONE TOO. TRIED TO REACH ASSOCIATION CHAIRMAN AND COMMITTEEMEN BUT ALL UNAVAILABLE AND REFUSE COMMENT. CHECKING PAPERS TONITE FOR POSSIBLE FOLLOW-UP STORIES MONDAY AM AND ALSO PM PAPERS TOMORROW. WILL AIRMAIL SOONEST. REGARDS ADAMS

Stanton read the teletype three times. Then he laughed. "May I keep it?" he said. "It's quite an epitaph, isn't it?"

"You can keep it, but why the epitaph?"

"Oh, nothing. They canceled the close-up, I hope?"

"Canceled it! Are you being funny? There's talk of using that shot of you smashing the model as picture-of-the-week, in our very next issue."

"Then I'll sue," he said. "I'll sue for damages."

"Oh, Stan! After I told them it was a wonderful idea." She squeezed his hand and smiled at him with friendly malice. "I thought you'd be pleased, Stan. I hoped you'd appreciate it."

"Hah!"

"The close-up of Stanton Wylie is going ahead on schedule," Nancy said. "I wrote almost a thousand words about you today. When I started, I thought it would be easy, but it wasn't. Most of it sounded like a schoolgirl's diary, and I kept erasing things and tearing up pages, and —oh, Stan!"

Their kiss lasted through one red light on Fifth Avenue and through another on Madison, but the taxi driver was an elderly, congenial philosopher who kept his eyes on the windshield and made no uncouth remarks, even when the cab braked to a stop in front of Nancy's apartment, and the meter ticked up another nickel for waiting time. . . .

On the sidewalk she said, "Mr. Wylie, I've been keeping a secret from you, and it's too big for me to save for myself."

"Yes, Miss Mainwaring?"

"I adore you, Mr. Wylie. You were sure to find out, sooner or later, but I thought I'd tell you now, to save time, so to speak."

"Miss Mainwaring, I love you—so to speak."

"Do you, Mr. Wylie? Do you, really and truly? You wouldn't deceive a poor working girl, would you?"

"Heaven will protect you," Stanton said gravely.

"That's what I've been told," Nancy replied with equal gravity. "And up to now it's been all too true."

"Miss Mainwaring, I begin to see you in your true light. You're a spider, aren't you?"

Nancy put the key into the lock, opened the door, curtsied. "Here's my parlor, Mr. Fly. Won't you come in?"

Stanton replied by taking her in his arms, kissing her, and then lifting her and carrying her across the dark threshold.

"Why, it's charming!" Stanton said, glancing around the apartment when Nancy switched on the lights. The living room was small, but comfortably arranged and scrupulously tidy. The floor was covered with a champagne-colored rug. There was a pair of love seats upholstered in a dull gold brocade fabric; a mahogany coffee table between them; end tables supporting gold-shaded lamps mounted on antique French apothecary jars; a Winthrop desk with a Revere bowl on the open leaf; a wide, ceiling-high bookcase solidly tapestried with heavy, important-looking volumes.

"Very, very nice," he added. Nancy was pulling back the curtains and raising the Venetian blinds on the windows which overlooked the avenue. "How long have you been living here?"

"Since before the war." She turned and noticed the way his expression changed. "Yes, it was Ted's and mine," she said. "The first and only place we called home.

"Sit down and make yourself comfortable while I investigate the liquor supply," she went on. "It seems to me I have a bottle of Scotch left over from my last debauch. . . . No, you stay there, Stan," she said, as he started to follow her into the bedroom toward the kitchenette. "I enjoy playing hostess."

Stanton remained in the living room, and, quite without meaning to, found himself taking inventory of the number of things in it which served as silent reminders of Nancy's husband. That bookcase filled with fat volumes bearing medical titles—those would be his books. The set of old prints caricaturing medicos of a bygone age would be his, too. The silver cigarette box on the coffee table had his initials, and so did the small silver loving cup which now served as a receptacle for pencils and pens on Nancy's desk. . . . When he looked past the folding doors into the bedroom the first thing he saw was a photograph in a leather frame on her dresser, and he didn't need to ask himself who it was.

Nancy returned with two highballs, and sat down beside him on one of the love seats. "Here's to you, Mr. Wylie!" she said, clinking glasses with him.

"Here's to us, Miss Mainwaring!" Stanton replied.

"I wonder," Nancy said. "Now I want to be told all about everything—starting with the bruise on the face."

"Well . . . I spent the afternoon with Mrs. Billy Paige, otherwise known as Dreamboat McKenna."

"You didn't get into a fight with *her*, did you?"

Stanton shook his head. "No. That was about the only thing that didn't happen. It was a pretty wild afternoon."

He related the events of his visit to Dreamboat carefully and in detail, although he characteristically minimized his part in the street brawl. Nancy heard him through without comment, and when he had finished she looked at him and shook her head.

"My word, Stan, you certainly get involved in the damnedest things," she said. "It isn't safe for you to be out alone, is it? I ought to keep an eye on you all the time."

"Sold!"

"You know, that's quite a slick operation those peop' have got. Quite a twist to the old badger game. I wonder they report their ill-gotten gains on their income tax returns. And what would they call them, do you suppose?"

"Probably list them as 'miscellaneous.' "

"Mm, or maybe 'income from rents and royalties.' That would do it."

"What I can't understand is why they take the risk," Stanton said. "After all, Paige is well established."

"He's only been established a little while," Nancy said. "And if they actually have been broke all their lives, no amount of money would be enough for them now. Besides, there's very little risk. Almost none. They never ask the victim for anything—they're too smart for that. They simply put the victim in the position of bribing this Dreamboat not to do something she has a perfectly legal right to do. That's why it's so slick. If anyone's guilty, it's the victim."

"Yes . . . yes, that's true," he agreed. "Well, anyway, the main problem was settled—took care of itself, I should say——"

He was interrupted by the ringing of the telephone in the bedroom. It rang three times, and then Nancy stood up.

"I ought to have one with a cutoff switch," she said. "I'll bet it's your wife, Stan."

"Calling *here?*"

"Oh, I was very indefinite when I talked to her, but I said I *might* be seeing you this evening, and I expected to hear from you. If she called the office and they told her I'd gone home, she might try this number. She sounded frantic, I told you."

The phone rang again, and she looked at him and said, "Shall I answer it? Or tear it out by the roots?"

He frowned and shook his head. "I don't know, I . . . you think it is Betsy?"

The phone rang for the fifth time.

"I'll answer it," Nancy said. She walked into the bedroom and took the telephone from its black cradle. "Yes?"

Then she nodded, and covered the mouthpiece with her hand. "It is your wife. What do you want me to tell her?"

Stanton hesitated, and Nancy added, "I think you'd better talk to her. She's obviously desperate about something."

"Well, all right. I might as well get it over with."

"Yes, he's here, Mrs. Wylie," she said into the telephone. "Just a minute, please."

When he came into the bedroom Nancy again put her hand over the mouthpiece. "Shall I hide my head under a pillow and pretend not to be listening? Or would it be better to lock myself in the bathroom?"

Stanton shook his head. "It's perfectly all right for you to listen. In fact, I'd rather you did."

He took the receiver with a stolid, impassive expression, but inwardly he was nervous. Regardless of circumstances it was by no means easy to emancipate himself suddenly from all the ties and patterns which had been created through the years. He pretended a superior detachment from any thoughts or feelings about Betsy, but in point of fact her proximity on the telephone frightened him.

"Hello," he said.

"Stanton!" The way she pronounced the single word told him that she very recently had been crying, and that she was far from being in control of herself. Stanton realized it with a little shock. He was so accustomed to her usual poised and competent exterior that he couldn't quite visualize her in tears. He doubted whether he ever had seen her weeping.

"Yes," he said. "What is it?"

"Why aren't you here?" she demanded. "I've been trying to reach you everywhere."

"I decided to stay in town," he answered laconically.

"You've got to come right away," she said. Her voice shook with urgency. "On the first train you can get. Something dreadful has happened."

"It isn't Jerry, is it? Something the matter with him?"

"No . . . no. I can't talk about it on the phone, Stanton, but it's important. You've got to come home immediately."

After a pause, Stanton said, "But I have no intention of coming home. I'm quite happy where I am, and I intend to stay here. If you want to tell me what the trouble is, tell me now, or not at all."

"Stan, you don't know what you're saying!"

"On the contrary, I know perfectly well what I'm saying."

"I—what's got into you? I don't understand you."

"That makes us even, then," he replied. "Is there anything else?"

"There's everything else!" Betsy cried wildly. "You must be out of your mind!"

"Oddly enough, I've just recovered my sanity."

This time the pause was Betsy's, and after a moment of silence he said, "Yes? Are you there?"

"Stan, you must think you're playing a joke—either that, or you think I'm joking; I'm not. Listen to me, Stan." Her voice lowered, and she began to speak with great distinctiveness, as though to make sure he caught every syllable. "An hour or so ago I took a call from some perfectly awful woman in New York who claimed she was the wife of our friend Billy Paige."

"Our friend Billy Paige," he repeated.

"What?"

"Go on."

"She—this woman called in a perfect fury." Another pause; Stanton could picture Betsy sitting by the telephone, considering the choice of phrases. "Whoever she is, she'd picked up some unspeakable scandal in New York about the fact that—well, that I've been friendly with Billy for some time, and she said the vilest things and made the most awful threats. She said she was going to divorce Paige in New York and——"

"Don't bother to tell me. I know all about it."

"What did you say?"

"I said I know all about it," he repeated brusquely. "I know all about Mrs. Paige—she doesn't just claim to be his wife, she *is* his wife. And I know all about 'our friend' Billy, as you call him. And, my dear, I know all about you, too."

The silence prolonged on the other end of the wire, and finally he said, "Well?"

A small voice answered, "Stanton, I have no idea what you may have heard, but I want to tell you that——"

"Betsy," he interrupted, "I'm not going to listen to any ingenious excuses or explanations. I know all I need to know, and I don't want to discuss it."

"Can't we even talk?"

"We are talking."

"You mean—" there was another silence, terminating in a quick sob—"I'm to be tried and convicted and dismissed this way? On the telephone? I can't believe it."

"No?" he replied. "There were things I couldn't believe either. Part of your education, Betsy."

Another silence and another sob. "You mean, you aren't coming home? I'm not going to see you again? Is that it?"

"Yes," Stanton said, "that's it."

"Have you forgotten Jerry? What about Jerry?"

"I've thought about him, and I have some ideas. You'll hear what they are, in time. I'll see my lawyer tomorrow."

Now he heard broken agonized sobs, and he frowned and held the receiver away from his ear. For a moment he felt compelled to say something which would soften it and compromise it, because for an instant he had a bright vision of a lovely blonde in a bouffant dress, whirling in front of the bandstand in the ballroom of the Ritz; then another vision of a charming, laughing girl in a white piqué dress with a blue sash posing in front of the Doges' twisted columns on St. Mark's Square in Venice.

"You can't . . . Stanton, you can't . . ."

He waited, almost frightened by the sound of her voice. It was something utterly new to him, this note of pleading and pathos. He was accustomed only to that distinctive finishing-school accent of hers, and to a flow of fashionable talk as smooth and as unemotional as the surface of a frozen lake. But now she sounded like a despairing lost child. . . . He stifled the impulse to say something to comfort her.

". . . can't just leave me like this," she was saying. "We're married, Stanton. You can't . . ."

Vision of a lovely blonde girl, tanned like an almond, lying in such flushed, innocent sleep beneath the mosquito netting in a Venetian hotel room . . .

"What am I going to do?" she cried in desperation. "What shall I do about this awful woman you say is Mrs. Paige? What shall I do?"

Ugly vision of another girl, another hotel, another room.

"I don't know," Stanton said coldly. "You might try calling our friend Billy to see if he has any ideas. . . . Good-by."

Her plaintive sobbing was audible in the room as he put the telephone down. He sat for a time on the edge of Nancy's bed with his chin cupped in his hands, staring bleakly at the floor. He felt strangely weak, and strangely devoid of sensation, as though he had just passed unharmed through a moment of great danger and was only now beginning to comprehend that he had escaped.

Nancy was standing in front of the dresser on the opposite side of the room. She brushed her hair with slow, down-pulling strokes, and stared thoughtfully at herself in the dimly lighted mirror, pondering the strange molding of destinies by Mr. Bell's great invention. That call from Joe Harper, the *Life* close-up editor, the other morning . . . and now this. I wonder whether Bermuda's been interesting, the last few days? she said to herself. And I wonder, if I hadn't answered the phone when Joe called, and had gone to Bermuda, would I be the same person I am now? Would I be feeling the same way? Was it all bound to happen anyway? Would I have met Stanton on the Bermuda plane, or somewhere else? Or was it an accident that depended on my picking up a telephone? Ah, *"Quien sabe?"* as the Spaniards say. . . .

A pair of eyes regarded her steadily from the side of the dresser, seeming to compel her to look down at the portrait. She kept her eyes on the mirror while she brushed her hair, and then fussed for a moment with the cap of a perfume bot-

tle. But finally she did look down, with an expression between a smile and a frown, and her hand caressed the heavy
leather frame, which was curiously stitched with rows of
fine steel wire. I know, darling; I'm being a ninny, she said
silently. I'll stop.

Then she turned away from the dresser and looked at
Stanton, still sitting on the edge of the bed. "Of course, I
heard it all," she said. "You surprise me, Stan."

"I do?"

"Yes. You were quite brutal, you know. I wouldn't have
believed it, if I hadn't listened."

He glanced up quickly. "Well, she deserved it, didn't
she?" he demanded.

"Mm. Perhaps. Don't look so indignant, Stan. I was making a comment, not a criticism."

"It won't hurt her to have something serious to think
about, for a change." He spoke truculently, in what Nancy
interpreted as an attempt at self-justification. "It might even
do her some good; it might make her realize that she can't
——" He stopped.

"Can't what?"

"Oh—— Let's forget it, Nancy. Shall we?"

"All right. As you say."

"Why, what's the matter?"

"Nothing."

"Nancy!" He stood up so quickly that the recently forgotten pain throbbed hotly again across his face, and it
made him wince as though he had been struck.

"You ought to sit down, Stan."

"No." He walked over to the dresser. "What is it? Why
are you so distant, all of a sudden?"

Nancy sighed as she looked at him. "I'm not distant,
Stan. I'm right here, beside you, within arm's reach. I'm not
distant. I've just been thinking a little, about a few things."

The compelling eyes in the portrait on the dresser steadily regarded her, and she glanced down. Stanton followed
her glance, and when he saw the face in the leather frame
he slowly nodded. "Oh," he said. "That again."

She didn't reply, and Stanton turned away and started to
leave the bedroom. Somehow it seemed almost indecent for
him to be in there, just then, with that picture.

"Yes," Nancy said. "You go and sit down, Stan, and I'll bring us some more drinks."

This time when she came back with the highballs she didn't sit beside him, but instead took the other love seat, facing him. For a few minutes she sipped her drink and watched him silently. At length she said, "When did you make that decision about your wife? What led up to it?"

"I don't know that I'd call it a decision," he answered. "It just seemed inevitable, somehow. After I made sure that Jerry was safe, and this Paige business was settled, it all became perfectly clear. I knew what I wanted."

"Yes?" Nancy said. "What?"

"Two things. First, to be with you. Second, to go away somewhere. I don't want to hang around New York. I thought I'd go down to Bermuda with you, as a starter."

"As a starter," she repeated. "And then what happens?"

"Then—why, we could go anywhere we wanted. Maybe Rio. I've never seen Rio, have you?"

"No, I've never seen Rio."

"Well, it's supposed to be pretty wonderful. And from Rio——" He made a gesture which encompassed the world.

"You mean, we just float on a little pink cloud from one wonderful place to another, indefinitely?"

"As long as we feel like it, and the supply of wonderful places holds out. . . . We could always settle down, if we wanted to."

"It sounds like a dream."

"It doesn't need to be a dream at all. There's nothing to prevent us from doing it. Nothing."

She looked at him for a moment, and then laughed.

"What?" he said.

"I was thinking that long before we get to Rio my reputation will be split wide open at every seam."

"Then we'll sew it together again," Stanton said. "Because by the time we get to Rio I'll have my divorce, and I've always wanted to be married in a place like that, with a double-ring ceremony, strolling musicians to serenade us."

"Some girls *might* interpret that as a proposal, Mr. Wylie."

"Some girls would be awfully stupid if they didn't, Miss

Mainwaring. I'm asking you to marry me, if I need to make it plainer."

"But this is so sudden, Mr. Wylie," she said demurely. "I'm quite overwhelmed, really I am."

Stanton grinned at her. "Miss Mainwaring, this coyness! It ill becomes you, a full-blown woman of the world!"

"Please, Mr. Wylie!"

"You're not overwhelmed at all. You're not even surprised. And why should you be?"

"Stan!"

"I won't try to make a speech about it, because you know what happens when I make speeches. In basic English, I love you. I'm asking you to be my wife."

"But Stanton——"

He stood up from the love seat and scrutinized the highball glass for a second, holding it in front of one of the lamps mounted on old apothecary jars. Those might be Ted's too, he reflected. And what of it?

"It may sound abrupt," he continued, still looking at the glass, and talking away from her. "There should be a buildup, I suppose. I ought to tell you that I think you're beautiful; I do. I should say that your voice sounds like music; believe me, it does. Your hair, and your eyes—brown magic, should I say that? And the way you walk, the color of your skin, the way you smile, the shape of your hands, the excitement of your figure, the warmth of you——"

"Stanton!"

He looked at her and smiled. "But you know about my speeches. To tell you all that, I need Cyrano behind me in the garden, prompting me and giving me the lines. But, since Cyrano isn't here, I'll have to do it alone and say it by myself."

"I'm not Roxanne," Nancy said. "And there's no garden."

"And no Cyrano to give me pretty speeches."

"You've done very nicely on your own, Stan."

"Well then—I love you; I need you; I want you to be my wife. Will you marry me?"

Nancy stared at him through a long moment of trying to sort out some confused and tangled thoughts, and getting nowhere with them. She tried to say something, but gave it up and shook her head helplessly. "What's the matter now?"

he said. "It couldn't come as such a shock. I've been leading up to this ever since I met you on the train."

"I . . . I'm slightly dazed," Nancy said finally. "I'm beginning to see that you really mean it all—even about the wonderful places and the pink cloud."

"Of course I mean it!" Stanton exclaimed in an outraged voice. "Don't you know I fell in love with you the minute I set eyes on you?"

"It's a nice thought," she said with a smile. "At my age, love at first sight is pretty unusual."

"But I thought you—well, agreed with me that there was something special between us? Don't you?"

"Yes, dear, of course I do. I told you, I adore you, Stan." Nancy placed her highball glass on the coffee table and stood up. She moved close to him and put her hand on his arm. "I was just trying to realize that this isn't fantasy. . . . You make it sound so beautifully simple, Stan. We go to Bermuda. We go to Rio. We get married and live happily ever after, floating around on a pink cloud from wonderful place to wonderful place. It's as easy as that."

"Yes, it is," Stanton said. "Why not? Hell's bells, there's little enough enjoyment of living left in the world, and precious little time for whatever bit remains! We might as well take what we can find, while we're able to."

"Yes, you have a point there. . . . But Stan—not that I want to climb down from our pink cloud, or anything—aren't there one or two details that sort of get in the way? For example, your son?"

"I'll work that out tomorrow with the lawyer," Stanton said. "We'll arrange some suitable division of time, and visitation, and so on. That will solve itself as we go along," he added confidently. "You'll like Jerry."

"It seems to me you're being terribly offhand about him," Nancy demurred, "just leaving it up to a lawyer like that. I thought he was your main concern in this whole business?"

"He is," Stanton said with a frown. "But I don't know. He doesn't need me. He's more his mother's boy than mine —always has been. Next year he'll be away at school, and he's at an age when I don't mean much to him. I've just been a fifth wheel around the family, anyway, although I didn't wake up to the fact until lately. It'll be all right. Jerry will manage. Why, even if we're in Europe or South America, with air service what it is he could join us for vacations. No, don't worry about Jerry."

So that disposes of that, Nancy said to herself. Or does it?

"Well, what about your career?" she asked. "What happens to the business?"

Stanton laughed harshly. "What business?" he said. "After last night in Chicago, there is no business. I couldn't look a client in the eye, much less face the people in the office." He suddenly thought of little Miss Rice and the way she had begged him for a copy of the speech. "I'll let my assistant handle the business."

"But you can't just let everything go, Stan."

"Why not?" he said with a shrug. "It's my business. I can do whatever I please with it."

"Yes, I didn't mean that. I was talking about all the fine things you were planning to do. What happens to them? What happens to the City?"

"You saw what happened to the City last night."

"No, I didn't, Stan. I saw what happened to a plaster model on a table—not the City."

He sighed and shook his head. "I told you, Nancy, my heart isn't in it any longer." He shrugged again, this time wearily. "I lost something—that's all. Maybe with you I'll find it again sometime."

Ah, but it wouldn't work that way, Nancy thought. It wouldn't work that way at all. As I well know.

"You really think you can quit?" she said. "Kill it, and throw it all away, just like *that?*" She snapped her fingers. "I don't believe it."

"I tell you, my heart isn't in it," Stanton said. "Something's gone, and I don't care any more. Don't you understand? If I were a pianist and had my hands cut off, you wouldn't expect me to play the piano again, would you? . . . It's the same thing, if you'll visualize an idea instead of a pair of hands—do you see?"

Nancy gave him a long, queer look. She was biting her lip, and her brown eyes were infinitely sad.

"Let's not talk about it any more," Stanton pleaded. "Let's get back on the pink cloud and make some plans. I think I'll call the air line, and find out if I can get space to Bermuda, on your plane. Do you know what flight it is?"

Nancy shook her head. She might have been on the verge of tears.

"Darling, what?" he exclaimed. "Why don't we forget all this and concentrate on ourselves?" He started to put his arms around her, but she backed away from him.

"Why, Nancy——"

"No, not now, Stanton," she said in a very low voice. "I have to decide something, dear. Let me be, for a minute, will you?"

She turned to the window and stared out over the city, now commencing to stir and rustle again after the torpor of Sunday afternoon. Lights were blinking in the apartment houses and hotels along the avenue; blinking on to signal weary arrivals from country week ends; blinking off to signal ebullient departures—after a lazy, yawning day with bed, newspapers and the radio—for a late restaurant supper, or a show at the nearest Loew's. A few couples strolled carelessly along the sidewalk, unhurried, and even the taxis seemed to be proceeding at a relaxed pace. A huge balloon of light hung captive above the city, but it was soft and diffused, and nearly all the shops along the avenue were dark. And there was a silence, of a comparative sort. A bus started its roaring ascent of the three-block incline below the apartment. A faint rumbling came from the Third Avenue Elevated. Half a block away, a doorman whistled for a cab in front of a hotel canopy. Somewhere in the sky four engines thrummed and vibrated on the wings of an airplane, outward bound, which crossed the bubble of light over the city and diminished so rapidly that the eye still traced its silver path after it had vanished beyond the edge of the ocean.

Still—a quiet Sunday evening; almost pastoral, for Manhattan. Yet even in the quiet there was an indefinite sense of mobilization of energy for the start of another Monday, another week. The giant was finishing his nap, and while still rubbing his eyes with one hand he already was reaching with the other for the switches and levers and valves which would pour out the energy for another cycle, another week. . . . Gulliver would sit up in bed on Monday morning and observe with satisfaction how the pygmies rushed through the city with such sweat, noise, speed, energy and desperation. Nancy stood at the window for a while and then turned.

"Stanton," she said. "I've thought about it."

"Yes? Shall I call the air line now?"

Nancy shook her head. "Darling, there's nothing in the world I'd rather do than say yes, and I just can't."

Stanton looked at her in complete astonishment.

"Stan, I'm not going to play any games with you. I really and truly do adore you—at least, I can't even look at you without wanting to throw myself at you, and most of all right now—and I don't need to tell you that I wouldn't be bothered by any thought of conventions. So when I say 'no' it's against every single impulse that I have, urging me to say 'yes' and just fly away with you, to the ends of the earth, or the moon, or wherever you wanted to go. So, you see, I have to fight myself very hard to say 'no,' and the only thing that gives me the courage to do it is that I do love you so much. . . ."

"I don't understand you."

"Let me try a different way, then. Stan, if you were just a nice, agreeable, ordinary man, of no value or importance, I'd probably say 'yes' without giving it a thought, because it wouldn't matter where you were or what you were doing—or if you ever did anything. But you *aren't* that man, and you do have value and importance—great importance—and what you do matters a great deal more than you imagine. I suppose, if you really go ahead and quit everything and throw yourself away, there's nothing I can do to stop you. But at least, I shan't be a party to it. I won't be a contributing factor. Because you have a tremendous job to do, Stan, and if you back down from it there's going to be an awfully disappointed girl named Nancy Mainwaring."

"What do you mean?" he asked. "What job?"

"The job of being the sort of person you are, Stan, and staying that way. The job of hanging onto a dream that you have, and communicating it as well as you can to other people. The job of trying to bring some reason into this world that you complain about so much, while there's still a chance for it to survive. The job, in short, of being, in your own fashion, a rather great man."

Stanton said nothing.

"You know, Stan, for an intelligent man, you have some peculiar blind spots," Nancy went on. "You've talked to me a lot about the atom bomb, and slums, and ugliness, and all the other things that worry you, and now you sound as though you put them in the same category with hurricanes and earthquakes and tidal waves and volcanic explosions—great natural disasters, inevitable and unavoidable. They aren't that at all, you know, and you didn't think so on the train, either. They were brought about by people, and they can be brought under control by people—provided the Stanton Wylies of the world lead them to do it."

He smiled a little. "That's a large order," he said. "Am I supposed to handle it alone?"

"Of course not. The point is, you're one of the few, the very few, who stands out from the crowd and above the crowd, with something more than the crowd mind and the aspirations and ambitions of the crowd. . . . Stan, have you ever seen a crowd of people writing a book, composing a symphony, painting a portrait, or doing anything else worth while, unless they were led and directed by someone better than themselves? No, you haven't, and you never will. I'm not talking about the Feuhrer principle. I'm saying that whatever capacity people have for creative endeavor—which is the source of all progress—doesn't just flow spontaneously from a bubbling spring; it's evoked by the example of the rare few. I surely don't need to remind you that most of the progress of the race has been due to the malcontents who refused to accept the status quo and did something about it, and to the impractical dreamers who were derided and hounded through the streets and burned at the stake because they were rash enough to believe that the dead level of the mob could be raised. . . .

"You've called the City an impractical dream, Stanton, and so it may be. But it's the kind of dream the world has lived by, in spite of itself, since the beginning of time, and the kind of dream that's more badly needed now than ever before. You can't lose it, Stanton—or yourself, because whether you like it or not you have a responsibility beyond the fulfillment of your personal desires. In one sense, your life doesn't belong to you at all. It belongs to humanity, and at this particular moment you can't be spared."

Stanton gazed at her in silence for a long time. "You're very eloquent," he said at last. "I didn't realize you . . . felt that way about things."

"Well, I do, Stan, and if I'm not mistaken you do too."

"Suppose," he said quietly, "suppose—I'm not saying I will—but suppose I did make another stab at my work, instead of going away. And suppose it was all right. Then, could you and I—?"

She replied with a wan smile, shook her head. "No, Stan."

"But why?"

"Because that's only part of your job. The other part is your family, and it's perfectly clear that one meshes with the other."

"What do you mean?"

"I mean—" she again had the sensation of choking as she spoke—"I mean, I think you ought to go back to them."

He looked stunned. "But—good Lord!" he exclaimed. "I can't go back!"

"Why can't you?"

"Because—why, because of everything!"

"No, because your wife had an affair with an actor. That's the reason."

"Isn't that enough?"

"I don't think so."

"I don't understand you at all!" he cried. "How could I possibly go back to her, after what she's done?"

"Because if you look at it in perspective, it's very unimportant, compared to keeping your family together and maintaining a home for your boy. You sat there and blandly told me that he's at an age when he doesn't need you, that he's more his mother's son than yours, and that you've just been a fifth wheel around the place. I say, Poppycock! Show me a child his age who doesn't need a father and a home intact, and you've shown me a freak. You know it as well as I do. And if you *have* been a fifth wheel—which I doubt—it must be your fault."

"You expect me to live with an unfaithful wife?"

"Stan, your feelings are natural and understandable— also very conventional, I might say. You're reacting the way you always were taught to react about this particular problem, the way you're reminded to react every time you see a movie or read a magazine story. 'The wicked woman has sinned, and must be punished. Marriage is impossible with her, after this.' So someone goes off to Reno in high dudgeon and gets a divorce—as though that solved anything—and the lives of two or three or four or five people are knocked off the tracks, with the result that our population of socially and emotionally displaced persons grows. And for what?"

"It's easy enough for you to say all this."

"I knew you'd come to that. I'm not the injured one, so it's easy. Believe me, sir, it is not. I'm talking against myself, Stanton. I'm talking myself down. I'm talking myself straight out of the one thing I want most in the world—you. No," she added quickly, before he could interrupt. "Let me go on. Let me finish. I've never been too impressed with the ideal of absolute monogamy as the be-all and end-all of marriage. It may be fine, in the abstract, and it may be fine for great numbers of people, though I doubt it. I'd rather have a husband who once in a while slept with a girl if he felt like it, and let it go at that, than a husband who never slept with a girl but always thought about doing it, even when he was sleeping with me. Of course, if I knew about the girls, I'd be angry, and upset, and resentful—just as you are. But most of it would be the protest of my own wounded ego, not the fact of infidelity itself. And I'd like you to tell me truthfully how much of your own feeling about your wife is the fact of her unfaithfulness, and how much is wounded ego. Or—let me put it another way, Stan. Suppose when we met on the train Friday you hadn't known anything about your wife and the actor. Suppose we met, and talked, and liked each other and felt a warmth and a kinship—whatever it is that does exist between us—and suppose it seemed right and natural for us to sleep together. We might have, you know. I wanted us to."

"Yes," he said. "If it hadn't been for the conductor."

"Exactly. You might have hated yourself in the morning, but it wouldn't have automatically ended your marriage and broken up your home. You wouldn't have felt that because of sleeping with me you no longer were a fit father, or even a decent husband. You wouldn't have thought it important enough to tear your home apart, or even disturb anything in it."

"There's no comparison," Stanton said. "None at all. You're talking about one thing that might have happened. I'm talking about the way Betsy went about it."

"Yes—and why, Stan? Have you asked yourself why? I haven't met her, and I don't know anything about her except that you've made her out to be a child. And a very selfish child, as she's proved by the way she's behaved. But perhaps she never had much chance to be anything else— had you ever thought about that? Have you encouraged her to grow up? I would judge not, from some of the things you've said. On the contrary, you seemed rather proud that she *was* a child."

"In other words, it's all my fault. Is that it?"

"Now you're being the child, Stan."

"Well, I can't see why you're so keen to excuse her."

"I'm not excusing her at all. I'm simply asking you to consider the relative importance of things. Look, Stan, you told me yourself that you had a better-than-average marriage for fifteen years. You have a son. You have a home. The Wylies are a going institution. Against that is the fact that your charming but infantile wife has had a silly little affair with a professional glamour boy who makes a career out of women. That just isn't a good enough reason for smashing a family to pieces, and I think if you did you'd always be sorry for it. Not that your wife shouldn't be held to account," she added. "I certainly would put her through a course of sprouts of some kind, and obviously she needs firmer handling in the future than she's had before. But you look big enough to keep her under control."

Stanton looked at her with a perplexed expression, and shook his head. "I'm completely befuddled," he said. "Here we are, two people who claim to be in love with each other, talking this way. It's crazy. Why do we do it?"

"Because of the job you have to do," Nancy said. "And it now seems to devolve on me to persuade you to do it."

"I wish I understood what happened to make you become so . . . dedicated, if that's the word," he said.

Nancy didn't answer for a time. There was a curious clouded look on her face, and her eyes seemed to be fixed on some far-away point in space. "I think I could tell you," she said at last. "If you'd let me."

"Why do you say 'if I'd let you'?"

"Because the thing that happened happened to Ted," she said. "And I know you don't like to hear me talk about him. However," she added after a pause, "perhaps I will tell you, anyway, if I can."

"If you can?"

"It's not easy," she said. "I've never told anyone before. I never thought I'd be able to. But I'll try. It may explain several things to you."

She turned and walked into the bedroom, to the bureau. For a moment she stood there, with her hand resting on the leather frame of the portrait of her husband. Her face wore a desolate expression. "Dear God!" she murmured. "What am I doing to myself? And why must I do it?" Then she picked up the portrait and went back to the living room. She placed the picture on the coffee table and sat down on the love seat.

"That's Ted," she said simply. "It was taken a few months after he went into the Army. In his own way, he was a rather great man, too. You know the way we met, at the meeting in Chicago. . . . And we fell in love almost as suddenly as you and I did, Stan. We were married in a matter of weeks, and I don't suppose two people in the world ever were happier—while it lasted. He was my first love, Stan, and I can't tell you how devoted I was to him." Her voice trembled, and Stanton saw the tears welling in her brown eyes.

"Don't," he said gently, reaching for her hand. "Don't go on, Nancy. Don't torture yourself."

Nancy shook her head. "I—I'll be all right," she said. She spoke in a quick, husky voice, and kept her gaze fastened on the picture. "I told you he was a doctor," she continued, pointing to the metal caduceus which gleamed on the lapel of the uniform. "A little after Pearl Harbor, he got a commission in the AAF, and they sent him down to the School of Aviation Medicine at Randolph Field in Texas. After that, he moved around from Randolph to Wright Field, to Thunderbird in Arizona, to Selfridge in Michigan, and for a while he was in Washington, so we had a chance to be together for a little. I took a leave of absence from the office and tried being an Army wife, but it didn't work very well, because they kept shifting him so often, I'd barely catch up with him one place when he'd be ordered off to another. . . .

"Then he went overseas—to England, with the Eighth Bomber Command. We kissed good-by one morning, as if he were only going downtown for the day, and I went back to my job at *Life* and spent my spare time trying to educate myself about being a doctor's wife. I read those books in that case over there, and a good many more besides, and I even audited some medical courses at Columbia. . . .

"We had so many lovely plans, about what we were going to do, after the war. Ted wasn't sure whether he wanted to stay in New York, or maybe go into practice in some small town somewhere. I didn't care, one way or the other, as long as we could just pick up where we left off and go on with what we had started when he came home. . . .

"I really did learn a bit about medicine—or thought I did, at least. I wanted to be able to keep up with him, as well as I could, and when he came home and started practicing again, I hoped I'd know enough maybe to be of some help to him later on. Probably it was silly, but it was the only thing that made sense to me, because Ted was all I thought about. . . .

"I never told him, and I've often wondered what he would have said. It was going to be a surprise, you see. I was going to surprise him one fine day by saying something like 'Yes, Doctor, it's obviously a perforated intestine, and of course you'll do a resection at once, won't you?' and then bowling him over by knowing what I was talking about. . . . You see?"

"Yes," Stanton said quietly, "I see."

"He came back a few times—always very quick trips, and it would have been easier for both of us if he hadn't come at all, because when he went away, it . . . Then . . ."

Her eyes never left the portrait, and her hands were gripped together so tightly that her knuckles gradually were turning white. But her voice seemed to become smaller and retreat into the distance, and somehow, while she talked, it took on a remote, disembodied quality, as though she had fallen into a hypnotic trance.

"I think I told you that he was especially interested in the respiratory diseases. He did a lot of work on high-altitude flying—oxygen deficiency, nitrogen bubbles, and such things. Then they gave him a project—making a study of fatigue under actual combat conditions. He and an assistant or two would go along on bombing missions and take temperature and blood-pressure readings, heart and respiration, and so forth, and sometimes they'd test the effects of new medicines, or drugs, or special foods. . . . It . . . Ted always made a joke of it and said he was just going along for the ride, but of course he was in as much danger as anyone else. He went out on missions, and came back from them.

"And then . . . then there was the one he didn't come back from—a raid on Bremen in April of 1943, a hundred and fifteen B-17s out to plaster the Focke-Wulf plant, and Ted going along for the ride. He'd written me such a happy letter an hour before they took off. It was on my desk at the office that morning—he always addressed them to the office because the mails are earlier there. He didn't say much about what he was doing then—it was mostly about us, and what we were going to do together, and when I finished reading it I had such a wonderful, warm, looking-forward-to-it feeling. . . . He ended the letter before he meant to, with a little postscript about having to close now because he was going off for another ride with the boys . . . and that afternoon the telegram came from the War Department."

She paused. Sounds from the street filled the room; the distant groaning of a bus on the avenue, and the fainter rumble of the elevated. Then there came the merest echo of a female call for "Taxi, taxi!" The starting cough of a cold long-parked automobile; the small grating rattle of garbage cans being readied on the pavement for the dawn patrol of sanitation department trucks; the dull, fading note of a ship's horn on the East River; an obscure, muffled shout from someone, somewhere on some dark street; the gentle sigh of the night breeze, fingering the ends of the window curtains and stirring the scraps of paper in the gutters.

"I've never remembered anything about that afternoon, after I read the telegram," she said, and her voice now seemed farther away than any of the sounds of the city. "And the next few days are a blank, too, a kind of etherish fog. I know I kept going to the office every morning, and they kept sending me home. I don't know why. Everyone was very sweet and considerate, and they whispered after me when I passed them in the hall. . . . They even sent flowers. Boxes of flowers came here—*here*—and I opened them and looked at them, and took out the flowers and put them in vases until I didn't have anything left to hold them, and more boxes came, and I wondered why I was getting so many flowers. . . .

"Then the fog cleared away—too soon—and I began to realize what had happened—gradually, over a long time. For a while I kept telling myself that it was a mistake, it had to be a mistake, and whenever I answered the phone or opened the mailbox I expected word that it *was* a mistake. The love we had for each other was too real and too deep just to *go*, that way, and the plans we'd made together stretched so far ahead . . . it wasn't possible that they could simply vanish.

"Well, that phase passed, too, and I discovered how dangerous it can be to love someone as much as I loved Ted. You spoke of having a vacuum in your life, Stanton. In my case it was close to obliteration. I quit. I gave up. I had no purpose, no meaning, no ambition—nothing. Short of actually committing suicide, I did my best to kill myself—the part of me that *knew*, at last, that it was all over and done with. How I tried to run away! How I threw myself at the men! How I plunged into one frantic affair after another! And the parties I went to, and the parties I gave! And the whisky I swilled! I made a beautiful spectacle of myself, Stanton! I was always late at the office, and for months I couldn't turn out a decent piece of work of any kind. I'll never know why they didn't fire me—pity, I suppose. It all just went on and on and on, with me headed straight for the undertaker or the psychopathic ward. . . .

"And then—" she paused again, and the silence in the room was like something tangible—"then it happened. So casually, it's hard to believe. I was sitting in the office one day, nursing my usual hang-over, and the telephone rang. It was a long-distance call from Washington, from an air-corps colonel who had been on General Eaker's staff during the war. He'd known Ted pretty well, in London, and he'd come to see me once, to say the usual things that people say to young widows. I scarcely remembered him, and I couldn't understand it when he said, 'Miss Mainwaring, could you come down to Washington right away?' I naturally said no, of course not, why should I? And he said—over the telephone, mind you, as though he were inviting me to a cocktail party—he said, 'Because I have something here of vital interest to you. I think you ought to listen to the way your husband lived the last few minutes of his life.'

"Well, it turned out that they'd found the plane. This was months after V-E Day. The plane had crashed several miles outside Bremen and landed in a swamp. Most of it was covered up. Of course, it was a wreck, shot full of holes and half burned up, wings torn off the fuselage, and sections scattered around the swamp. . . . But one thing they recovered intact. This." She ran her hand along the rows of fine steel wire intricately stitched around the leather frame which held his photograph. "Do you know what it is?"

Stanton shook his head.

"It's from a wire recorder—of course you know what that is. There weren't very many of them then, but they'd put an experimental model on board Ted's plane. The recorder was smashed in the crash, but the wire was still there. It's a complete record of every speech and every sound made in that plane from the take-off to . . . the end. . . ."

Nancy sighed, and continued: "What would you do, Stanton? I didn't think I could take it. I thought if I listened to anything like that I'd break down for good—not that I hadn't done quite a job of it already. But that would be too much. That would be too much. That would really crack me in small pieces. I told the colonel I couldn't face the idea. . . .

"The next day he called me again. I told him the same thing—that I just couldn't do it. It would be like going through Ted's death by proxy, and I simply didn't have the guts. I remember what he said, because he sounded so earnest: 'Ted was one of my best friends. I know how much he loved you. I think you owe it to yourself—and to him.' "

For a moment her voice broke, and she passed a hand across her forehead.

"I . . . finally I went. I forced myself to go. I flew down, one morning, and the colonel met me at the airport and took me to the Pentagon Building. He had a recorder in his own office, and I sat in a chair and he turned it on. I nearly fainted when I heard Ted's voice coming from the wire, so clearly that he might have been there with me, and while it was going on I held onto the chair arms so hard that I broke half my fingernails. It was like being on a roller coaster, I remember. . . .

"I listened to the whole thing. The name of the plane was the 'Romping Rhino,' and the way they all joked and carried on, leaving England, it was hard to believe that it wasn't some sort of a romp, instead of serious business. Even when they were over Heligoland Bight, heading for Bremen, they kept on talking about the baseball season, and a poker game some of them had been in that afternoon, and —of course—girls. They were passing chocolate and cigarettes and thermoses of coffee around, and in the midst of this social hour there was Ted with another doctor, making their studies of flight fatigue in that crew. . . .

"Then the talk began to get more serious—and a lot more technical. Pilot to Navigator, Pilot to Bombardier, Pilot to Gunner, and so forth. They were testing things. I'm not telling it well, Stanton. I don't think anyone could, without the background sound effects. All the talk was recorded on top of one roar from the plane's own motors, and another roaring from the other p'anes around it, and a lot of rattling around with ammunition cases. . . . The gunners let go with a few practice bursts . . . there was a kind of thumping in the distance; it sounded like a bass drum in a football stadium, but it was antiaircraft fire, and it was getting louder and louder. The pilot of Ted's plane was talking to one of the other planes in the group . . . 'Roger . . . Willco.' The navigator said something like 'I thought this was going to be a milk run, and here we are on Purple Heart Corner.' You could feel them all tensing. 'Hey, you down there in the greenhouse——' . . . 'Left—steady—left— Jesus, look at the fires! We don't have a target.' . . . 'Easy, easy—right—steady—hold it! On target.'

"And then there was more of the thumping, much louder and closer, and the most fearful racket you could imagine —explosions, whistling sounds, this terrific pounding and thumping going on, machine guns popping everywhere, and more and more engines roaring in the background. I heard one voice saying, 'Four—no, six—M.E.s coming up at four o'clock—some more ahead and over . . . Bombs away!" Then the loudest noise of all. First, a tremendous blast, and a sound of metal being punctured, and then something that made me think of shaking a lot of marbles around in a tin box. . . . Next, you could hear the wind rushing into the cabin of the plane, and somebody said, 'Jesus, it's cold in here!' And somebody else said, 'Don't worry, it's going to warm up soon.' And a second or two later there was a new kind of noise—not so loud, but the worst one—fire; and some hissing when they turned on the extinguishers. . . .

"They didn't have a chance, and they all knew it. Most of the right wing was shot off, two engines were gone, the controls were useless, and even if they'd had time to jump, the plane already was so close to the ground that their parachutes wouldn't have opened. The noise of the wind and the fire was growing stronger in the cabin, and there was this pack of fighter planes all around them, and machine-gun bullets making a sieve out of the bomber. . . .

"And, do you know, all those men behaved in the strangest way? They were lost, and they couldn't do a thing to help themselves, and nothing made a bit of difference. So what do you suppose they did? They stayed on the job, the ones who were still alive. Up to the very last second, they kept on doing the things they were supposed to do. I heard the pilot saying that three fighters were closing in, and he was going to ram one of them if he could, and then a gunner answered that he'd take care of the other two. The radio operator was dead, and the navigator was badly wounded. I heard him cursing about his left leg. . . .

"Then I heard Ted's voice. He'd been wounded himself, and he sounded very weak, but he was trying to do something for the navigator. He mentioned a tourniquet, and then he kept asking the other doctor for a morphine Syrette. But I suppose the doctor was dead, too, because there wasn't any answer. Then there was a final roar, and silence.

"That was all," Nancy added. "There were no heroics. No one tried to act like Superman. No one attempted any fine speeches, and if they did any praying they prayed alone, and to themselves. But it was the very quietness of the way they behaved, the absence of theatrical gestures, that made it so—well, magnificent was the only word I could think of.

"Even then, while I was sitting in the colonel's office trying to collect myself, I remembered something Ted had once told me during the course of a long discussion we were having about the state of the world. He said that the condition of nations only reflected the condition of the individuals living in them, and that if the individuals started to break down, sooner or later the nations would too. Conversely, if individual man could be counted upon to do his job, the ills of the world in time would disappear. . . .

"There's no more to tell, Stanton, except, perhaps, that it was a very different Nancy Mainwaring who meekly crawled back to New York that afternoon. And she's been a changed person ever since. I won't go into the way I soul-searched and upbraided myself for the pathetic way I'd been behaving. You can imagine. But things suddenly straightened themselves out for me, and I got back to being a reasonable facsimile of what Ted would have wanted me to be. So, Stan —now do you see?"

Stanton regarded her in silence. Her story had had the peculiar effect of making him feel puny and inadequate, and his mental state was one of extreme confusion. His gaze crossed the depths of her brown hair, lingered on her oval, ivory-tinted face with the full, firm mouth, and the snapping eyes placed at the slight, tantalizing angle, then followed the lines of her body down to the silken gleam of her legs. He shook his head a couple of times, as if he found it difficult to comprehend that it was actually she who had been speaking.

"Of course I see about Ted," he said at last. "He was a hero, and, as you say, a great man. But about us, I don't know. I don't know."

"Stan, you know I'd be bound to judge all other men against Ted, don't you?" Nancy said. "I love you because you remind me so much of him, and believe me, dear, it's no casual love, but a real one. And I can't accept less from you than I learned to expect from him."

"You're certainly honest about it," Stanton muttered. He sighed wearily. "I can't seem to think clearly. In fact, I can't seem to think at all. I can't decide anything, sitting here, looking at you this way." He rose heavily from the love seat. "Maybe if I go outside and walk around——"

Nancy stepped up to him and put her arms around him and for a moment nestled against his collar. "Maybe that would be best," she said, in a queer, small voice.

Then she turned away from him quickly and stood looking out the window with her head bowed, so that he wouldn't see her tears.

She remained at the window for some little time after the door closed behind Stanton, and then she saw him emerge onto the sidewalk and stand there irresolutely. He took a few lagging steps toward the uptown corner of the avenue; stopped; looked back; then took a few more steps. "Good-by, darling," Nancy murmured.

Her face was working with the force of potent emotions when she retrieved the portrait from the coffee table and carried it into the bedroom, and she set it down on the bureau with a bang. In the same instant she had an impulse to abandon herself to wild crying, and an equally strong urge to begin smashing and tearing things and give herself over to a pent-up torrent of rage. She looked at herself in the mirror with a mingled expression of scorn and fury.

"So, Nancy, you've done it again," she said in a voice that was harsh and brittle. "You've done it again." She nodded disgustedly at her own face. "Everybody's little mother. The heroine of every situation. The noble, self-sacrificing soul. Why don't you join the Salvation Army and be done with it, you do-gooder? And for what? For what?" she demanded bitterly. "Who told you you had to save the world? Don't you have any right to anything for yourself? Doesn't your own happiness count at all? You had it here—or the best chance for it you'll ever have again—right in this room, and what do you do with it? You send it marching straight through the door, and away forever."

Then she stopped, trembling, overwhelmed by a new thought. Perhaps she hadn't after all; there was a chance. Perhaps he hadn't been convinced. Perhaps she had failed in her earnest attempt at persuasion, and in so failing succeeded for herself. Maybe——

In a kind of frenzy she hurried back to the window, opened it and leaned out. She couldn't see him anywhere, but there were more people on the avenue now; he might be part of the crowd. Nancy slammed the window shut and ran to the door, ran down the flight of stairs to the street, bursting forth so precipitously that she collided with a leisurely couple strolling past. She gasped some sort of apology into their astonished faces and nearly broke into a run toward the corner where she last had seen Stanton.

He wasn't there. The side street was empty, and among the dim figures proceeding along the avenue she saw no one who looked like him. She had a moment of indecision. There were so many people, and the avenue was lighted so duskily. . . . He might have changed his direction.

Then she crossed the street and resumed her nearly running pace for another block, and another after that. She threaded back and forth across the sidewalk to avoid running into people, but bumped some of them and left behind her a little trail of following glances and comments which ranged from the indignant to the amused, to the speculative.

And then there was a small eddy in the crowd ahead, and part of the street was clear of people for a moment, and she saw Stanton walking with a slow, deliberate, somnambulistic gait, with his hands thrust into his pockets, and his head bent, eyes following the cracks in the pavement. Nancy wanted to cry out, and wave, and rush up to him. "Go on!" she told herself exultantly. "Bring him back. Tell him—tell him you didn't mean it, you take it back, it wasn't true—anything. Give yourself *one* break, Nancy. But hurry!"

And she tried to hurry, but more and more people seemed to get in her way, and for some reason she couldn't see them very clearly, and a traffic light changed and she had to wait for several cabs to round the corner. . . . By the time she had gained enough ground to be able to call to him, she saw that he had stopped in front of a dusty old red brick church which she had passed so many times it was as familiar as a postbox, but never had visited. The evening service had just ended. A few members of the congregation lingered and chatted in dark clusters on the steps, and three bars of yellow light from the open doors of the church fell softly across the sidewalk. Stanton was standing in one of them, and even

220

at the distance Nancy saw something in his expression which made her hesitate. The Lincoln lines were engraved so deeply on his forehead that they made shadows. He shook his head, perplexed, and slowly started climbing the steps.

Nancy stopped in the shadow of the corner of the church, beyond the periphery of the light, and watched him as he approached the center door. A young, fresh-faced rector in a black robe approached, and she heard him say, "Yes, won't you come in, my friend?"

"I wondered——" she heard Stanton say. "I know it's late, but I wondered if I might listen to a hymn."

"Hymn?"

"Yes, *Ein Feste Burg*—'A Mighty Fortress.' "

"Why, we've finished the service. I don't know. I was about to close the doors and lock up." The young rector looked confused. "Our organist——"

"I need something," Stanton said. "And I think that might help."

The rector studied him for a moment, and nodded. "Please come in," he said. "I'll see."

Stanton followed him into the church.

"Last night we were requesting "I Could Write a Book" in the Parakeet in Chicago, Nancy thought, "and tonight——"

She stood just outside the middle door. She looked at Stanton kneeling in the empty church, and at the rector and another man talking in front of the organ. The organist glanced back across the vacant pews, nodded, and moved to the stool and sat down. He turned one knob on the keyboard and pulled out another. The church vibrated with a preliminary hum, and then the slow, majestic chords rolled out:

> *A mighty fortress is our God,*
> *Whose goodness faileth never.*

Nancy waited until the hymn ended and the organ was silenced. She watched Stanton slowly rising from his pew, and the young rector approaching him and then walking with him toward the door. Then she retreated to the shadowed corner beside the church. She could hear him talking to the rector, thanking him, and a moment later he came down the steps and paused on the sidewalk while the church doors closed behind him and the three bars of yellow light were blotted out, one by one. For a moment he looked thoughtfully down the avenue, and Nancy was certain that he would—— But he turned and started in the opposite direction, toward Grand Central and the train which would carry him to Westport.

She followed him as far as the curb of the nearest corner. There she stopped, and gazed after him until he finally disappeared. In spite of herself she cried a little, very quietly, and people going by stared at her with open amazement. A bus stopped, and a pair of girls emerged, one of them saying, "Sure, I like him all right, but every time I go to a show with him we got to sit in the *bal*-cony. Hey, look it! What's eating *her!* Will you look at that!"

A mellow gentleman of chivalrous disposition studied her from a brief distance, shaking his head and clucking to himself over the sight of this handsome, brown-haired girl standing alone, in tears, on a corner of Madison Avenue that fine Sunday evening. Impelled by a laudable desire to give aid and comfort, he started to approach her, and even got as far as raising his hat. But when he was close enough really to see her face something caused him to turn aside.

Possibly it was the fact that although she was crying, an odd smile, quite indefinable, was on her face. It might have been a smile of triumph, for Nancy was looking up at the sky, and beyond the spreading fan of light above Manhattan she saw the cold stars buttoned like rhinestones against the infinite blackness, and it seemed to her that they now formed a vast constellation which outlined the soaring sweep of a tall white city blazing in proud splendor against the night.

It was an optical illusion, of course—something to do with the refraction of the rays from the street lamp through her tears—but a persistent one. She was certain it was there, so certain that her crying ceased, and her smile became one not only of triumph but of elation.

"Darling, you know," she said to the sky, oblivious of the restless sea of people surging about her, "you set an awfully high standard for a girl like Nancy."

Chapter 12

Hᴍ," ꜱᴀɪᴅ Mr. O'Mara on Tuesday morning. "Hm."

The elegant legs of the assistant managing editor extended from the leather sofa in Joe Harper's office in the Time & Life Building and were, as usual, encased in trousers pressed to the sharpness of guillotines. And while he read the manuscript his face, as usual, was a scene of patient, superior boredom. With a final "Hm" he tossed the mimeographed pages across to Joe's desk, and unfolded himself from the sofa.

"It——" He shook his head. "Something's wrong. Something just isn't there."

Joe looked at him, and said, "Like what?"

O'Mara contemplated the ceiling with a wise expression and pressed finger tips against his right temple.

'I . . . can't . . . quite put it into words. It doesn't matter, anyway," he said. "The people upstairs want the piece, so we'll run it. But I still don't think it belongs in the magazine."

"Now wait a minute," Joe said. He glanced at Nancy Mainwaring, who sat on the window ledge looking at both of them—and at neither one. "The piece was done in a rush, and Nancy gave up her vacation to accommodate the schedule. I think she turned out a damned fine job, considering the time, and everything. If you want to make a criticism, at least be fair about it."

O'Mara gave Joe a thoughtful look and mentally entered his name in his private list of undesirables. "Very well," he said. "Since Miss Mainwaring is with us, I thought I'd spare her feelings."

"Don't mind me," Nancy said.

"Nancy's been around long enough to be able to take any legitimate criticism from anyone without getting her feelings hurt," Joe said.

O'Mara shrugged lightly. "Very well," he said again. "The trouble with this piece is that it sounds like research. It might have been written from the morgue clips. You get no sense of really *knowing* the subject when you've finished reading the close-up—that's what I complain about. And with due apologies to you, Miss Mainwaring, and with full appreciation of your efforts, I must say that I've found the same thing to be true of every piece written by a woman writer on this magazine. The research is fine, but the final product—— Well, in this case, this close-up of this Stanton Wylie—to be frank, it sounds flat. It sounds as though you'd never even met the subject, much less *lived* with the subject, if you know what I mean."

There was a long silence in the office. Then Nancy dismounted from the window ledge. "That does it," she said. "That really does it. Joe, I'm going down to the Holland for a cup of coffee. Come with me?"

Joe nodded, and they left the office without speaking to O'Mara. He expounded his opinions of this gentleman while they were riding down in the elevator, and when they reached the lobby he said, "Let's forget the bastard. You can, anyway. Tomorrow night you'll be in Bermuda."

But Nancy shook her head. "No, you're wrong," she said. "I canceled it. I'm not going."

Joe looked at her, and didn't reply. He knew her well enough—and was wise enough—not to.

"As a matter of fact, I'd like another assignment," Nancy said. "I want something to do. I couldn't face Bermuda, at the moment."

"Serious?"

She nodded. "Very."

"We-ell," Joe said in his slow way, "there *might* be a good one for you. There's a woman out in Medford, Oregon, who——"

"That's for me," Nancy said, without waiting to hear the rest. "That's my story."

THE END

www.ingramcontent.com/pod-product-compliance
Lightning Source LLC
Chambersburg PA
CBHW020443270626
47155CB00022B/1347